MARRYING
the
MATCHMAKER

Books by Jody Hedlund

A Shanahan Match

Calling on the Matchmaker
Saved by the Matchmaker
A Wager with the Matchmaker
Marrying the Matchmaker

Colorado Cowboys

A Cowboy for Keeps
The Heart of a Cowboy
To Tame a Cowboy
Falling for the Cowgirl
The Last Chance Cowboy

Beacons of Hope

Out of the Storm: A Beacons of Hope Novella
Love Unexpected
Hearts Made Whole
Undaunted Hope

Orphan Train

An Awakened Heart: An Orphan Train Novella
With You Always
Together Forever
Searching for You

The Bride Ships

A Reluctant Bride
The Runaway Bride
A Bride of Convenience

The Preacher's Bride
The Doctor's Lady
Unending Devotion
A Noble Groom
Rebellious Heart
Captured by Love

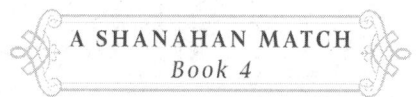

A SHANAHAN MATCH
Book 4

MARRYING *the* MATCHMAKER

Jody Hedlund

BETHANYHOUSE

a division of Baker Publishing Group
Minneapolis, Minnesota

© 2026 by Jody Hedlund

Published by Bethany House Publishers
Minneapolis, Minnesota
BethanyHouse.com

Bethany House Publishers is a division of
Baker Publishing Group, Grand Rapids, Michigan

Printed in the United States of America

Library of Congress Cataloging-in-Publication Data
Names: Hedlund, Jody author
Title: Marrying the matchmaker / Jody Hedlund.
Description: Minneapolis, Minnesota : Bethany House, a division of Baker Publishing Group, 2026. | Series: A Shanahan match ; 4
Identifiers: LCCN 2025015414 | ISBN 9780764244377 paperback | ISBN 9780764246128 casebound | ISBN 9781493452538 ebook
Subjects: LCGFT: Fiction | Christian fiction | Romance fiction | Novels
Classification: LCC PS3608.E333 M37 2026 | DDC 813/.6—dc23/eng/20250624
LC record available at https://lccn.loc.gov/2025015414

This book is a work of fiction. Names, characters, places, and incidents are the product of the author's imagination or are used fictitiously. Any resemblance to actual events, locales, or persons, living or dead, is coincidental.

Cover design by Jennifer Parker; Image of couple by Lee Avison / Trevillion Images

Baker Publishing Group publications use paper produced from sustainable forestry practices and post-consumer waste whenever possible.

26 27 28 29 30 31 32   7 6 5 4 3 2 1

1

ST. LOUIS, MISSOURI
JULY 1849

She'd done it. She'd finally sold a story.

Trying to remain as composed as possible, Zaira Shanahan stepped out onto Seventh Street and closed the door of the newspaper office behind her. She only managed two strides before she clasped her hands together and released a squeal of delight.

Her dreams were coming true. She was an official author.

Well, her pseudonym, K. S. Flanders, was the author . . . which didn't bother Zaira too much. The fake name was just a technicality. All that mattered was that she was being published.

Thankfully, Mr. Knapp hadn't pressed her to reveal more about who K. S. Flanders really was and had accepted that the fellow was a friend who wished to remain anonymous. If the newspaper owner had suspected Zaira was K. S. Flanders, he hadn't said anything when he'd offered her a weekly column. Maybe he'd decided people would be more willing to read episodes from an unknown man than from a nineteen-year-old woman, especially the daughter of one of St. Louis's most prominent families.

Whatever the case, Zaira wasn't complaining.

"A weekly column." She couldn't keep a wide smile from blossoming. "Just think, by Sunday all of St. Louis and beyond will be reading my story."

Oh, sweet saints. Her stomach flipped like a steamboat paddle wheel. She had four days to write and deliver the next installment. Sure, she could use some of what she'd already written. Mr. Knapp had mostly liked it. But he'd given her a short list of edits to pass along to K. S. Flanders—edits that included adding more intrigue to leave readers anticipating the next segment. He'd also requested that the feelings between the heroine and her love interest be more realistic and contain more depth.

He'd agreed to publish two chapters. After that, he would gauge the public's response before approving more. It went without saying that if the story wasn't well received, K. S. Flanders would have a short publishing career. But if the two segments got good reviews, then she'd be able to keep on publishing in the weekly column.

She took several more rapid steps away from the *Daily Republican* office—which was housed in a temporary building since the old one had been destroyed in the fire that had ravaged St. Louis only a few months ago in May. As she caught her reflection in the window of the law office next door, she halted again and admired the young woman she was becoming.

She, the middle Shanahan child, who often got lost in the crowd of her five siblings, was growing up and doing something with her life, something she loved, something that gave her purpose.

She straightened her shoulders and lifted her chin. The fashionable straw bonnet with the wide brim framed her distinct, Shanahan heart-shaped face with high cheekbones and a dimple on her chin. Even though she'd done her best to tame her long, curly red hair into a chignon, the humidity of the hot July day had teased some shorter strands into escaping, so she looked less elegant than she'd hoped.

The summery green of the ribbon on her hat was the same shade of velvet trimming her gown, a romantic color that matched her eyes and also made her skin and hair come to life. Not only that, but the gown was flattering to her figure and made her appear older and more womanly.

She released a happy sigh, gave her petite frame a nod of approval, then turned away from her reflection. As she did so, she collided with a man hurrying down the boardwalk from the opposite direction.

"I beg your pardon." The fellow reached out to steady her. As his hand circled her forearm, he froze.

She shifted and found herself facing Bellamy McKenna, the Irish matchmaker. His easy smile disappeared and was replaced by a scowl, and his dark brown eyes narrowed beneath his tweed flatcap.

It didn't matter one iota that Bellamy was peering at her as though he'd just had a run-in with a dirty rat. With his dark hair, tanned skin, and chiseled features, he was still the most gorgeous man in St. Louis, and nothing could mar his utter beauty, not even his obvious irritation.

As her sister had always said, Bellamy was a heart-stopper and looked more Italian than Irish. While that was an accurate description, Zaira likened Bellamy to a Celtic warrior from the old myths. He was strong and full of valor and unwilling to back down from a challenge. At the same time, he was charming and witty and savvy with a bit of enigma, a puzzle that needed solving.

Every single Irishwoman in St. Louis wanted to be the one to *solve* Bellamy . . . including Zaira. There was no sense in denying it. Doing so would be like denying that the stars came out at night.

The trouble was that Bellamy was not attracted to her. Not even a tiny bit. In fact, he seemed to dislike her more every time he saw her.

She had a feeling his contempt was because she knew about his little—or perhaps not-so-little—secret. And he wasn't keen on her bringing it up once in a while.

Regardless, she enjoyed teasing him and didn't intend to stop. It made life more interesting, and she was all about making life interesting, since more drama meant more fodder for her stories.

"Well, well, well." She gave him another once-over. Usually, he wore black trousers with a white dress shirt and black vest. But today he had on a matching suit coat that lent him the air of a gentleman. "If it isn't Mr. W. B. M. himself."

Bellamy glanced quickly around the nearly deserted street. For midday, the quiet was eerie without the usual carts and drays and wagons rumbling by. Only a handful of men loitered in front of a barbershop a few buildings away, talking together in hushed tones as if they were at a funeral.

Maybe they were. The city seemed to be dying more every day that the cholera epidemic lingered. The death toll last week had risen to over seven hundred people. And if her parents knew she'd ventured downtown into the danger, they'd lock her in her room at their country home, Oakland, and never let her out.

Bellamy's eyes turned almost black as his gaze returned to her. "You shouldn't be here."

"Afraid I'll tell everyone your secret?"

"You should be afraid I'll be telling everyone yours." His voice was low.

Whenever she talked with Bellamy, her blood hummed with an energy she loved. "What exactly do you think my secret is?"

"You know that I know."

She wasn't sure if he really knew about her publishing efforts or if he was bluffing. Either way, she suspected he wouldn't say anything to her parents any more than she'd say something to Oscar.

She nodded at the canvas he was holding, hidden behind brown paper. "Which one do you have there? The field of wildflowers?"

That had been her favorite of the paintings she'd seen in his studio in the shed.

Bellamy's eyes only narrowed on her all the more. "Go home and stay there."

The first time she'd noticed him coming out of Templeton & Evans Gallery back in the spring, she'd been surprised to say the least. She hadn't expected a man like Bellamy to be interested in art. But he'd most definitely been carrying a canvas, although it had been covered and she hadn't been able to see what it entailed.

Secretly, she'd followed him to the shed behind Oscar's Pub, where he'd stowed the canvas away. When he'd gone into the pub, she'd snuck into the shed and investigated long enough to discover not just that canvas but others—incredibly beautiful paintings of landscapes around St. Louis. Each of them had the initials W. B. M. in the corner. All she'd needed to do was return to Templeton & Evans to find several more of those paintings with the same initials. They'd been for sale, and the price tags on them hadn't been cheap.

A few weeks later when she'd been trying to sell another one of her stories, she'd seen Bellamy coming out of a different art gallery, and her curiosity had gotten the best of her. She'd gone right up to him and asked him if he was an artist with the name W. B. M.

Instead of staying calm and unruffled like he usually did, he'd been flustered and defensive. His reaction had given her the answer she'd been looking for—that Bellamy McKenna was a very talented artist.

"You need to nip along, Zaira," Bellamy said. "The city isn't safe."

"Aw-w-w." Zaira cocked her head and gave him what she hoped was her most flirtatious look. "It's so nice to know you care about me, Bellamy. I feel so special."

He scoffed, his eyes now flashing with danger—a danger that invaded her and marched into her veins.

Similar to previous interactions with Bellamy, she didn't understand the emotions he brought to life in her, but she liked the excitement and thrill of their nearness and their conversations.

"Don't be daft." He leaned in farther, his face only inches from hers, his gaze riveted to her mouth. "You know you're just a little lass playing grown-up."

Something in the way he was studying her mouth sent a sizzle through her, one that scorched her insides and made her inhale sharply.

At the quick rise of her chest, Bellamy's attention dropped to her bust. The style of her summer gown was cut low, leaving the swell of her chest showing above the lacy edge of her bodice. His gaze seemed to reach out and caress her skin, and she drew in another breath, this one more pronounced than the last.

Was this what desire truly felt like?

She'd tried to write about it realistically. But maybe it was impossible to portray something she'd never experienced firsthand. Did she need to facilitate a relationship with someone like Bellamy so she could experience more depth of emotion the way Mr. Knapp had suggested? Maybe she could have her first kiss? For research purposes?

She wouldn't mind making Bellamy her subject. Her thoughts spun with all the possibilities even as her gaze snagged on Bellamy's mouth. With such a handsome mouth—one with a ready grin—he was probably a very good kisser.

"Stop, Zaira," he growled.

"Stop what?"

"Stop flirting with me every time you see me."

She took a rapid step back, his words like a splash of cold water against her overheated body. "I'm not flirting."

"Oh aye. It's easy to see that you like me." His voice held too much swagger. "But nothing will ever happen between us."

How was it that Bellamy could read people so well? Almost as if he could get into their minds—her mind—and see every single thought.

It was slightly mortifying. But thankfully she didn't embarrass easily. Instead, she forced herself to smile brightly. "I didn't expect anything to *happen*, Bellamy. But since you brought it up, maybe that's what you're hoping for."

He released another scoff. "Ach, now I understand why there's talk of your da coming to me soon to find you a match."

She hadn't heard that talk. But with Kiernan now happily married to Alannah, maybe her da was ready to start the matchmaking process for the next of his children. If so, she'd have to find a way to dissuade him and buy herself more time.

"You tell them I'm too young for a match." Her smile faded. "I'd like to wait until I'm at least twenty-one." Even if her mam had been younger than her—only eighteen—when she'd married Da, surely there was no hurry.

Bellamy shrugged and finally took a step away from her. Without his presence overwhelming her, she allowed herself a full breath.

"It's not my job to question *when* a person gets married." Bellamy carefully adjusted the canvas he was carrying. "'Tis only my job to question *who* a person marries."

She arched a brow. "Seems like you're having a hard time with even that lately."

He arched his brow back.

"The week of finding Deirdre Whitcomb a match is coming to a close." She knew about Senator Whitcomb's visit to Bellamy and the weeklong deadline for finding a match for his daughter. Everyone in St. Louis and the surrounding countryside had heard about the challenge. No one understood exactly why the match was so important. Some speculation abounded that a much older politician wanted to marry Deirdre and Senator Whitcomb couldn't turn the fellow down without ruining his political career.

Bellamy blew out a tense breath that told Zaira the young matchmaker hadn't yet been able to find anyone Deirdre would accept. With only one day left before the week's end, Bellamy was likely to fail. And if he failed in this important match, he would lose the confidence of the community—a confidence he'd just started to gain after the matches he'd formed for three of the Shanahan siblings. In fact, if Bellamy was unsuccessful with the senator's daughter, then Oscar wouldn't let his son take over as the official matchmaker, at least not for a while.

"I'm friends with Deirdre," she said.

"Is that a fact?"

"Oh aye." Well, maybe *friends* was a stretch. But Zaira did have the same social circle as Deirdre and was familiar with the young woman since they'd grown up together.

"So now you think you'll be telling me the kind of man Deirdre needs?" Bellamy's lips quirked with the beginning of a smile—an arrogant one that said he didn't believe Zaira had any information to offer.

"I can help you, Bellamy. But if you don't think so, then go ahead and keep looking for a match. I'm sure you'll figure it out since you're so smart."

"I will figure it out just fine, so I will."

She shrugged and gave him her most innocent smile. "Good luck." She turned and began to walk away. She could feel Bellamy's gaze trailing her, the heat of it scorching her skin. It wasn't fair that one man could affect a woman so intensely. Why couldn't she have that effect on him? Instead, she only seemed to annoy him.

She made a point of walking as gracefully as possible for a few more steps before she turned, pressing her hand against her chest, to the spot where he'd been staring a few moments ago.

He was still watching her, and his attention shifted to where she was holding her hand, just as she'd intended. "If you change your mind and want the name of the love of Deirdre's heart, you know where to find me."

She didn't wait for his response. Instead, she continued down the street.

Aye, she was going to use Bellamy McKenna for research whether he wanted it or not.

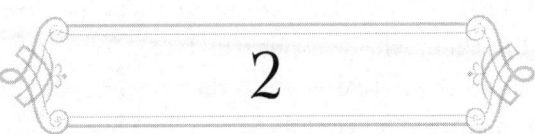

2

*T*oday is the day, Bellamy." Oscar's voice boomed
through the apartment, stirring Bellamy to wake-
fulness.

He stretched on the sofa where he slept most nights. Even
with his eyes closed, the bright daylight coming in the open
windows indicated that it was at least midmorning.

A shadowy presence stepped above him, one containing
the waft of strong coffee. "You better have a good and decent
fellow lined up for the senator's daughter."

What a great way to start the day, with Oscar nagging him
just as he had all day yesterday.

"I've got it under control, so I do." Bellamy draped his
arm over his eyes and pretended to sleep so Oscar would go
away and leave him alone.

"Ach, it doesn't look like you have control of anything."
Oscar's loud slurp filled the quiet of the apartment. "Least
of all that young woman."

Bellamy inwardly sighed. The only word Deirdre Whitcomb knew was *no*. She'd said it to at least twelve candidates

he'd presented to her, including an old flame he thought she still cared about.

Even using his unconventional methods, Bellamy hadn't convinced her to fall for any of the men. And rightly so, if he was honest with himself. None of them had been good for her. But then, who was her true love?

His thoughts jumped back to the conversation he'd had with Zaira yesterday when he'd run into her on his way to one of the galleries.

Even just thinking about that woman again sent a jolt of heat through his gut. Ach. Whyever did she have to be so beautiful every time he saw her? Not only had her rosy cheeks and bright green eyes been prettier than usual, but the gown she'd been wearing had molded to her body, showing every blessed hill and valley of her figure.

Thankfully her stunning red hair had been mostly tucked out of sight. Because whenever it was down, he could hardly think coherently around her and usually made a total bumbling blaggard of himself . . . Although he'd acted like a bumbling blaggard around her yesterday, too, letting himself get carried away with staring at her.

"Well?" Oscar hadn't budged from the spot beside the sofa.

"Doncha be worrying." Bellamy forced his thoughts from Zaira to Deirdre. "I have just the right man for her."

It wasn't entirely a lie. He might not know the right man, but Zaira did.

"Oh aye. I can help you, Bellamy. But if you don't think so, then go ahead and keep looking for a match. I'm sure you'll figure it out since you're so smart."

He'd have to humble himself and tell Zaira he'd been

wrong and that he needed her help after all. He nearly groaned at the prospect of doing so. Not that he was opposed to apologizing. He'd had to do his fair share of that over the years. But the idea of having to admit he was wrong to Zaira was like having to eat dirt.

Oscar took another noisy slurp of coffee. "I don't need to be reminding you that everyone is watching how you handle this. Everyone. And if you don't form the right match, you'll be setting yourself back."

Bellamy was just beginning to earn his reputation as a good matchmaker, and he couldn't afford any mistakes now.

Aye, the stakes were high.

Part of him wanted to shrug and pretend he didn't care. He had his artwork, and that fulfilled him. He'd sold a decent number of paintings already as W. B. M., which stood for William Bennett Moore. Bellamy had chosen the name of an American because no curator wanted to buy paintings from an Irish immigrant. He'd discovered that in his early days of trying to gain interest in his work.

Only after switching and taking a new identity had his paintings started to sell. Until the cholera outbreak, he'd been doing well. Mr. Davenport, the curator at Templeton & Evans, had started to ask about Mr. Moore having a show at the gallery. Of course, Bellamy had told Mr. Davenport that Mr. Moore was not open to the idea, that he was too unsociable.

Regardless of the opportunities starting to open up, Bellamy had anticipated inheriting the matchmaker role for most of his twenty-two years. Every oldest son in the McKenna family had taken up the job through the centuries—

his da, granda, great-granda, and more as far back as they could recall to the Middle Ages and even beyond.

Bellamy couldn't be the first to walk away from it or, worse yet, fail at the job. No, he had a responsibility, and he took it seriously.

Not only that, but he'd learned over the past six months of helping the Shanahans find their matches that he was good at pairing couples. He hadn't been sure at the beginning with Finola Shanahan. But once he'd started down the road of matchmaking, he'd realized that the matchmaker blood ran thickly through his veins. He'd loved every moment of finagling and scheming and planning. He'd even enjoyed the challenges and overcoming the difficulties.

More than anything, he'd felt an incredible sense of satisfaction when he'd been able to bring two people together in real love relationships that would last forever. The McKenna matchmakers might be unlucky in finding love for themselves, but they had a magic touch when it came to finding love for others. That was all that truly mattered. If Bellamy could spend his life helping others succeed where his own family had fallen short, then maybe he could make up for all their mistakes.

Oh aye, he was ready for the full responsibility of matchmaker, had dreamed of the day when he would take over for Oscar. But if Bellamy didn't prove himself with the senator's daughter, no one would want to come to him. It wouldn't matter that he'd had success with the Shanahans.

No, everyone would hear of his failure and assume he didn't have what was needed to be a matchmaker. They would likely take matters into their own hands and form matches without any help. Already many among the younger generation were doing so and forgoing the wise input of the matchmaker. After time, a new generation would believe the role of the matchmaker was no longer necessary, and it would fade into oblivion as an antiquated relic of bygone years.

If he didn't prove that a matchmaker was capable and necessary, then the loss would be his fault, at least in St. Louis.

Bellamy blew out a noisy breath, opened his eyes, and met Oscar's probing dark gaze. The older man's face was ruddy and perspiring, and the day had barely begun. His thick gray hair was combed into submission but wouldn't stay that way for long. At sixty, he was slowing down, the years of living by the philosophy that "it was never too early for a decent draught" showing in his heavy paunch and big veinous nose.

"Did you hear me now?" Oscar's voice boomed louder.

"How can I be forgetting the consequence of failing when you've told me a few dozen times a day for the past week, so you have."

"Instead of being direct with the lass, have you tried a subtle approach?"

"Aye—"

"The matchmaker is all about being able to feel the pulse of a relationship, expecting the unpredictable, and not controlling love—only guiding it."

"Naturally."

"She might be grazing in the same pasture every time and need help seeing that the grass is greener elsewhere."

Bellamy knew the job of the matchmaker was to keep the lass from getting stuck on the same kind of men and turning her out to a new pasture with someone she might not have expected but who was actually better for her.

Bellamy stifled a sigh. "I've heard your advice plenty and am doing it just so."

"Then get yourself up and make haste." This time Oscar lumbered away from the sofa through the tidy but sparsely furnished apartment. With two bedrooms and a main living area, the place was spacious enough for all of them, though Bellamy didn't have his own room. He didn't mind, since he wasn't in the apartment often.

A moment later, Oscar exited and started down the creaking steps to the pub.

Bellamy pushed himself up until he was sitting on the edge of the sofa. With the late hours they worked at the pub every night, they usually weren't early risers. Bellamy kept even later hours painting in the shed, so it wasn't unusual for him to sleep away the mornings, sometimes not getting up until almost noon.

But today, he knew as well as Oscar that he was wasting time abed when he still had the looming challenge of finding a partner for Deirdre Whitcomb.

Somehow everyone had learned of the senator's challenge and of Bellamy's confident response that he would find a match for the man's daughter. If only the senator had given him longer than a week.

But Bellamy had discovered the senator was getting pressure from Senator Snyder, who held the position of majority leader and was a powerful man. It had taken only a little asking around for Bellamy to learn that most of the younger senators did Snyder's bidding or ended up with ruined reputations and short political careers.

The rumor circulating around St. Louis was that Snyder wanted to marry Deirdre. But since he was a widower in his forties, Deirdre had refused, and her father didn't have the heart to force her into the marriage. He'd come to Bellamy to form a love match for his daughter, probably hoping a hasty marriage to a man Deirdre loved would provide a feasible excuse for why she wasn't available to Snyder.

Regardless, Bellamy was failing the mission. Now he had no choice but to talk to Zaira and see if she could help him.

"So?" Jenny's question came from the kitchenette off to the side of the living area.

Bellamy rested his elbows on his knees, then buried his face in his hands. He loved his sister, but he wasn't in the mood for a lecture from her this morn any more than he'd been needing the lecture from Oscar.

Her agile footsteps crossed the room toward him. She stopped in front of him and held a cup of coffee low enough that the waft of the strong brew rose to fill his senses.

He took the mug from her. "Thank you."

She smoothed a hand through his hair just like she'd always done since he'd been a wee babe. "You're a grand man, Bellamy McKenna. Doncha be forgetting that because I sure won't be."

With twelve years' age difference, Jenny had been more like a mother to him than sister. In fact, Jenny had been the one to raise him for most of his childhood. She'd fed and clothed him, rocked him to sleep when he'd been fussy, hugged him when he was scared, and kissed his scrapes when he'd been hurt. She'd been there for him every step of his life with a fierce, motherly love he'd never gotten from their mam.

The only thing he'd gotten from Mam was his love of painting. During the rare times when Mam had been around and available, she'd taken great pleasure in teaching him how to paint. She'd always come to life when she held a paintbrush in her hands. Her melancholy had disappeared for a short while, and in those moments, she'd been someone he'd admired and someone he'd wanted to be like.

If only Oscar had accepted her for who she was, painting and all. But he never had supported his wife's talent or efforts. He'd only criticized her and made her feel bad about painting, the same way he had with Bellamy.

Bellamy had long ago determined that he didn't care what Oscar thought of his painting. Oscar could criticize him all he wanted, but it wouldn't change Bellamy's desires or plans to paint. He intended to carry on and do everything his mam had dreamed of and never been able to accomplish.

Jenny's fingers smoothed back his hair again before she cupped his cheek. "You know that even if you make this match, you'll still have to do the one thing you don't want to if you plan to solidify your place as the next matchmaker."

He knew what she was referring to—the pressure for the matchmaker to get married. It wasn't necessarily a requirement, but most people would be more willing to take marital advice from a married matchmaker than from a single one. Bellamy understood the logic. He just hoped to prove he was different.

He offered his sister a half grin. "So, you're trying to scare me away from following in Oscar's footsteps, are you?"

Her beautiful brown eyes regarded him seriously. She had such pretty features, but over recent years she'd grown more haggard, especially her eyes, which had taken on a perpetually tired and sad look.

Bellamy suspected some of the sadness had to do with the

fact that she'd never been able to have any children of her own. Now that she was nearing her midthirties, perhaps the reality of her childlessness weighed more heavily. Whenever he asked her about it, she always denied that she wanted children, claimed that raising him had been enough for her. But he suspected if given the chance, she'd take a baby or two of her own.

She bent and kissed his forehead, then straightened. "I'm just wantin' you to be happy, Bellamy."

He offered her a grateful smile. "I know. And I thank you, Jenny."

She pressed both hands to his cheeks and held him in place. "Regardless of what you think, you weren't meant to do this life alone."

She was hinting again at his need to take a wife, but he ignored it. "That's why I have you."

"Oh aye. You'll always have me." She held him for a few more seconds, her eyes still sad. Then with a sigh, she released him and started toward the door.

He wanted to reassure her he'd be fine without a wife, but he'd already done so on other occasions. Yet she still persisted in pushing him toward marriage.

She was as well aware as he that every matchmaker in their family had problems with their spouse leaving, cheating, or divorcing them. Their marriages had apparently started with renowned love and passion, but each one had eventually combusted with disaster.

Bellamy wasn't sure why the matchmakers were lucky with others but so unlucky in love for themselves. A part of him suspected his family was cursed, and that no matter how hard he might try to avoid the curse, he'd end up unlucky too.

Curse or no, he couldn't put off marriage forever. But he intended to delay it as long as he could—hopefully for years, until he was older and more mature. Maybe after growing in his matchmaking skills, he'd eventually have the discernment to choose a partner wisely and be able to break the unlucky streak or curse or whatever it was.

For now, though, he wasn't rushing into anything. No matter what Oscar or Jenny might say, he was waiting to get married.

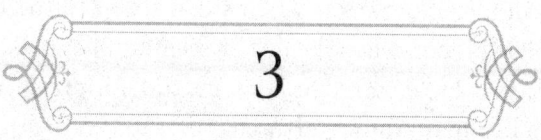

3

*B*ring *more depth of feeling to the romance.*"

Zaira tapped her pen against her lips and stared out at Dover's Pond. Mr. Knapp's editorial suggestion had played round and round her mind for the past hour that she'd been trying to rewrite the romantic scene between the heroine and the man she loved and wanted to marry. The two shared only a short kiss, but no matter what Zaira put down, she ended up crossing it out.

She tossed her pen onto the manuscript pages, then let herself fall back into the long grass and wildflowers that surrounded the pond. With her skirt hiked past her knees and her feet already dangling in the pond, she swished the water as she peered up at the vast blue sky.

She had to get this next segment perfect. If she failed to deliver what Mr. Knapp and the readers wanted, she would lose her opportunity to be a published author. In fact, her writing career could be over.

To get it perfect, she had to infuse more emotion into her story. But to do that, she needed to experience romance for herself, and she needed the practice of being with a man.

During her sheltered life, she could count on one hand the number of times she'd been alone with a young man who wasn't her family. Maybe twice? Three times at the most, if she counted the occasion when she'd stood in the hallway with Coyle Nooan when the rest of their families had lingered in the parlor. He'd stared at her with stark appreciation, but he hadn't said anything personal.

"Ugh." Zaira splashed a foot in frustration, sending droplets over the bare skin of her legs and knees. "No wonder I can't write realistically." There was so much of life she had yet to live, so many emotions she hadn't felt, so many things she'd never done.

When it came to the romance in her story, how could she possibly write with more depth when she'd never been in love, never even come close?

She closed her eyes and puckered her lips. What would a kiss feel like? As she touched her fingers to her lips, she tried to imagine soft lips against hers. It would be tickly and sweet and would make her feel cherished, wouldn't it?

But even as she tried to guess what a kiss would evoke in her, she sighed. "Oh, Zaira, you're pathetic."

"I'd have to agree."

As her eyes few open, she released a squeak and bolted to a sitting position.

There, standing only a few feet away, was Bellamy Mc-Kenna. He had a vest over his shirt, which was rolled up at the sleeves. His hands were stuffed in his trouser pockets, and his flatcap was donned at a rakish angle.

Beyond him near the covered pavilion, he'd tied his horse. How had he approached without her hearing him? Had the rustling breeze and the buzzing of the cicadas masked his arrival? Or had she been too distracted to notice him? Too caught up in imagining what a romance would be like?

Had he seen her kissing the air?

From the smirk tugging up the corners of his lips, she guessed he had.

A flush swelled into her cheeks, but she merely lifted her chin and glared at him. "You shouldn't sneak up on people like that."

"Maybe you should be paying better attention to your surroundings. What if I'd been someone nefarious?"

"Nefarious?" She lifted a brow. "My, my, we're using big words today."

"Believe it or not, a person doesn't have to be a writer to use big words."

She hadn't known for sure if he was aware of her writing pursuits. But he'd obviously deduced it. Either that, or he'd gone into the newspaper office yesterday after seeing her step out of it and had wheedled Mr. Knapp into telling him what she was up to.

The best thing to do was pretend she wasn't surprised and act as though she wasn't perturbed by him in the least.

"Oh aye." She tried to form her lips into a smirk of her own. "Using big words has more to do with intelligence or the lack thereof."

"Naturally I'm very intelligent."

She scoffed. "And, of course, I'm not a writer any more than you are a painter."

His dark gaze hardened, and his jaw flexed.

Why didn't he want anyone to know about his painting? As a man, he couldn't possibly have the same obstacles that she had as a woman, could he?

Perhaps he'd taken a false identity because of family, which was another reason she used her pseudonym. Of course her family and friends knew she loved to read and write stories. And her parents were satisfied with those pursuits . . . as long as they remained firmly in the hobby arena.

She would be expected—just like her two older sisters—to get married and have babies. Not that she was opposed to getting married and having babies. She just wasn't ready quite yet. She wanted time to write and publish first, before her life became busy with everything else.

The truth was, if her parents knew she was starting an actual career as a published author, they wouldn't approve. Such aspirations weren't acceptable for a lady of an upstanding family like the Shanahans. And after the trouble her other siblings had caused over the past six months, Zaira refused to burden them with additional scandal.

For now, it was best to let them believe she was their "easy" daughter, the one who "complied" and "never caused trouble." Those assumptions allowed her to go unnoticed much of the time and have freedom to do as she pleased. Maybe they would never have to know about her publishing. Maybe she could keep her pseudonym forever.

Whatever the case, she needed Bellamy to understand that if he didn't respect her privacy, then she wouldn't be able to respect his.

His brooding eyes held hers.

She wanted to stay irritated, but the longer those dark eyes peered at her, the tighter her lungs grew, until she felt breathless. My, but he had such beautiful eyes, so expressive and rich, especially with such thick lashes surrounding them.

"So . . ." He was the first to break their intense connection by looking away.

She tried to draw in a breath, but as his gaze landed upon her bare feet and legs, her lungs squeezed shut again.

He ought to cast his sights someplace else as any gentleman would do under the circumstances. He should give her time to pull down her skirt and petticoat to hide her indecent exposure, especially since he'd caught her unaware.

But Bellamy McKenna was no gentleman. He was a rake, and he did as he pleased by taking his time in perusing every inch of her exposed legs.

She wanted to be outraged or, at the very least, scold him for his lack of good manners. But as his attention lingered over her pale skin, a strange warmth fanned to life low inside—a warmth that spread, a warmth that filled her with pleasure, a warmth that she didn't want to stop.

Was this similar to the feelings Mr. Knapp had referenced? If so, she clearly needed to experience more of it, and Bellamy was the perfect candidate to help her. She'd already decided that yesterday after their encounter. The attraction she felt for him was too undeniable and too delicious.

The trouble was, Bellamy would never agree to help her with research for her stories . . . unless they could strike a bargain—a bargain in which they both got something they needed.

And she knew exactly what he'd come for.

She couldn't keep a smile from tilting up her lips. "So, Bellamy McKenna. What brings you out to visit me on this lovely summer day? I gather it's not so you can ogle me, although you're doing a fine job of that so far."

He smirked in response. "Oh aye. I am doing a fine job, am I not?"

Too fine if the warmth continuing to flow through her was any indication. If he refused to be a gentleman and stop looking, then she had to put an end to the indecency. She lifted first one foot and then the other, setting both into the grass, and then pulled her skirt down over them.

As she did so, he finally lifted his gaze to meet hers. For just an instant, the dark brown of his eyes glowed with a barely banked heat—a heat that reached across the distance between them and sparked against her, sending tiny flames skittering over her skin, just like it had done yesterday and on other occasions she'd been near him.

Did he feel the heat too? Or was she just so enamored with him that she would take any look or word he was willing to give her and add more meaning to it than he intended?

She tucked her skirt more firmly around her legs. "What can I do for you?"

"I think you know."

"Do I?" She tilted her hatless head, her braid dangling over her shoulder and down her chest. Of course she knew he was there to get information about Deirdre Whitcomb. But Zaira wasn't about to make this easy on him. He deserved to work for whatever she gave him.

He scanned the surrounding woodland, thick with the foliage of brambles and briars and wild berries. Would the picturesque landscape end up in one of his paintings?

His gaze touched on each lily pad in the pond and the long cattails growing along the far end before settling on a log near the pier and a turtle sunning itself there.

"You told me you could help me with Deirdre." His voice

was soft and free of the arrogance that usually filled it. "I'm sorry I turned you down. I could use your perspective, if you're willing to give it."

A tiny needle of guilt pricked Zaira. She should help him because it was the right thing to do, not because she needed something in return. But she had only three days left to re-write the next segment of the story that included the kiss. And she had to get everything right or perhaps lose out on her chance to continue publishing.

Slowly she pushed up, shaking out her now-damp skirt. She didn't hassle with donning her stockings and shoes, but she did make a point of tucking her feet out of sight underneath the hem of her skirt. She wasn't sure why she was bothering, especially now that he'd already seen not only her feet but also her calves.

"You do actually know who Deirdre cares about, do you not?" His voice contained a note of exasperation. "I'm running out of time to make the match, so if you're not knowing, be kind enough to say so."

"I said I'd help you, Bellamy." She took a step closer. What should she ask him for first? "And yes, I know who Deirdre admires."

"Who?"

She moved again, this time putting herself directly in front of Bellamy and leaving only six inches—or less—between them. "If I give you the name, I'd like something in return."

His eyes rapidly narrowed. "What?"

She halved the distance so now only three inches remained. She was close enough she could hear his breathing.

If he was intimidated by her nearness, he wasn't showing it. He didn't move and didn't react, not even in surprise.

She had the urge to walk her fingers up his arm and across his chest as she'd once seen her oldest sister, Finola, do with her husband, Riley. Finola had finished her finger-walk at Riley's top button, then had fisted a hand in his shirt and pulled him down for a kiss.

Zaira guessed such a move would be entirely too bold. Nevertheless, she had to keep going. Too much was at stake if she acted shyly.

Sucking in a steadying breath, she reached out and laid her hand on Bellamy's arm.

His gaze snapped there like he'd been stung by a hornet. "What are you doing, Zaira?" His voice was low and full of warning.

Warning of what? She shrugged as nonchalantly as possible. "I need to do some research for my writing. And I'd like your help."

He stared at her hand for several long heartbeats before lifting his eyes to hers again. "What kind of research?"

She hadn't really thought through her plan. What exactly did she want Bellamy to do? Hug her? Perhaps kiss her? That surely ought to be enough to help her understand romance, wouldn't it? "I was thinking one hug and one kiss."

"Holy mother." He took a step back and shook his head, a strange panic filling his features.

She grabbed his arm. "Please, Bellamy. I wouldn't ask if it weren't important."

He was still shaking his head, his eyes wide.

"Okay, no hug. Just a kiss."

"I'm not kissing you."

"It won't mean anything. It's not like I want to have a relationship with you. In fact, I don't even like you."

The panicked look seemed to ease from his features. "You don't like me?"

"No." Maybe she liked him a little. Or a lot. But she didn't *want* to like him. And that was mostly the same thing, wasn't it?

He studied her as though he was reading her thoughts, probably realizing her denial had been too adamant.

"Okay," she said. "I admit I find you a smidgen attractive. But I don't want to marry you or anything close to that."

"So, you'll help me with Deirdre if I help you with your research by kissing you?"

She bit her bottom lip. She wanted to tell him yes, that was the only way. But she wasn't so desperate that she would deny him help if he really was opposed to kissing her. "Listen, Bellamy."

He was staring at the bottom lip she'd just worried between her teeth. And the brown of his eyes was dark and melted and dangerous.

She couldn't keep from releasing her hold on his arm. Something about him was so magnetic that she was liable to be drawn in and lose herself to him if she wasn't careful.

"I'm listening," he whispered, a small smile beginning to tug at the corners of his lips.

Did he think she was silly? Maybe she was, but she didn't care. "It obviously has to be a good kiss and one full of feeling. But that's all."

He nodded slowly. "How long does it have to be?"

"I don't know. How long are kisses supposed to last?" See, this was why she needed to do the research.

He shrugged, his smile turning sly. "It can last as long as you want."

"Then let's agree to a time limit."

"What will be sufficient for your research?"

"Half a minute?"

His brows shot up.

What did that mean? Was half a minute too long or two short? Probably too short, if the kissing of her married siblings was any indication. "Then two minutes."

"Two minutes of kissing?"

"You're right, that's too long. Maybe one."

He crossed his arms, the muscles in his forearms taut. "And when would you like to do this one-minute kiss?"

"The sooner the better. I need to turn in my next segment in three days."

He hesitated. "So, your story has a kissing scene?"

"Just a brief one, and the editor says it needs to be more realistic."

"Does it now? And you think kissing me will help you convey that?"

"Aye." She actually didn't know, but it was worth a try.

He glanced around again, probably checking if they were alone.

Which was a good idea. She needed to make sure no one—especially her two younger brothers—was near to witness her bold behavior in kissing Bellamy McKenna. She didn't want word getting back to her da and mam that she was a loose woman.

Oh, sweet saints. She pressed a hand to her chest. Would kissing Bellamy make her a loose woman? Maybe she shouldn't kiss him.

"What about a hug instead of a kiss?" Her question came out rushed and wobbly.

He stuffed his hands into his trouser pockets. "You decide. 'Tis your research."

"Then let's stick with a hug."

He shrugged as if either a kiss or a hug was all the same to him. Maybe they were. And maybe she was having a moment of worry for nothing.

"So now that we have that worked out," he said, "will you be telling me the man for Deirdre?"

"We haven't picked a time or a place for the hug."

With an exasperated sigh, he stepped forward and reached for her. "Let's get this over with."

She batted his hand away. "Eww. No. I won't hug you like this, not with that kind of attitude."

His brows shot up again.

"It has to be romantic, sweet, tender, and full of emotion."

"That wasn't part of the bargain."

"Oh aye, it was implied. What good is a hug if it doesn't have any romance to it? Then I may as well go hug my mam."

He shoved his hands back into his pockets. "Fine. You're right."

"Of course I am." She sniffed, then turned up her nose at him. "We'll meet here at the pond tomorrow at this time, and you can hug me then."

"Why not now?"

"Because I want to be dressed for the occasion and in the right mood."

This time he looked at her like she'd grown antlers out of her head.

She supposed she was being a bit dramatic about it. But

she loved drama, and the anticipation of meeting up with Bellamy secretly tomorrow for a romantic hug would certainly inspire her writing.

"I can't wait for tomorrow to discover Deirdre's match."

"Zach Meier."

Bellamy's forehead furrowed, and she could see him trying to place the name.

"The Meiers own the breweries—"

"Aye, I am just a wee bit familiar with the Meiers."

Of course he would be, since they likely provided much of the beer sold at Oscar's Pub. "Deirdre met Zach last summer when a group of us went to the horse races together. He was sitting near us and introduced himself to her. I could tell right away they were meant for each other."

"Could you now?" Bellamy's tone held a slight note of sarcasm.

"You're not the only one who has a gift for finding true love. I happen to have an excellent instinct too."

Bellamy was silent several heartbeats, as though trying to decide whether to believe her. "Zach Meier's family is German and Protestant." He spoke with a finality that said the matter was settled.

"They fell in love with each other." She picked up her manuscript and pen in one hand and her stockings and shoes in the other. Then she started toward the path that led back to Oakland. "Love doesn't respect boundaries based on a country of origin or a way of worshiping. True love pushes past all that, Bellamy. And you know I'm right."

She waited for him to argue with her. But he didn't say anything. When she glanced over her shoulder a moment later, he was striding to his horse.

4

ellamy pushed his horse faster, urgency driving him. From the galloping close behind, he knew Zach Meier and Mr. Meier were still following him.

They were almost to the levee, and Bellamy prayed they weren't too late, that Senator Whitcomb hadn't left with his family yet. While Bellamy had been at Dover's Pond with Zaira, the senator had sent word to the pub that he was taking his family out of the city to a place safe from the crowds and cholera. The Whitcombs were leaving midafternoon on a steamer heading north to Iowa, where apparently Mrs. Whitcomb's sister lived.

The senator had thanked Bellamy for his efforts but had indicated that he wasn't waiting any longer. Even though Bellamy still technically had the rest of the day to arrange a match, the senator had given up on him and now probably hoped to delay dealing with Senator Snyder's proposition by hiding his family away.

Bellamy didn't blame the fellow. The possibility of finding a match for Deirdre hadn't looked too promising, not after all her rejections that week. But after speaking with Zach Meier, Bellamy conceded that Zaira had been right about the pair. He could see that the sharp-thinking man was exactly what the indecisive Deirdre needed. Zach was also good and kindhearted, even if he was German and Protestant. Maybe Zaira was also right about those things not mattering so much when it came to love.

Bellamy hadn't told Zach or his father why he needed them both to come with him to the levee. Instead he'd insinuated that it had to do with a shipment of malt that the newly formed Public Health Department was considering confiscating because of the speculation that malt was one of the contributors to cholera.

The Meiers intended to get to the malt first, since they didn't believe it had anything to do with the cholera. Bellamy didn't think it did either. But the consumption of malt was one of many theories floating around about the cause of the deadly disease. In the desperate quest to bring the epidemic to a halt, people were willing to try just about anything, especially because each day the disease seemed to run more rampantly.

As Bellamy veered his horse onto Front Street, the levee spread out before them bordered by the long row of warehouses in the process of being rebuilt after the recent city fire. The drays pulled by mules and horses milled about among the stacks of merchandise, bales of hemp, hogsheads of tobacco, and the many other goods brought to St. Louis every day.

The waterfront wasn't as busy as usual—fewer dockhands, businessmen, and passengers. There were fewer steamboats too. Even so, dozens of them still lined the shore of the Mississippi River, their tall smokestacks coughing out cinders and black coal smoke.

It hadn't taken much investigating for Bellamy to discover which steamboat the Whitcombs were traveling on. It usually wasn't hard to get information. The people coming and going from the pub provided a wealth of it, or at the very least offered a name or place where he could seek out what he needed.

Now he scanned the smaller packets for the name *Prairie Princess*. He found it almost right away. Thankfully, the passengers hadn't yet boarded and were waiting near the gangplank while their luggage was being loaded.

He headed directly toward the steamboat and could hear Zach and Mr. Meier on his trail.

Bellamy spotted the senator in a top hat and fine white suit, his long sideburns and slick mustache giving him a distinguished air. Beside him his wife stood underneath a parasol, her yellow-and-white lacy gown the latest fashion. Deirdre was chattering with one of her younger sisters, and they, too, held parasols and wore bright summery gowns.

Deirdre wasn't necessarily a pretty girl, especially compared to a stunning beauty like Zaira Shanahan. But she was lovely in her own way. Bellamy needed to get a view of her face when she first glimpsed Zach. Then he would know for certain if the match was meant to be. The eyes were almost always windows into a soul, and expressions often spoke louder than words.

As he reined in near the Whitcomb family, he positioned his horse so he could see both Deirdre and Zach.

"Good afternoon, Senator." Bellamy nodded at the gentleman.

The senator nodded back. "Bellamy McKenna."

In that moment, Deirdre caught sight of Zach, and her conversation with her sister came to an immediate halt. Her eyes widened and seemed to take in the young man hungrily, as though she hadn't ever expected to see him again and now couldn't get enough of him.

That was a grand sign.

Zach and his father were reining in beside Bellamy, but their attention was on a warehouse farther down the levee, the one that usually housed the malt and other brewing supplies.

The senator's brow furrowed. "You did get my note, didn't you, Bellamy?"

"Oh aye, that I did."

Deirdre still hadn't taken her gaze from Zach.

Bellamy cocked his head toward the Meiers. "I saw you as I was passing by with the Meiers and thought I'd make sure you're certain you're ready to be done with the matchmaking."

Mr. Meier finally fixed his attention on the Whitcomb family. He gave the senator a nod before turning his anxious gaze upon Bellamy. "Should Zach and I ride on ahead?"

"You've met the Whitcombs, haven't you?" Bellamy asked.

At the name Whitcomb, Zach's head whipped toward the family, and his gaze flitted over everyone until he found Deirdre. Something in his expression changed, came to life, but also filled with a quiet pain.

The reaction was the final confirmation Bellamy needed. It was clear Zach cared about Deirdre but didn't think he could ever have her. Perhaps he'd even heard about the matchmaking for her over the past week but hadn't come forward as a candidate because he didn't think he had a chance of winning over her parents or his, not when the Germans and Irish in St. Louis didn't get along.

Well, it was time to push the fellow to a fight—this one a fight for the woman he loved.

"I've heard of the senator but never met him." Mr. Meier tipped his hat first toward Senator Whitcomb, then his wife. "Nice to meet you, Senator. Ma'am."

"This is Zachary." Bellamy waved a hand at Zach. "He runs half a dozen breweries here in St. Louis with his father. We're here to make sure the supply of malt doesn't get confiscated."

"Pleased to meet you both." The senator spoke the words perfunctorily, doing his duty to remain friendly with constituents even though he obviously was in a hurry to take his family out of the city.

Deirdre was still staring at Zach with stars shining in her eyes.

Zach offered her a smile.

She gave him a tremulous one back.

"Zach and Deirdre." Bellamy pretended to suddenly remember them. "If I recall correctly, the two of you have met before, haven't you?"

Deirdre nodded, her smile widening. "Yes, we've known each other since last summer."

Zach hesitated with a sidelong look at the senator before responding. "I have had the pleasure of making Miss Whitcomb's acquaintance. You have a lovely daughter, Senator."

"Thank you." The senator smiled at Deirdre, but upon seeing the way she was peering up at Zach, as if the sun, moon, and stars revolved around him, his smile faded. He glanced sharply back at Zach, who met his gaze head-on without faltering.

Good for him. Bellamy inwardly cheered the fellow on, praying he wouldn't back down. A little competition would help push Zach into the fight. "I've been working with the Whitcombs this week in trying to find a match for Deirdre."

Zach's eyes rounded, enough for Bellamy to realize the young man actually hadn't gotten the news about the matchmaking. Now that he knew, would he step up on his own and make an effort to win her? Or would he need a nudge? Maybe even a shove?

"We're taking a break from the matchmaking," the senator said to Zach. Did his voice contain a warning?

"Oh aye." Bellamy made his voice as casual as possible. "Deirdre had a dozen men who are interested in her."

"A dozen?" A note of dismay tinged Zach's tone.

"Deirdre is quite the catch, so she is."

Zach returned his attention to Deirdre. "I agree. She is very much a catch."

The young woman's cheeks flushed, and her eyes filled with obvious pleasure at Zach's compliment.

"You're not a half-bad catch yourself." Bellamy infused his tone with humor, hoping to mask the seriousness of his hint.

Mr. Meier had raised his brow and was now paying close attention to the interaction happening with the Whitcomb family.

"You've done well for yourself." Bellamy spoke quickly before Mr. Meier could interject any negativity. "From what I've heard, your breweries are so profitable that you've been investing in real estate both inside and outside of St. Louis."

Zach shifted in his saddle, clearly not quite comfortable talking about his wealth. "That's right."

Zach's father's expression turned more severe as though warning Zach to walk away from the young woman, that this wasn't the time or place to start working on a match.

But Bellamy couldn't let the matter slip away. Not yet. At the very least he had to ensure that the two young people were seriously considering each other before the conversation came to a close.

"Ach, I'm surprised you haven't been snatched up yet by some lucky lady." Bellamy grinned broadly. "Maybe you'd like me to be helping you find a match. I'd have a long list of interested families."

"Maybe . . ." Again Zach looked at Deirdre.

Mr. Meier shook his head. "I appreciate the offer, Bellamy. But we'll find Zach a good Protestant woman."

At the word *Protestant*, everyone seemed to stiffen, including Zach.

They might as well get the differences between the two families out in the open now rather than later. Bellamy crossed his hands casually, resting them on his thigh. Then he watched Zach, waiting for the young man to take the lead in the conversation. Something in Zach's posture said he didn't agree with his father. And Bellamy was hoping he'd say so.

Before Zach could speak, Deirdre's father frowned. "What's wrong with a Catholic woman? They make excellent wives too."

Perhaps Senator Whitcomb wasn't opposed to social and religious differences. As a politician with constituents of all races, cultures, and denominations, maybe the senator had already learned to set aside personal preferences for the greater good of the community. If so, the match would be easier if at least one set of parents was open to the merging of two cultures.

Zach met the senator's gaze levelly. "There's nothing wrong with Catholic women, Senator. And my father knows that I don't have a preference toward Protestantism or Catholicism."

Mr. Meier shook his head. "There are too many differences—"

"If we love God first and foremost, that's all that really matters."

Bellamy nodded at Zach. "Well said."

Zach released a tight breath, perhaps drawing courage from Bellamy's affirmation. "In fact, I would be willing to convert to Catholicism for the right woman—"

"I won't allow it." Mr. Meier's countenance was growing stormier.

The senator, on the other hand, was studying Zach with keen interest—an interest Bellamy recognized in a potential father of the bride. Mr. Whitcomb clearly appreciated an open mind as well as a man who was willing to compromise. And he was seeing that in Zach.

"With all due respect," Zach said firmly to his father, "I plan to choose the woman I marry."

"Your mother will be even more opposed to a match with this family—this woman." Mr. Meier cocked his head in Deirdre's direction.

Inwardly, Bellamy gloated. Just what he'd wanted—one of the family members bringing up the match first so the idea appeared to be theirs and not his.

"If Mother opened her mind, she would love Deirdre."

"Of course, anyone would," the senator interjected while staring at Mr. Meier. "Deirdre is the most agreeable woman I know, next to my wife, that is." He smiled fondly at his wife.

Standing beside Deirdre, the middle-aged woman returned his smile before patting Deirdre's arm tenderly.

Deirdre's eyes were brimming with undeniable hope.

On the river behind them, the *Prairie Princess* gave a long whistle, beckoning the passengers to board.

"Time for us to go." Mr. Whitcomb took his wife's hand.

Deirdre, her gaze locked on Zach, didn't immediately turn. Zach was watching her too, and something seemed to pass between them—something Bellamy could only describe as heated sparks.

Something that reminded him of the heated sparks that had flared in a similar fashion between him and Zaira earlier.

Mr. Meier's frown was still in place, but he said no more.

At this point, Bellamy knew he didn't need to speak again either. He'd done his job in bringing the couple together and had planted the seeds for a match. Now the union would need to unfold in its own time. It wouldn't happen today. But it would eventually.

In the interim, he'd look like a failure for not finding the senator's daughter a husband by the allotted time. But at least in the long term, Deirdre would end up with the right man—the man she loved—and that was truly all that mattered.

With a final nod toward the senator, Bellamy picked up his reins and guided his horse toward the warehouse. Without Zaira's input, he wouldn't have been able to facilitate this "accidental" meeting. He was in debt to her and owed her everything she'd asked of him.

But no respectable man would ever carry through with her bargain, not when she'd asked him to meet her alone and kiss and hug her. Of course, she'd changed her tune and asked for only a hug. . . .

For research purposes.

He nearly laughed out loud again as he had earlier. What sane man would be able to resist kissing her once he had her in his arms? Not him, that was for certain. That meant the best way to avoid the entire situation was to stay away from her—far, far away.

Would she be mad that he'd broken his part of the bargain? Naturally so.

But he wouldn't let a little fear of Zaira's reaction push him into doing something daft.

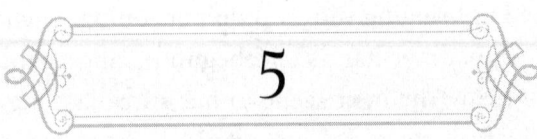

5

*H*e wasn't coming.

Zaira ceased her pacing to glance around the pond. Again. But only the same dense woodland greeted her as it had during the past hour of waiting.

She fisted her hands on her hips and glared at a doe and her two fawns grazing on the opposite side of the pond. "You're a scoundrel, Bellamy. A big, big scoundrel."

A strange disappointment sliced into her. No, she wasn't sad about not getting a hug. Well, maybe a little. Because she couldn't deny she'd been dreaming for the past twenty-four hours about what it would be like to stand in Bellamy's embrace.

More than that, though, she was upset he hadn't carried through with his part of the bargain. She thought he was a man of his word—honorable and true and trustworthy. Even if he'd changed his mind about hugging her, she'd expected that he would at least meet her at the pond and tell her she had to come up with a different exchange.

Not that she wanted anything else . . .

Had he sensed her ardor? Was that why he'd broken their bargain?

Maybe it was for the best. After all, it was improper for a lady to be alone with a man and hug him. Women of her status and upbringing simply didn't encourage such things.

She dropped her hands and began pacing again. She'd tried rewriting the next scene in her story last night, had hoped the feelings and depth would come to her without experiencing anything with Bellamy, but she'd failed miserably at coming up with new and exciting material. She'd only put down more drivel.

"I wouldn't be here either if I didn't need it," she said, trying to assuage herself.

She hadn't heard any news from the city on whether or not Bellamy had succeeded yesterday in matching Deirdre Whitcomb. Maybe he'd failed and therefore assumed the bargain was obsolete.

But that was the thing about bargains—they didn't become obsolete. He had to do his part regardless of how things had turned out for Deirdre's match.

She paced several more times along the pond's edge before lengthening her stride toward the path that led to Oakland. She would go back to the house and tell her mam she was riding into the city to take Alannah and Kiernan produce from the garden. Mam had just complained earlier in the morning that the newly married couple needed the fresh food, that it would help them stay safe from catching cholera while they resided in the city for a little longer to enjoy some privacy.

While in town, Zaira would *just happen* to ride past Oscar's Pub. She'd stop and find out why Bellamy hadn't followed through on their agreement. Surely doing so wouldn't hurt her or cause any trouble.

Zaira hurried across the road and down the lane to the sprawling Italianate-style home surrounded by the tall oaks that gave Oakland its name. She quickly located her mam in the library. Mam opposed her going into the city—just as Zaira had predicted—even with the offer to visit Alannah and Kiernan and find out how they were faring.

Somehow, though, Zaira managed to outtalk and out-maneuver her mam. She was, after all, the sneakiest of her siblings and could get away with much more than anyone else. It wasn't something she was proud of, but it was a skill she utilized to her advantage.

A short while later, she was mounted and speeding along the dirt road that led into the city. Once she entered the outskirts of St. Louis, she headed down St. Charles's Street in the direction of the big sign with *Oscar's Pub* in bright green calligraphy, contrasting the white background.

Young ladies like herself didn't enter pubs. But as she reined in outside the two-story building in the heart of St. Louis's Irish district, she pushed aside all the rationale that told her to wait and to send in a message for Bellamy to come outside and speak with her. She didn't want to chance Bellamy sneaking out the back door and avoiding her. No. She needed the romantic interaction with him today, soon, if she hoped to turn in her next story segment on time.

Without giving herself the chance to overthink her plans, she tied up her horse, then headed directly to the front door of the pub. As she opened the door a crack, she threw off her straw bonnet, patted her loose curls, and then pinched her cheeks to bring color to them.

With what she hoped was an alluring smile, she pushed the door wide and stepped inside.

The dimness of the room greeted her first, along with the strong scent of cigar smoke and beer. As she closed the door behind her, the low hum of conversations around the room tapered to silence.

From what she could tell, only a dozen or so people were present, mostly older men who were smoking and playing cards. A lone fellow at the bar counter had paused mid drink to stare at her. In a pale face with a purplish nose, his eyes seemed dark but not dangerous. His reddish hair was standing on end, and his garments were rumpled.

Bellamy wasn't in sight, but his paintings were. They graced the walls, each containing landscapes as beautiful as his other paintings. The difference was that these didn't portray local scenery. Instead, they resembled what she imagined Ireland would be like. Perhaps they were of Ireland, and perhaps Bellamy had painted them when he was younger and still lived there. After all, Bellamy had immigrated with his family when he was twelve, which was only ten years ago.

Bellamy's sister, carrying a platter filled with steaming bowls, entered the pub from the kitchen area. At the sight of Zaira standing near the door, she halted, her eyes widening. The tray wobbled, and the bowls on it clattered together.

Although Zaira didn't know Jenny well, she'd seen her occasionally over the years at parades, mass, and other gatherings. She was quite a bit older than Bellamy and didn't have any children of her own, which was a shame because she'd always seemed to mother Bellamy so sweetly.

Jenny set the platter onto the bar counter and continued to stare at Zaira, clearly not expecting a woman to be there.

Zaira fumbled backward a step. Maybe she ought to leave. Before her fingers connected with the door handle, Bellamy breezed into the pub from the kitchen too. He was carrying another platter, probably the noon meal for everyone there. After all, it was about that time of the day. And now half her day was wasted.

If her manuscript segment hadn't been due tomorrow, she wouldn't care what time it was. But with every minute that passed, her nerves were stretching tighter. So much was at stake with this next part of the story, and she had to get it just right.

Bellamy rounded the bar and strode toward one of the tables without acknowledging her presence.

He might try to avoid the coming confrontation, but she wasn't the type of woman to step aside quietly and let any man ignore her. "Bellamy McKenna, you're a scoundrel."

He kept his eyes on the thick mutton stew as he began to set the bowls around the table in front of the men. Its rich flavor with a hint of Guinness permeated the air.

He was wearing an apron over his shirt and trousers, but nothing could hide his lean, muscular frame. His dark hair was slicked back, and his jaw had a slight layer of dark scruff as if he hadn't taken the time to shave today.

It was a shame Bellamy was always so good-looking *and* genuinely caring about people. It was easier to dislike handsome men when they were mean and arrogant.

"Bellamy," said the older man at the bar counter, "the young lady is talking to you and said you're a scoundrel."

"I have ears, Georgie." Bellamy set another bowl down.

"They must not be working."

"Oh aye, they're working just fine."

"It's your mouth that's not working."

"It's working fine too, so it is."

Georgie made a humming noise at the back of his throat as he stared at Zaira again. "Then I guess it's your eyes that aren't working. Because you cannot see that a beautiful lass is here for you."

Bellamy gave what could only be described as an exasperated sigh and shake of his head. He finished setting the last bowl down before he turned to face Zaira. "What I see is a bothersome lass."

Georgie's grin spread wide, revealing a mostly toothless mouth. "She's *bothering* you all right."

The other men in the room guffawed.

Although Zaira wasn't quite sure what Georgie was referring to, Bellamy tripped over a chair leg.

Maybe her presence there was affecting him more than he was letting on.

The realization sent a shot of energy through her. If she was going to get him to follow through on the bargain, maybe she needed the men in the pub to join her in nudging Bellamy into action. She didn't necessarily want him to hug her in the middle of a pub since it wasn't exactly romantic, but where else would he do it? Out on the boardwalk or on the street? No, a small audience inside was better than outside, where anyone might walk by.

"Bellamy McKenna, we made an agreement, and you failed to uphold your part of it."

He was swiping up random coffee cups left on the tables and setting them on the now-empty platter. "The match didn't go through."

"But the information I gave you was correct, wasn't it?"

Bellamy hesitated enough that she knew it was.

"Then you owe me regardless."

He scoffed. "I've canceled the bargain."

She wasn't prone to easily losing her temper like her red-headed da and older sister Enya. But at the moment, her temper felt like a wild beast in a cage, and for some reason Bellamy had a way of poking the beast so it longed to be unleashed.

She fisted her hands at her sides.

Bellamy tossed her a dangerously crooked grin, one that almost seemed to mock her. "Go home, Zaira Shanahan, and stop trying to play grown-up."

Play grown-up? Now he'd really done it. He'd not only poked the beast, he'd set it free. "I don't need to play grown-up." She started toward him, a thud to each of her steps. "Because I already *am* grown-up."

At her approach, he narrowed his eyes upon her.

Back at the bar counter, Jenny hadn't moved from where she'd placed her tray. Her round eyes were watching every one of Bellamy's moves. And so were Georgie's.

Zaira guessed the other men were enjoying the interaction too. She might as well make this as dramatic and interesting as possible. No sense in the whole scene being boring.

She didn't stop until she was in front of Bellamy. Before he could react, she took the platter from his hands, practically tossed it on the table, and then clasped his hands in hers. She didn't give him time to react or pull away. Instead, she jerked him forward so that he stumbled against her. In the same motion, she slid her arms up around his neck.

His eyes widened in surprise. He obviously hadn't expected her to force him to carry through with their agreement. But she was, even if she had to initiate it all.

She locked her hands in his hair, digging her fingers in

deep. Then, before she could allow herself to second-guess what she was doing, she stood on her toes and pressed a kiss against Bellamy's lips.

He remained as still and cold as a marble statue and didn't bother to put his arms around her.

His lack of response only fueled the redheaded temper again. She knew nothing about kissing, but she was determined to make the most of the moment, especially now that she'd started it. With an enthusiasm she'd witnessed when her older siblings kissed their spouses, Zaira moved her mouth against Bellamy's, opening up and capturing his lips with hers.

She could admit she loved the hardness of his mouth and the firmness of his lips. She loved the strong length of his body so near to hers. And she loved the smoothness of his hair in her fingers.

Aye, she was conscious of her audience. And aye, she could hear a faint warning bell at the back of her mind telling her she was taking things too far. But she was too mad to care and too stubborn. She was kissing Bellamy, and that was all there was to it.

Besides, Bellamy wouldn't push her away in front of the customers. She was betting his pride would force him to interact with her just a little.

"Give it back to her!" came a call from one of the men.

"Unless you don't know how," said another.

"Maybe that's why he failed in the senator's match. Because he doesn't know how to kiss."

She could feel Bellamy's muscles tense, the comments obviously needling him. Still, he didn't move.

She leaned toward his ear and whispered one word. "Coward."

Then she started to lower herself and pull away. Should she raise a hand and slap his cheek? Or should she toss him a glare, then stomp out?

Before she could decide, Bellamy's arms snagged around her, he angled his head in, and his lips caught hers in a surge of emotion.

Passion.

Fire rippled through her body, especially the parts of her that were connected to Bellamy. Her flesh was scorched, her blood hot. And her lips? They felt suddenly cherished and desired and needed all at the same time.

This was what she'd been wanting, the emotions she'd needed to experience, the pleasurable connection she'd been waiting for.

Bellamy's hand at the small of her back pressed her hard. Was he just pretending? Or did he feel everything too?

She honestly didn't want the kissing to end, wanted to keep on going, wanted to keep the closeness with him.

But in the next instant, he pulled back abruptly, letting go of her and taking a rapid step away. He tossed a glare toward the men he'd just served. "There. Are you satisfied I know how to kiss?"

The men were beaming as if they'd just been given the greatest show on earth.

"Oh yeah!" shouted one.

"That's the way it's done," called another.

The calls bordered on lewd, but Zaira was trying to live in the moment and let the experience saturate her senses. Her lips were swollen and warm. Her blood was pumping at double the speed. Her nerves tingled with a need to be touching him again. And her heart . . .

She splayed a hand over her chest to capture the rhythm of the wild beating. Her heart was tapping out a song of its own—a new melody she didn't know but wanted to hear more of.

Would it be possible to do more research with Bellamy? With this kind of emotion flowing through her, she would constantly have a source of inspiration, wouldn't she?

"Thank you, Bellamy." Her voice was breathless.

His dark gaze collided with hers, sending more heat crashing over her. What was this? They weren't kissing or hugging, and she still felt like they were. Was it possible to facilitate passion even without physical contact?

Did she even want to?

"It's done." Bellamy's whisper was so low she could hardly hear it. "And it better not happen again."

6

*H*e'd just kissed Zaira Shanahan. In public.

What in the wee devil had he done?

"Whoo-ee!" Georgie slapped his hand against the bar counter. "I always knew that when Bellamy found the right woman, he'd be a goner."

Bellamy was standing close enough to Zaira that he could see the hurt in her eyes at his comment about not kissing again. He meant it. He couldn't kiss her again. But he didn't have to be a donkey's hind end about it.

"He's a goner!" Georgie shouted again. "Madly in love."

"Who's madly in love?" The door of the pub opened, and Oscar stepped inside. The midday sunshine outlined his bulky body and poured past him into the dimly lit room.

"Bellamy's madly in love." Georgie's grin was much too big for the occasion. "And he just kissed Zaira Shanahan."

Bellamy couldn't deny he'd enjoyed the kiss. Any denial would be a total lie. From the moment Zaira wrapped her arms around his neck and moved against him, his body had flared to life with a need for her so intense that he hadn't been able to resist kissing her back. Oh aye, he'd tried not to, had tried to think about other things, had tried to pretend she wasn't there, had tried to ignore her luscious lips and her hot breath and her soft body.

But he hadn't been able to think about anything but her. The longing for her had risen so strongly that it had cut off his heartbeat and breathing, leaving him incapacitated and able to do only one thing—kiss her back.

Just once. That's all.

"Well, it's a good thing Bellamy's ready for love." Oscar threw the door open wide. "Because it's time for the matchmaker to be finding a match."

"So it is," someone echoed.

Oscar stepped back outside and cupped his hands around his mouth. "Let it be known!" he shouted in his loudest voice to the passersby. "I'm now accepting offers for forming a match with Bellamy! Spread the news far and wide through the Kerry Patch and beyond!"

As he shouted it again, Bellamy wanted to roll his eyes at Oscar's theatrics, but he folded his arms instead.

Zaira had taken another step away from him, putting a table between them. She was even more beautiful now than she'd been when he'd stepped out of the kitchen with lunch for everyone. In fact, he'd nearly stumbled at the sight of her. With her long hair down and her cheeks rosy from the heat and her green eyes so vibrant, he'd had a hard time preventing himself from stopping and staring at her. But he'd forced himself to walk past her and deliver the food.

Of course, she hadn't been willing to let him snub her. And she'd been right. He shouldn't have canceled their bargain. It hadn't been noble of him. If he'd done as he said, then he would have avoided having her come to town and seek him out in a public display that was sure to cause gossip.

He didn't necessarily mind the gossip about himself. He was more worried about her reputation. Even if she was maddening, he didn't want people speaking ill of her.

Oscar waved at several people, shouted something more, then stepped back inside. "After failing to match the senator's daughter," he said as he made his way toward his corner table where his leather journal sat, "Bellamy has no choice now but to form a match of his own. 'Tis the best way to be saving his reputation as the new matchmaker and showing himself to be responsible."

Since the meeting between the Meiers and Whitcombs yesterday, Bellamy had talked about Zach Meier being interested in the senator's daughter. He'd hoped the news would alleviate some of the censure that might come his way for failing to find someone for Deirdre in a week's time. But most people were focused on his inability to close the deal and make something happen.

Whatever the case, Oscar was being too pushy. "There's no need to be rushing—"

"Oh aye, there's a need." Oscar scraped out his chair and plopped down.

Zaira was inching her way toward the door. She was probably hoping to leave without any more notice. Her parents likely had no idea she'd come to the pub. If they discovered her presence here, they would be angry with her, even scandalized.

"No more putting off marriage, Bellamy." Oscar opened his ledger. "You have to be proving to everyone that you know all about love and marriage and relationships."

All the dormant frustration inside Bellamy swirled into a growing storm. Oscar had no right to preach about proving things he knew nothing about. He hadn't loved his wife the way she'd needed, and his lack of sensitivity and hardheadedness had driven his wife to drink and eventually desert their family. If Oscar couldn't make a marriage work, why did he think Bellamy could? Especially when he was well aware the McKenna matchmakers were unlucky in finding true love?

"The match between Zach Meier and Deirdre will eventually work out. I felt the *thin breeze* between them." Bellamy tried to infuse his statement with a determination he wasn't yet feeling inside.

A thin breeze was usually one close to the ground that most people missed but that signified a change in weather. The same was true in relationships. Other people might miss the thin breeze—the slight changes in a relationship—but not the matchmaker.

"Thin breeze or no, you still have to be seen as responsible." Oscar leafed through his ledger, scanning each page as he did so. "And there's no better way to be learning about love than to experience it for yourself."

Zaira had reached the door and started to open it.

"Stop right there, young lady." Oscar didn't look up.

Bellamy hadn't been sure if Oscar had even noticed her presence. But the old matchmaker was obviously still as keen as he'd always been—one of the traits Bellamy had inherited.

Zaira paused.

"I hear Bellamy's in love with you."

"That's not true!" Bellamy's denial came out too forcefully, and once spoken, he wished he could pull it back and say it again more casually.

60

As it was, Oscar paused in perusing his ledger and raised a brow at Bellamy.

"Oh aye, it's the truth." Georgie picked up one of the bowls of stew still sitting on Jenny's platter. "We all saw the way he just kissed Zaira Shanahan."

Zaira lifted her chin and met Oscar's gaze bravely, as though she intended to take full responsibility for all that had happened between them.

"It wasn't really a kiss," Bellamy said, trying to figure out a way to save Zaira from being drawn into the situation. "And it didn't mean anything."

"Whoo-ee!" Georgie called out again almost gleefully. "If that wasn't a kiss, I don't know what is."

Several of the other men chortled and made comments under their breath about how it was definitely a kiss.

Oscar already had the mistaken impression that Bellamy liked Zaira—or at least was attracted to her. No doubt, now after discovering they'd kissed, he would start planning a wedding right away.

Bellamy needed to set Oscar straight. "I'll not be marrying Zaira. So don't even say it."

Her narrowed eyes shot to Bellamy. "Bellamy McKenna, you're arrogant for thinking I would marry you. Because the fact is, I wouldn't consider it, not even if you were the last man standing in St. Louis."

Her voice was filled with a derision that took him off guard. He wasn't used to women disliking him. Before he could think of a response, she flung open the door the rest of the way, stepped out, and then slammed it shut behind her.

With the echo reverberating in the silence, Georgie tried

for a whistle through his toothlessness. "You blew that, Bellamy."

He shrugged. "I'm not getting married, especially not to her."

Oscar was quiet, staring at the closed door. All eyes swung to him. Everyone was waiting for his final say about the kiss with Zaira. As if that mattered.

Bellamy started toward the bar counter, suddenly needing to get away from the scrutiny and the gossip and the pressure. As he moved past Georgie and rounded the counter, he could see in the large mirror behind the bar that Oscar was watching him now.

"Fine." Oscar's voice boomed through the pub. "If not her, then you'll have to choose someone."

"We'll see about that, won't we now?" Bellamy halted beside Jenny, avoiding her gaze, which was full of a hundred questions. Oscar had already told him the Shanahans would be looking for a match for Zaira soon and that James Shanahan would want his youngest daughter to have a profitable match with someone in her social class, especially since her brother Kiernan had recently married a poor housemaid.

It didn't matter to Bellamy. He wasn't considering Zaira or anyone. And Oscar would learn that soon enough, because no matter how stubborn Oscar was, Bellamy was more stubborn. No matter how savvy Oscar still was in finding matches, Bellamy was equally as savvy and would find a way to outwit him.

He held Oscar's gaze in the mirror for another moment. The glint in Oscar's dark eyes said that he intended to win the coming battle.

Bellamy forced a grin in return, one he hoped conveyed

that he also planned to win. In fact, he had no intention of losing. He'd rather stay single than doom himself—and more importantly doom his future wife—to a lifetime with an unhappy marriage.

The door of the pub swung back open, and Bellamy couldn't stop himself from anticipating Zaira's return to sling another comment at him.

The breathless, sweating person that stumbled through the door wasn't Zaira. He was Mr. Boland, the watchmaker from the corner shop down the street. Had he run all the way to the pub?

"Oscar!" the spindly man called as he bent over and gasped for air. "I'm here to be the first to offer my daughter in marriage to Bellamy."

Before Mr. Boland could catch his breath, a second man bumped into him from behind, Mr. Flemming, who owned two boardinghouses in the Kerry Patch as well as several rental homes. A burly fellow with a severe expression, he lifted his flatcap from his head and scowled at Mr. Boland. "I would have been the first if you hadn't pushed that cart in my way."

Folding his hands on his protruding belly, Oscar reclined in his chair, a grin settling over his countenance. "Come on in. I'm ready to start the meetings." As Oscar spoke the words, he looked directly at Bellamy. "Let's find my son a match."

7

*S*he'd been foolish to kiss Bellamy in the pub two days ago.

Zaira sat primly on the wicker chair on the veranda in the shade, her mind unable to focus on the Sunday afternoon visit with Kiernan and Alannah at Oakland. Instead, her thoughts circled around to Bellamy and the realization that she'd been rash in kissing him so publicly.

Her parents hadn't heard about the kiss yet. If they had, they would have been irate and spoken to her about her indecency.

Seated on a chair beside her, Mam held herself with the usual poise, her petite frame perfectly positioned, her elegant summer gown perfectly fitted, and her brown hair perfectly parted down the center and looped over each ear. Aye, Lucinda Shanahan, with her dainty features and porcelain skin, was always a picture of perfection.

Da reclined in the wicker chair beside Mam with Kiernan and Alannah sharing the porch swing across from them. Kiernan and Da were built alike with wide shoulders and muscular frames. Both were dressed in low-cut vests and tailored frock coats with silk cravats and high starched collars that framed their smoothly shaven chins and cheeks. Both were also talkative and had carried most of the conversation so far since they'd gathered on the wide wraparound porch of the country home to avoid the stifling heat inside.

Her two younger brothers, Madigan and Quinlan, sat at the opposite end of the veranda, playing chess. At sixteen and fourteen, the two were rarely so quiet and still—only on the day of rest when they were required to cease from their usual activities. After returning from mass at the nearby parish church, they'd shed their cravats and vests and had unbuttoned the top two buttons of their shirts, which was as far down as Mam would allow them.

Without a breeze, the humidity was heavy, and Zaira wished she had the same freedom to undo her buttons, or at least to shed the frilled manchette cuffs at her wrists. Better yet, she would have taken off her petticoats or gone without her corset. But she held herself as gracefully as possible, even though she was sweltering under the layers of her heavy Sunday gown. She'd also done her best earlier to remove the ink stains from her fingers.

She was taking extra precautions today to be as ladylike as possible, hoping no one would think her capable of the kiss in the pub—if the topic came up.

If only she'd been more rational and had thought through the ramifications of her actions. But she'd allowed her anger at Bellamy to push aside all reason, wisdom, and logic. Now, if word spread about her kissing Bellamy, she'd cause another scandal for her family, which was exactly what she'd hoped to avoid with her venture into becoming a published author.

Why had she let Bellamy antagonize her? Had she really needed the research? Or had she just been looking for an excuse to see what kissing Bellamy would be like?

She stifled a sigh, then pumped her paper fan near her face, barely moving the muggy afternoon air but rustling the big leaves of the potted plant, one of the many that decorated the veranda.

From the swing, Kiernan pinned her with another disappointed look similar to the one he'd given her when he'd first arrived. That had to mean he'd heard rumors about her, didn't it?

If he knew about the kiss with Bellamy, how long before he told Da? How long before someone else shared it with Da while he was in town? How long before the neighbors learned the gossip and then brought it to Da's attention?

Zaira spread her hand over her churning stomach. She didn't want to cause her parents any grief. They'd considered her their easiest child since she was quick to comply, was always helpful and cheerful, and was also usually even-tempered.

But once they learned of her mistake, they would surely be mortified. She would lose her place as their sweet daughter, and she would be nothing more than an utter embarrassment to them.

Alannah reached for Kiernan's hand and squeezed it. He wrapped his fingers around hers in return. His features softened as he took in his wife's beautiful face framed by her pale blond hair. As her blue eyes connected with his, she seemed to be imploring him about something.

He released a tight breath and gave her an imperceptible nod before returning his attention to Da and the ongoing conversation about the Committee of Public Health that Riley, their brother-in-law, was helping to lead and the much-needed changes the committee was quickly trying to implement to curb the spread of the cholera.

Although Alannah had served as a maid first for Enya and then at Oakland, Zaira had never thought of her as a servant. It had been easy to see from the start that Alannah wasn't an ordinary woman, especially to Kiernan.

As an avid reader, Alannah was a skilled editor. If not for Alannah's help in editing, Zaira wouldn't have been able to garner Mr. Knapp's attention. In fact, Alannah had been the one to first suggest the need to enhance the authenticity and depth of emotions between her characters.

While Alannah's feedback had been helpful, the kiss with Bellamy had maybe been even more so. Zaira had used the feelings from the exchange with Bellamy to stir her writing, pouring out her heart and emotions into the story. When she'd turned it in and Mr. Knapp had skimmed it, he'd offered her a genuine smile and told her that readers would enjoy the next chapter by K. S. Flanders and that he was happy to keep working with the fellow.

Zaira had left the office elated . . . but only until she'd passed by Oscar's Pub and witnessed a dozen or more fatherly aged men lined up outside. She'd only had to inquire of someone passing by to know that Oscar was serious about finding Bellamy a match and half of St. Louis's Irish community had come out to talk to Oscar about it.

Of course, Bellamy was a catch for his influence and standing in the community, and it was no surprise that every single woman on the western side of the Mississippi was in love with him. How could they not be with how handsome, charming, and kindhearted he was? She'd already been half-way in love with him, even before experiencing that kiss with him at the pub. Now despite her intentions to hold off on marriage, she fancied him even more.

"So, what other news from the city can you tell us?" Da tapped his cigar into the crystal ashtray on the wicker table beside him. A chunk of ashes fell off before he lifted the cigar and took another puff, the sweet but spicy waft of tobacco lingering heavily in the air.

Kiernan glanced again at Zaira, and this time, the accusation there was more than she could bear. Oh aye, he'd definitely heard about the kiss that had transpired with Bellamy. But he'd likely been tasked by Alannah not to say anything, which would account for why he'd remained silent about the issue.

Yet, how long could he stay silent before blurting the truth?

Zaira needed to talk to him before that happened.

She pushed to her feet, and a moment later both Kiernan and Da stood politely too, as was done in the presence of a lady. But was she a lady anymore after her indecent behavior?

"Kiernan, would you like to take a short stroll in the gardens?"

He raised his brow at Alannah, as though seeking her permission.

She squeezed his hand. "Oh aye, take all the time you need." The offer was gracious, especially since Alannah wasn't entirely comfortable with Da and Mam and was still adjusting to her changing role in their family.

Da and Mam were likely adjusting to that changing role too. It would take time for them and the community to see Alannah as more than a maid. But at least they were being kind to her.

Kiernan held out the crook of his arm to Zaira. She took it, and together they descended the front stairway and meandered across the manicured yard toward the side of the house. Mam's flowers along the house had wilted in the summer heat, but the raised herb beds as well as the vegetable garden were still doing well.

"So you're enjoying married life?" Zaira asked as they rounded the corner and the front veranda disappeared from sight.

Kiernan glanced over his shoulder and then turned his full glare upon her. "What were you thinking, Zaira? Kissing Bellamy like that?"

"I figured from the scowls you kept giving me that you'd heard."

"Everyone left in St. Louis has heard."

She pressed one of her hands to her forehead. "Oh bother."

"*Oh bother* is right." Kiernan didn't slow their steps but instead seemed to pick up the pace as though he was anxious to get her as far away from any listening ears as possible.

"I didn't mean for it to happen." Technically she'd gone intending to only hug Bellamy. The kiss had taken things too far. Regardless of what she'd planned, she should have dragged him out into the alley, maybe even into his shed studio first. If only he hadn't been brash and stubborn, and if only she hadn't overreacted.

The muscles in Kiernan's arm flexed. "Does that mean Bellamy took advantage of you? Because if he did, so help me, I'll teach him a lesson he won't soon forget."

"No, the kiss was my fault." She wished she could explain to Kiernan that she'd done it to add more realistic emotion to her story. But she didn't think Alannah had shared anything about her secret writing life with Kiernan.

"What happened?" Kiernan shook his head. "No, never mind. I don't want to know. It doesn't matter. All that matters is that we do what's right moving forward."

"What is the right thing, Kiernan?" Zaira looked up at her older and wiser brother. "What should I do?"

"That's exactly what we need to figure out." Kiernan's voice contained his usual authority.

She stooped over the fence and plucked a ripe cherry tomato from one of the plants. The garden spread out beside the summer kitchen, a low brick building that was white-washed like the house. The barn with the conveyances and livestock stood behind the kitchen and was bordered by meadows of wildflowers and a woodland.

It would certainly be a pretty landscape for Bellamy to paint.

She gave a curt shake of her head. She didn't want thoughts of Bellamy to invade her at times like this. She needed to put him from her mind once and for all. But how could she when she found herself reliving their kiss every quiet moment she had? And how could she when she was filled with an undefinable longing to kiss him again?

Of course she wasn't planning on kissing him a second time. Once had been sufficient to learn about realistic romantic feelings, hadn't it?

She popped the cherry tomato in her mouth and savored the rush of sweetness.

Kiernan had halted and was studying the house, as if the stately home with its large windows and balconies and expansive porch held the answers to all their troubles.

"I'm worried about Mam and Da finding out," she said softly.

"And I'm worried about another scandal."

With Kiernan's marriage having caused a stir in St. Louis society, they'd been less warmly received at mass this past week. They also hadn't had any invitations to visit friends or be a part of any gatherings—although that could be attributed to the cholera.

While Zaira had never given much thought to their family's status and reputation, Kiernan had always cared much more. Although he was learning to put less emphasis on what people thought—especially about his marriage to Alannah—he still had businesses to run and couldn't afford more problems.

Kiernan's brow furrowed in thought. "So Oscar is looking to match Bellamy."

"Oh aye. Oscar was very vocal about it when I was there."

"To salvage Bellamy's reputation because he failed with the senator's daughter." Kiernan wasn't asking. He clearly already knew everything.

It was too bad Bellamy hadn't been able to make the match between Deirdre and Zach Meier. Maybe Bellamy's timing hadn't been right. Or maybe other issues were at play—like the family differences. Whatever the case, Oscar was indeed pushing Bellamy into marriage. "Bellamy doesn't want a match for himself. He was actually quite opposed to it."

Kiernan shook his head, irritation in his eyes. "It doesn't matter if he's opposed. We'll work out a deal with him."

"Work out a deal?"

"Since each of you needs a match, you'll choose each other."

Zaira could only stare at her brother. She didn't realize her mouth was hanging open until he nodded at it. She closed it, swallowed, and then tried to formulate a coherent thought. "That's impossible . . . I would never . . . He would never . . . We don't like each other and don't get along—"

"This will all be temporary, just until all the rumors about the two of you fade." Kiernan nodded as if the matter was settled. "After a month or two, you can both go your separate ways and tell people it didn't work out. By then everyone will have forgotten about Bellamy's failure with the senator's daughter. And no one will be thinking about the kiss you and Bellamy shared."

Zaira's mind began to spin with what Kiernan was proposing. "So, you're suggesting I have a pretend relationship with Bellamy?"

"Do you want to avoid upsetting Mam and Da?"

"Very much so."

"They won't be happy to hear you and Bellamy kissed, but it won't bother them as much if you're matched with him."

"But the McKennas? Would Da agree to another match outside our social circles?"

"In all the matchmaking meetings that Oscar has held this week, he's let it slip that he has quite a bit of wealth. Even so, I think Da is learning, like me, that happy unions take more than money and family status to work."

This whole plan was taking things too far. "I don't like it, Kiernan. Essentially I'll be lying to Mam and Da."

"It'll be like playing a role in a theater production . . . just until the gossip dies down."

She hesitated. It didn't feel right. Although she wasn't sure why because she was already lying to her parents about her publication efforts.

Kiernan glanced in the direction of the front of the house as if to remind her they needed to return to the others before someone came looking for them.

Could she really play a role with Bellamy? And pretend to have a match with him? The plot might not be truthful, but it was interesting. It would be full of drama and excitement and would give her plenty more inspiration for her stories.

Her blood began to thrum faster at just the prospect. Did she dare agree to such a plan? It was bold and would likely be fun. And surely they could keep it harmless. After all, who would it hurt? Not her or Bellamy. Not Mam or Da. It would help keep her family from more disgrace.

"Well?" Kiernan's tone was demanding.

She shrugged one shoulder. "Even if I agree to it, Bellamy won't."

Kiernan stalked back toward the side of the house. "Don't worry about him. I'll make sure he agrees."

She raced after Kiernan. "Wait. I don't want you to bully him into it."

"He deserves to be bullied after kissing you."

"Let me talk to him before you do."

"I'll be the one confronting him first."

"Then just talk to him and nothing more." She grabbed on to Kiernan's arm.

He didn't stop walking.

"Please, Kiernan." She tugged on him, trying to pull him to a stop.

With a sigh, he halted abruptly, his jaw twitching.

"If this is going to be believable, shouldn't I move back

to the city?" That would make things easier for turning in her weekly segments to the newspaper. She would be able to write in peace and then deliver the drafts without having to find excuses to ride into the city.

He shook his head. "With as bad as the cholera is getting, I'm contemplating moving Alannah to Oakland."

"At the very least, let me come with you for a few days, just until I can talk with Bellamy and see if we can work out this arrangement."

Kiernan studied her face, as though sensing there was more to her request than she was letting on. "Fine. You can come home with us for now. But you'll be returning to Oakland with Alannah soon."

She smiled and then clapped her hands together. She hadn't realized how much she missed the busyness of the city, the interesting people, and the tension and conflict that played out on the streets. As much as she loved the beauty of the countryside, the city was where she found the life and inspiration for her characters and plots.

She would relish the time back. She might even relish feigning a relationship with Bellamy.

8

Desperation drove Bellamy out of the pub and into the kitchen. As soon as he was out of sight of the crowd, he bent over and tried to drag a breath through his tight lungs.

If he had to listen to one more father try to convince him to marry his daughter, he would go mad. He couldn't do it any longer.

The lingering scent of Dublin Coddle—the dish they'd served for supper with its creamy mixture of potatoes, onions, bacon, and sausage—filled his senses.

He needed a moment alone and was relieved that with the sun having set a short while ago, Jenny and Gavin had already gone up to the apartment. As usual, before retiring for the night, they'd moved the big cauldron of leftovers to low heat on the back of the stove for any latecomers to the pub. But most of the patrons on a Sunday night ordered drinks and weren't here to eat.

Tonight, the fellows were also here to talk with Oscar about the match—the match Bellamy didn't want. In fact, he'd made it clear again to Oscar after morning mass that he wasn't planning on getting married anytime soon.

Oscar had merely waved his large hand and said the timing didn't matter, that Bellamy could have an extended engagement—a year, even two. Oscar claimed that once Bellamy was in a relationship and headed toward marriage, that's all everyone needed to know, and they would think of him more favorably again.

The assurance had eased Bellamy's worries a little, and he'd pushed through the evening as best he could.

But now . . .

Bellamy straightened and stared past the disheveled kitchen. Dirty dishes and empty mugs were piled high on the worktable, and breadcrumbs and potato peelings littered the floor. The coal bin was nearly empty, and the bucket for water was drained dry.

Jenny and Gavin needed a kitchen boy who could help them with the mundane tasks. As business had increased and the popularity of the pub had gained momentum, the two had continued to shoulder the majority of the work. They weren't as young and energetic anymore and couldn't keep up the way they used to.

As much as Bellamy tried to help them in the kitchen, he also had more than he could handle pouring drinks and delivering the meals to the tables. Even though the spread of cholera and the slowing of business had alleviated a wee bit of the stress, the pub had been busier than ever for the past two days since Oscar's announcement.

"Ach." Bellamy rubbed the back of his neck, trying to ease the ache that had taken up residence there since the moment he'd kissed Zaira Shanahan.

It had been a mistake to kiss her. Pure and simple. He'd regretted it ever since. But that hadn't stopped him from thinking about that kiss. She'd been so pliable and responsive, hadn't pulled back or been hesitant. Instead, she'd been inquisitive, bold, eager, and full of emotion.

She'd been everything he'd imagined she'd be. Not that he made a habit of imagining sharing intimacies with Zaira. But there had been a time or two recently when his imagination had been all too vivid, and he'd envisioned her in all her fiery beauty, and he'd wondered if touching her would scorch him since the mere sight of her alone always did.

All it had taken was one kiss to learn that, aye, touching her had scorched his flesh all the way to his bones, and the heat still hadn't gone away. It burned through his blood like a fever, one he could only hope would cool with time, especially if he avoided her.

He guessed he wouldn't be able to avoid her forever. After all, the St. Louis Irish community was close-knit, and they were bound to run into each other. But when James Shanahan sought out the matchmaker for Zaira, Bellamy would have to let Oscar handle that one.

At the opening of the back door, Bellamy drew in another breath as Jenny hurried inside, her eyes wide, almost frantic. "Bellamy," she said with a glance out into the alley, "you have to nip along with all haste."

Bellamy tried to peer out the door past her, but the last of light left from the sunset didn't reach the shadowed alley that was surrounded mostly by tall buildings.

"Hurry with you now!" She closed the door and rushed toward him, directing him toward the front room of the pub.

Bellamy planted his feet and refused to go with her. "Whyever for?"

His sister looked again toward the back door as though she expected wild barbarian warriors to barge in at any second. "Kiernan Shanahan is out there and bid me to come get you."

"So . . . ?"

"So he looks angry enough to kill you."

Bellamy straightened, a strange resignation sifting through him. A part of him had been expecting someone from the Shanahan family to arrive and confront him for kissing Zaira. Even if technically she'd initiated the kiss, he could have backed away and put an end to her shenanigans before the kiss could go anywhere. Instead, he'd bent in and taken full advantage of the situation. He deserved to be called out for doing so.

If Kiernan wanted to reprimand him, so be it.

Bellamy took a step toward the alley door.

"No!" Jenny whispered harshly. "You need to nip along into the pub. You'll be safest there."

"I'm not running away and hiding from Kiernan." Bellamy broke free of his sister's grasp and started across the kitchen. "I'll be facing him like a man, so I will."

"William Bellamy McKenna." Jenny spoke his full name as sternly as she'd done when he'd been a boy and getting into trouble.

He didn't stop, though. He wasn't a boy anymore. He was a man. The truth was, he'd gotten himself into this predicament, and now he would be the one getting himself out of it.

As he opened the door and stepped into the growing darkness, the fancy Shanahan barouche parked outside the door was easy to see. And so was the brawny figure of Kiernan Shanahan as he leaned against the front wheel.

The driver was nowhere in sight. Perhaps Kiernan had sent him into the pub to afford them some privacy. Or so he could murder Bellamy without any witnesses.

Bellamy closed the kitchen door to keep Jenny from interrupting them, and then he strode straightaway toward Kiernan.

Kiernan pushed away from the wheel and stood stiffly, his fists balled at his sides. Jenny had been right. His expression did indeed radiate a murderous anger.

Bellamy didn't stop until he was close enough for Kiernan to take a punch, if that's what he chose to do.

And aye, that's what he chose. In the next instant, Kiernan's fist swung up and connected with Bellamy's jaw.

The sting radiated through Bellamy's head and down his spine. But he held himself in place, determined not to move or cower no matter how many hits Kiernan might take.

Kiernan didn't waste time in taking a swing with his other fist, this time into Bellamy's gut. The punch was just as hard as the first and nearly knocked the air from Bellamy.

The door of the carriage swung wide open. "Kiernan Shanahan, you stop beating up Bellamy right now." The voice came from the barouche interior and belonged to none other than Zaira herself.

"Stay inside," Kiernan called as he shifted back enough so he could raise a fist and plunge it toward Bellamy's nose.

At the impact, pain reverberated through Bellamy, and blood seemed to explode everywhere.

Zaira called out again, and from the corner of his eyes, he could see her step down from the carriage.

"Stop this instant, Kiernan." Zaira's voice held belligerence. "We agreed that you would talk and nothing more."

"I agreed to confront him." Kiernan rubbed at his knuckles, which would be bruised now too. "And I am confronting him. With my fists."

Even in the shadows of the alley, Zaira's beauty was as bright as a flaming sunset. She wasn't wearing a hat, and the red of her hair was darker tonight, almost auburn in the evening. Her delicate features were creased with earnestness, making her more striking. And her eyes were wider than usual, highlighting her long lashes.

Kiernan growled and started to raise his fist again—probably because Bellamy was ogling Zaira.

"No!" Zaira's sharp plea cut through the air, and she grabbed on to her brother and clung to him so he couldn't do any more harm.

Not that Bellamy cared if Kiernan battered him a wee bit more. Maybe if he showed up in the pub battered and bruised, he'd deter some of the fathers from wanting him for a son-in-law.

Kiernan glared at Bellamy for several long heartbeats before he lowered his arm. Even then, Zaira didn't let go of him.

Alannah hesitated in the door of the carriage, probably wondering if she should hold Kiernan back too. Of course Alannah was there. But why was Zaira? She shouldn't be in the city. She should have stayed at Oakland. Where she would be safe. And where he wouldn't have to worry about running into her.

"Let me talk to Bellamy." She pushed her brother toward the carriage door, and he didn't resist her. Or maybe he was no longer resisting because Alannah was reaching for him, her hands on his shoulders and then on his chest.

As Alannah guided him up into the carriage, Kiernan went along eagerly, didn't even seem to see Bellamy any longer. He had eyes only for his wife—eyes filled with a desire that told Bellamy that Kiernan was very happy with Alannah, just as Bellamy had expected he would be.

Bellamy couldn't keep from releasing a taut breath. He'd had to do some fine conniving in order to bring about Kiernan and Alannah's match, much more than he'd needed to do for Enya and Sullivan. But Bellamy was good at it. In fact, he'd been good at bringing together Zach and Deirdre too, even if he'd had a little help from Zaira and even if the match wasn't finalized yet. How many more people could he help find true love if he was given the chance?

He knew Oscar was right in trying to find him a bride, that doing so would increase his standing and trustworthiness in the community. People would start seeking him out for his advice and wise counsel the same way they did Oscar. It would show him to be responsible in the matter of love. After all, if he couldn't move things along in the matter of love for himself, why would people come to him to move things forward for them?

But how could he tie any woman to himself and the McKenna matchmaker bad luck?

Zaira gripped his arm and began to lead him away from the carriage. Like Kiernan, Bellamy was being dragged along and helpless to resist. Because he couldn't resist Zaira. He let her guide him, following after her, his hunger for her increasing with every step he took.

When she stopped beside the shed, he had the urge to pull

her flush and wrap his arms around her. It was almost as if he'd been waiting the past two days since last holding her for the next chance to do so. But that was ridiculous, because he was never going to embrace or touch or kiss her ever again.

As she pushed him against the shed wall, she already had a handkerchief in hand and was lifting it to his nose to ward off the bleeding. He needed to stop her. He could take the handkerchief for himself.

But as with before, he was helpless to resist. He let her touch the delicate cloth to his nose and gently press it there. Her thumb brushed against his lips, and she quickly moved it away. Even so, the touch seared into him, just as all her other touches had done.

"I'm sorry, Bellamy." Through the shadows, she was examining his face as boldly as she'd always done, which, if he was honest with himself, he'd always liked. He liked that she wasn't pretentious or shy or even coy. She was merely herself and didn't care about impressing him.

She dabbed again just as gently. "Kiernan is being a beast."

"If you were my sister and a fellow kissed you, I would be doing the same thing, so I would."

She just gave a shake of her head. "We both know I started the kiss and that you're not at fault."

"I could have stopped it."

"You did."

"I should have stopped sooner." He couldn't keep himself from glancing at her mouth, all too near, all too pretty, and all too kissable.

As if seeing the direction of his thoughts—or perhaps his gaze—she dropped her attention to the top button of his vest. Were her cheeks turning rosy? Was she thinking of their kiss again too?

A burst of heat fanned to life in his gut. And suddenly the air between them seemed charged and full of sparks.

Ach. This was no good. He didn't need or want to have chemistry with any woman, least of all a stunning woman like Zaira.

"We need to make a deal, Bellamy." She glanced around as if ensuring they were alone. The back door of the pub was opened a crack, and Jenny was peeking through, obviously worried about him. But they were far enough away, he hoped, that she wouldn't be able to hear his conversation with Zaira.

He took the handkerchief from Zaira. He had the feeling Kiernan was behind this deal, whatever it might be.

"We already had a bargain once," he started, "and look how that ended up."

"We both need each other."

"We do?"

"Oh aye. Both of our reputations are being questioned."

The heaviness that had been in his chest pressed down harder. Even though he'd warned the men in the pub the other day to stay quiet, they'd talked anyway, and word of the kiss had spread faster than a steamboat fire.

"Are people giving you a hard time?" If they were, it was his fault for not doing a better job in silencing the rumors.

"My mam and da haven't heard about it yet."

"And you don't want them to be finding out?"

"I'm afraid it's inevitable, don't you think? With the way the gossip has traveled already, 'tis only a matter of time before they learn of it."

He wanted to apologize. The words were on the tip of his tongue. But he held them in.

"But," she continued, "if I am matched with you, how can they get angry about a kiss?"

"Matched with me?" He shook his head and took a rapid step back. "Ach, no. That's not an option—"

"Hear me out." She placed a hand on his arm, probably to keep him from bolting.

He actually did want to bolt as far from her as he could because he couldn't consider a match with her. Not in a hundred years for a hundred different reasons.

"You need a match too, to save your reputation as the matchmaker."

"Doncha be worrying. I'll be finding a match on my own just fine." Or at the very least, he'd have a say in a few of the lasses Oscar narrowed down for him.

"We'll help each other out."

Being with Zaira wouldn't help him. It would only complicate matters. "Naturally you're attracted to me and want to be with me, but I just can't—

"Eww." She shoved against his chest this time. "Eww, no."

"Eww no, what?"

"Eww no, I'm not attracted to you."

"You sure kissed me like you were."

"It was for research, Bellamy. That's all." Her voice sounded exasperated. "I don't like you. And you don't like me. That's why a match between us would be so perfect."

He straightened and looked down at her more carefully. Though night was closing in, he could see the earnestness in her face. She'd made the declaration about not liking him before. Did she really mean it?

"You're too self-important for my taste," she stated, as if seeing the question in his eyes.

"Is that a fact?"

"It is." She peered up at him with her wide, honest eyes.

He could see no deception there, no games, no hidden motivation.

"Kiernan suggested that we stay in the match for a little while, and then eventually when the gossip dies down, we can go our separate ways, and no one will be the wiser."

Bellamy slid a glance in the direction of the barouche only to glimpse Kiernan with his arms around Alannah, kissing her as if he needed to in order to keep living.

At the sight of such passion, Bellamy's body tensed with sudden desire of his own—a strong need to be with a woman. After all, he was a man in the prime of his life and those kinds of needs were natural. It's just that he was usually able to pay them no heed, put them from his mind, and move on with life. All he had to do was remind himself of how disastrous his parents' marriage had been, how disastrous his grandparents' marriage had been, and how disastrous each matchmaker's marriage had been for generations. He wasn't repeating the mistake of locking into a marriage, chancing disaster of his own and hurting a woman he cared about.

But whatever Zaira was proposing, it was apparently only temporary.

"You'll be my fake fiancé, Bellamy." She lowered her voice to a whisper. "And I'll be yours."

Could such a plan work?

"We don't like each other," she persisted. "And we know each other's secrets. So it's actually a perfect arrangement."

Would it be a perfect arrangement, or would it only lead

to trouble? He was trying not to like her. But that didn't mean he could do away with all the attraction. It was much too strong, so strong that something inside warned him he needed to stay away from Zaira Shanahan instead of making an arrangement with her.

"What do you think?" She watched him with hopeful eyes.

He released a taut breath. "I think it's a dangerous plan."

"Dangerous?"

"It might not work."

She smiled. "You have nothing to worry about. I'm a grand actress."

"I'm not worried about that."

"Are you afraid you won't be able to pretend to be my fiancé?"

"I'm grand at acting too."

"Then what?"

Truthfully, he was afraid he wouldn't need to act, that being her fiancé would be too easy, and that he might even get carried away with his attraction to her.

He could feel her still watching him, waiting for his answer. With her looking at him like that, he had the overwhelming urge to bend down and capture her lips in a kiss. The need rose with such swiftness that suddenly he could think of nothing more he wanted to do.

And that was exactly why such a plan would never work.

He started to shake his head.

"Don't say no yet." The sincerity in her expression beckoned to him. "At least think about it."

He hesitated.

"Please?" Her whisper held a note of desperation he wanted to ignore but couldn't.

"Fine. I'll think about it and let you know." Without giving himself another chance to look at her, he started toward the kitchen door.

"You'll have to let me know soon, Bellamy." Her whisper chased after him, sending goose bumps over his skin.

If he was already having this kind of reaction to her after just a kiss, he had to stay away from her. Yet how could he, when she needed to repair her reputation and he was her only solution?

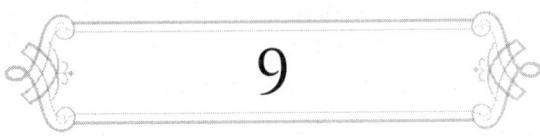

9

*Z*aira dangled from the second-floor balcony of her family's home. She gripped the wrought-iron railing with her bare hands even as she swung her legs around the side of the house. The toe of her boot caught in the trellis filled with ivy.

Sneaking out was as easy as always, maybe even easier because she only had Alannah and Kiernan to worry about and they were *busy*. Of course the family butler, Winston, was here too, but he'd already gone to bed.

She wedged her foot into the trellis firmly before hefting her body around to the side of the house. She grasped the trellis now with both hands and her other leg. She'd tucked the extra folds of her skirt out of the way, had learned to do that long ago so she didn't get tangled up.

Then without a moment of hesitation even in the darkness, she climbed down the twelve feet or so. When she had only a foot left, she let go and jumped the final distance, simply because she wanted to feel the exhilaration of escape . . . because that's what she was researching tonight.

Her character Frannie was sneaking out to meet with her love, and Zaira wanted to make sure she was writing realistically about the fears and concerns Frannie would have in the late hour of the night while creeping through the dark city streets.

In the story, the heroine would reach the rendezvous spot, the fellow wouldn't show up, and she later would learn he was imprisoned for a crime. Frannie wouldn't know he'd been falsely accused and would believe he was guilty. In trying to forget about him, she would force herself to accept a match with another man, only to later learn of her love's innocence.

It was the perfect twist to the plot, if Zaira could say so herself. But as usual, she was always looking for new ideas, and being back in the city would help.

Bracing herself against the house, she steadied her landing. Then she unhooked her skirt from the waistband, shook it out, and slid up the hood of her cloak. With a glance around to make sure no one had noticed her, she glimpsed only the deserted side yard that was bordered by a hedge. Through the shrubs, she could see the outline of the neighbor's house, but the windows were dark because the family, like hers, had left the city.

The truth was, she'd always been sort of invisible in her family. With all the busyness of having so many siblings, she'd sometimes been forgotten in the comings and goings and activities of everyone else. In her younger years, she'd sequestered herself away, acting out her stories. Then later, she'd taken to writing them down. So she supposed it had been easy to overlook her since she'd been occupied and content. She'd learned she could mostly do whatever she pleased, and no one would be there to stop her.

She honestly didn't need to worry about anyone seeing her tonight with how deserted the neighborhood was. But still, it was fun to pretend she was Frannie so she could refresh herself with all the sensory details and feelings that came with the nighttime adventure.

She crept low along the edge of the house, ducking when she came to windows. She had perfected the maneuvers, mostly the summer she'd been thirteen when she'd snuck out to meet with her schoolmates. They'd been daring and a little rebellious and congregated at a nearby park to giggle and talk and gossip about boys.

They'd only done so a handful of times because the last time had almost ended in disaster and had scared them from meeting again and rightly so. A group of rough-looking boys a couple years older than them had meandered into the park, noticed their little gathering, and began teasing them.

The teasing had started out harmlessly enough, but it had grown menacing. Zaira and her friends had finally run off, afraid the boys would chase them. Somehow in the running, Zaira had ended up near Oscar's Pub, and Bellamy had been outside in the alley.

She'd thrown herself upon him, shaking and sobbing. He'd guided her into the stable, letting her calm down before asking her what had happened. He'd been so kind and concerned and protective that night. He'd even walked her home and made sure she made it back up the trellis and inside before going on his way.

They'd never talked about that night. But after that, she'd noticed Bellamy in a different way than she ever had previously.

With a sigh, Zaira straightened and walked hurriedly

down the street in the direction that would lead to Oscar's Pub, all thoughts of reenacting Frannie's rendezvous falling from her mind. Ultimately, Zaira had one goal tonight: to confront Bellamy.

She had the feeling Bellamy wouldn't be happy to see her. The same way he hadn't been happy to see her last night when she'd ridden into the city with Kiernan and Alannah and tried to talk to him about the fake-relationship idea. She blamed Bellamy's cold reception on Kiernan's punches and not on the reality that Bellamy was never happy to see her.

Bellamy had handled the fight with as much composure and calmness as he conducted most things. He'd even given her the chance to explain the plan to have a pretend court-ship that could salvage both of their reputations.

The problem was that he hadn't been as enthusiastic as she'd expected. Instead, he'd rejected the idea right away. Then he'd said he'd consider it as he left her.

Had twenty-four hours been long enough to let him think?

She kept to the back ways as she raced along the mostly deserted streets and alleys to Oscar's Pub. When she reached the shed, she slipped inside and then shrugged out of her cloak. She finally allowed herself a full breath and a smile. She'd made it.

She struck the match she'd brought along, then fumbled with the lantern on the tall wobbly table at the center of Bellamy's studio. As the light sprang to life, she shivered with anticipation and just a little trepidation.

She spun slowly, taking in every inch of the tiny room Bellamy used for his artwork. Floor-to-ceiling shelves lined one wall and were overflowing with bottles of all shapes and sizes of beer and whiskey and other liquor. Another wall was filled with casks that contained more beer and ale.

The last time she'd been in the shed was with Alannah that terrible night a couple weeks ago after the gang attack at Kiernan's brickyard. Zaira had been too focused on Alannah's grief to pay attention to all the alcohol. She'd seen it all before anyway during her first time there.

But tonight she frowned at the sight. She wasn't necessarily opposed to drinking spirits. But after the research she'd done for her story on the problems associated with drunkenness, she did see the value in the American Temperance Society, which advocated for setting limits to the consumption of spirits.

The heroine in her book, Frannie, had a father who imbibed too freely and too often. As a result, he had a difficult time keeping steady employment and often lashed out cruelly at his wife and children. Frannie had witnessed too much heartache and longed to leave and marry Albert, the man who loved her. At the same time, she felt obligated to stay and provide for her mother and siblings since they relied on her.

Of course, Zaira had no experience with any themes of drinking or cruelty or hardship or other such aspects of her story any more than she had experience with romance. But she loved researching, especially the research into kissing.

Even though the repercussions of the intimate research were troublesome and she regretted being so bold, those few moments of pressing into Bellamy had been deliciously wonderful. When he'd started kissing her back, his lips had been hot and eager against hers, almost as if he'd wanted the kiss just as much as she had—which wasn't true, but it was fun to pretend that he had.

She closed her eyes and touched her lips just as she had a hundred times over the past couple of days, and she pictured Bellamy's face—the rigid lines of his jaw, the bottomless eyes, the rakish way his dark hair fell over his forehead. Just thinking about him stirred heat inside her—a heat that his kiss had fanned to life and now wouldn't be squelched.

But she had to squelch it. Because it was clear the only way he would agree to the fake relationship plan was if he was convinced she didn't like him.

Surely she could find a way to pretend she didn't feel anything so Bellamy would agree to a pretend relationship that might not be entirely pretend for her.

"Ugh." She rubbed her temple. How had her life gotten so complicated so quickly?

Her gaze snagged on a trunk tucked behind a barrel. The drips of paint on the side gave away the location of Bellamy's painting supplies.

She crossed to the trunk only to find it securely locked. She slipped a pin out of her hair, fiddled with the lock, and was rewarded a moment later with a click.

She'd learned how to pick locks when she'd been writing her previous novel and needed to write realistically about her character escaping from a dungeon. Of course, that novel and the one before that had been mere drivel—the inferior work of an amateur. Nevertheless, the efforts hadn't been wasted. Not only had she improved her writing skills through the process of completing the novels, but she could also pick a lock.

She raised the trunk lid to find a large box nestled inside. Carefully, almost reverently, she lifted the box from the trunk and set it on the table. As she opened it, she drew in a breath at the sight of a plentiful amount of paint tubes, brushes, rags, chalk stubs, a bottle labeled *turpentine*, and more items she couldn't name.

She emptied the supplies onto the worktable. Once they were all arranged, she found his easel hidden behind another barrel. Then on the top shelf, she located a canvas that looked like it was only half finished. She positioned it on the easel and stood back to admire it, just as she'd admired all of Bellamy's other paintings.

There was no doubt about it. He was a talented artist. It was just too bad—actually a tragedy—he had to hide what he did and couldn't take credit for the incredible paintings he was selling. But as with the last time she'd been tempted to say something to encourage him to be more open, she only had to consider her own duplicity with her published segments. Oftentimes, situations were more complicated than they appeared.

Bellamy would be downright frustrated to find out she'd gone through his painting supplies. But if she could rouse his irritation, maybe he would conclude he had nothing to worry about in forming a partnership with her. He'd understand that the two of them were enemies more than anything else. If he could see that, he'd worry less about any attachments forming between them during a fake match.

Aye, she was doing the right thing by coming tonight, and it had been a bonus to pretend for a few moments that she was her heroine sneaking out of the house undetected to meet with her love.

The story had been very fun to write, and the rewriting had been fun so far too. But Zaira had ideas for another story formulating, and she'd been eager to jot down the thoughts before she lost them.

She peeked through a crack in the shed door. The light in the kitchen window at the back of the pub was still burning. That likely meant Bellamy was tending to the few customers who remained at the late hour. She wasn't sure if he was planning to paint tonight. But when he finished his duties, he would see the light in the shed and come out to investigate. At least that's what she was counting on.

In the meantime, she would make herself comfortable and start working on plotting her next great novel. Since there were no chairs in the shed, she sat on one of the crates in the corner and formed a makeshift chair. With the lantern casting a glow over her, she pulled out the notepad she carried with her everywhere and began to jot down ideas.

She wasn't sure how much time had passed when the rattle of the door drew her attention away from the new story world and back to the present. Bellamy was finally coming.

Her heart hopped several beats—from nerves and not desire. But she forced herself to keep writing, pretending to be engrossed in the words she was penciling on the page.

The door opened slowly, and from the corner of her eye she could see Bellamy scan the interior and then find her.

She kept her head down and continued to write, although she had no idea exactly what was coming out any longer.

He sighed rather laboriously, then stepped inside and closed the door quietly behind him. She could hear him latch the lock before silence descended.

She *fastidiously*—she rather liked that word—scratched away with her pencil on the paper, also liking the sound the writing made, as if she were busy and inspired and caught up in the scene rather than writing a bunch of gibberish.

He leaned back and crossed his arms, obviously waiting for her to acknowledge his presence. Should she? Or should she wait for a few more moments?

While nibbling on her bottom lip, she pretended to reread the last sentence she'd written. Did she look deep in thought? She hoped so.

"I know that you know I'm here, Zaira." His voice contained a note of humor.

How had he figured it out? Inwardly she huffed.

It didn't matter. She would act as though she'd been too busy to acknowledge his presence. She crossed a random *t* and then dotted an *i* before laying her pencil down on the journal page and looking up at him. "Good to see you too, Bellamy."

"I never said it was good to see you."

If he thought his smirk and cocky attitude would annoy her, he was wrong. She loved his arrogance, and it only made her want to banter with him all the more.

"I know you didn't say it," she countered. "But I can tell you're ecstatic that I'm here."

He raised an eyebrow. "If you're thinking I'm *ecstatic* at the moment, then I can see how your writing realistic emotion might be lacking."

"Perhaps that's why I like to *practice*." She tried to infuse sultriness into her voice. "Maybe that's why I'm here."

When Bellamy's other brow rose, she guessed she'd failed to sound sultry and instead sounded like she was suffering from a stuffy nose.

"I know you didn't come to practice anything." Bellamy's voice turned wry. "Except maybe your acting skills."

She set aside her journal and pencil, then stood. "I came to watch you paint." She nodded at the table where she'd laid out his supplies.

He crossed to the table, opened his painting box, and began to place all the items back inside. "I'm sorry to disappoint you, so I am." Even though outwardly he remained composed, she could feel the tension emanating from him. "But you'll not be getting a show tonight."

This time she smirked. "Now who's practicing the acting skills?"

He paused in picking up a paintbrush before resuming at the same measured pace. "I assume your visit has to do with the other acting job you'd like me to take?"

"It does."

"The answer is still no."

Disappointment stabbed her and hurt more than she'd anticipated. She should have known what his silence all day meant. But she'd been hoping she could persuade him anyway. Was there still a chance, or did he have his mind so solidly made up that he wouldn't be budged for any reason?

The only thing that had seemed to give him pause last night was the fact that her own reputation was at stake. Could she play upon that?

It was worth an attempt. If that tactic didn't work, she'd have to talk with Kiernan again tomorrow and come up with another solution to her dilemma.

She gathered up her writing items. "You leave me with no choice, Bellamy."

He closed the lid on his art supply box, then leaned against the table as if he was settling in for the next performance.

She had to make it good. She paused, let her shoulders slump, and dropped her chin. "You know how strict my da is." She waited several heartbeats, hoping Bellamy would remember some of the gossip about her da—how he never let his daughters spend time alone with suitors, how he always required a chaperone, how he had stringent requirements for callers to sit on opposite chairs, and how he guarded their virtue religiously.

When Bellamy didn't respond, she released a long-suffering sigh—or at least hoped it came out that way. "Once Da learns of my—our—kissing, he'll never allow me a moment of privacy or freedom until I'm married."

"Naturally."

"He'll lock me away." She spun then and tried to remain stricken. "Probably in my chamber at Oakland."

Bellamy shook his head, almost as if he didn't believe her.

Was she laying on the drama too thickly? Perhaps she needed to be more realistic. "At the very least, he'll restrict me from leaving Oakland and won't let me go anywhere by myself." That was the truth. "Then how will I deliver my weekly manuscript segments to Mr. Knapp at the *Daily Republican*?"

A line formed in Bellamy's forehead, as though he was seriously contemplating her dilemma. "Maybe I could take them for you."

"Maybe." She pressed a finger to her lips, trying to maintain the seriousness of the situation. "My guess is he'll attempt to form a match for me right away to hide my indiscretion, just like he did with Enya."

"Your situation is far different than Enya's."

Her sister had been with child from a husband who had run off and abandoned her, and Da had been in a hurry to find a new spouse who would be willing to count the baby as his. Bellamy located just the right man at just the right time.

Bellamy's forehead furrowed deeper. Was he thinking the same thing?

"You wouldn't have me marry a stranger, would you, Bellamy?" She let sorrow infuse her voice, which wasn't too hard since the thought of marrying a stranger really was distressing. "You may have found someone quickly for Enya, but what guarantee do you have of finding me the perfect match so quickly too?"

He shrugged. "I have the luck o' the Irish, that I do."

"Surely you're not so lucky that you can accomplish the same feat twice." She fluttered her hand over her chest. Then she closed her eyes, hoping to make herself look more distraught.

He was quiet for so long she finally cracked open one eye only to find him smirking again. As she opened both eyes, he clapped. "Bravo. Grand performance."

This time she stomped a foot, unable to contain her irritation. She stuffed her journal and pencil into her pocket, then began to make her way toward the door, swiping up her discarded cloak from the top of a barrel where she'd draped it.

All the while, he watched her, his arms still crossed, his smile only growing.

"It was a mistake to come." She flipped up her hood, then unlatched the lock on the door. Though the night was still humid, she allowed herself a lungful of air before starting down the alley in the direction of her family's home on Third Street. The streets of St. Louis were dangerous at night, abounding with thugs and thieves, but she'd been careful on the way over, and she'd be equally as vigilant on the way back.

She made it only halfway down the alley before footsteps slapped behind her and a hand grabbed her arm, drawing her to a stop. She spun to find Bellamy towering above her. Though the darkness shrouded him, she could sense the tension in his grip.

"Doncha be thinking you can walk home alone this late at night," he whispered, his voice threaded with exasperation.

Was he thinking about that time when he'd walked her home many years ago after being chased from the park? Well, she wasn't that little naïve thirteen-year-old anymore. "I walked here alone just fine." She jerked her arm free and started on her way once more. She only made it two steps before he latched onto her arm again.

"I'll be going with you, so."

"No thank you. I'd rather be alone than be with you." She didn't need to act anymore. It was the truth.

10

*A*nimosity filled every word Zaira spoke.

Bellamy tried to see through the darkness and study her face. But her hood only added shadows, making it impossible to see anything. Which was actually good. Because if any man of low character caught sight of her beauty, she wouldn't be safe.

"I'll not be taking no for an answer." He clamped his fingers tighter around her arm so she couldn't break loose again. "I'm walking you home."

"And I'm not taking no for an answer. I'm walking alone." The animosity was still there, along with frustration.

Was she frustrated because he'd turned down her offer again at having a fake relationship?

She wiggled in an attempt to free herself from him once more.

"You're a stubborn lass." He didn't let go. "Do you know that?"

"It takes a stubborn person to recognize one."

He supposed he was being stubborn too. After another

night of listening to Oscar bargain with at least half a dozen more men, Bellamy should have been eager to accept her proposal, especially because he'd been more than a little annoyed after the last customer finally left.

When he'd stepped out of the pub a few moments ago, he'd been hoping to paint and relieve some of his stress. But at the sight of the light in the shed, he hadn't been surprised to open the door and find Zaira. He should have guessed she wouldn't accept his silent denial of her proposal, that she'd be back to get an answer.

"I'm sorry you had to come out tonight," he said softly. "I should have called on you earlier in the day instead."

"It's of no consequence to me." Her tone still held a bite to it.

"The truth is . . ." He drew in a deep breath and cast his gaze to the sky, as if that could somehow make it easier to say what needed to be said. "I'll accept your plan for the pretend match."

She stopped struggling against him and held herself motionless.

"'Tis the sound and reasonable way forward." All along, he'd known he couldn't deny her this, not if it would help salvage her reputation. Even so, he'd tried to put it off, tried to think of another way, tried to figure out something else, primarily because he was afraid—afraid of his own attraction to her and afraid he wouldn't be able to keep it locked away, especially if he had to spend any extended time with her.

However, that was his problem. Not hers. If she only wanted a temporary relationship and truly wasn't interested in him as a suitor, he would have his own ardor to worry about and not hers. The solution was to stay in control and not let down his guard when he was around her. He could do that, couldn't he?

"Are you sure?" she whispered back. "If you agree to it, then you can't keep fighting with me."

"I'm not keen on agreeing to it."

She snorted. "That's obvious."

"But I'll do it."

She hesitated for several heartbeats. "All right."

"All right." He breathed out the tension that had been building inside him since the night of the kiss and Oscar's pronouncement that he was seeking a match for Bellamy.

This arrangement with Zaira would buy him a little more time. Hopefully when they parted ways, he would have gained back the trust of the Irish community as a competent matchmaker. Then he wouldn't need to rush into marriage, and he could continue to wait for the right woman to come along.

Zaira seemed to relax even more, as if her worries had been alleviated too. "What comes next, Bellamy?"

He wasn't exactly sure. But he supposed if they hoped to prove to everyone that they were sincere, they would have to move forward with the same plans any other matched couple would make.

"I'll tell Oscar first thing tomorrow morn. Then we'll arrange a meeting with your da to pluck the gander." He didn't exactly like the idea of lying to James Shanahan. He didn't like the idea of lying to anyone. But what other option did they have?

"Do we need all of the formal steps?"

"I can suggest to everyone that we'd simply like to court for a while without signing papers."

"That would be better, don't you think?"

"Oh aye. But I have the feeling Oscar will be pushing for everything to be just so." Oscar would indeed want the traditional meeting—the plucking of the gander—to talk about the details of the match and what each family would be offering the other through the marriage union. He would also want the traditional meal—the eating of the gander—to celebrate the union.

"Then let's tell them we're only courting for now." Zaira's voice was suddenly hesitant. Was she also considering the seriousness of lying to everyone they knew? "We'll tell them we're not ready to be engaged, but we'd like to get to know each other better by spending some time together."

Would that work? Would such an agreement satisfy Oscar? Satisfy the Shanahans?

"A courtship wouldn't be as serious as an actual match," she continued, "and we wouldn't have to lie so badly, would we?"

A lie was a lie, no matter how big or little.

"Actually, what if we really do court each other?" she asked. "Just temporarily. We'll know it won't last forever, but we won't tell them that."

"It's still deceptive."

"Not if we act like a courting couple."

He stiffened. He hadn't liked the original plan to form a pretend match, and he didn't like the direction this new scheme was taking. "What exactly do courting couples act like?"

"If you need me to explain that to you, then you should abdicate your role as the matchmaker right here and now."

"I know how couples should act when they're in love with each other. But we're not."

"We don't need to be in love, not if we're telling everyone we just want to get to know one another better. But we have to make a show of acting interested in each other."

He palmed the back of his neck and the tightening muscles there. "Let's set some rules for what 'acting interested' looks like."

"You'll need to come visit me on occasion."

Fine. He could do that. They would have a chaperone, and he wouldn't have to stay long. "Anything else?"

"You'll have to be nice to me around other people."

"I'm nice to you already."

"No, you make it obvious you don't like me."

"If everyone assumes I don't like you, then whyever would they believe we want to start courting?"

"Because we kissed, and we want to explore if we have feelings for each other after all."

"That's a reasonable excuse." And it made sense.

"You'll have to talk to me without sounding irritated."

Was he really that much of a cad whenever he was with her? "'Twill be difficult"—he tried for humor—"but I'll try a wee bit."

"And maybe a gift or two?" This time her voice hinted at humor.

"That may be asking too much," he teased back. "But I'll see what I can do."

"See that you compliment me often."

"The same goes for you."

She paused. "Depending on how long this transpires, we may need another kiss—"

"I draw the line there." His heartbeat tumbled over itself

at just the thought of sharing another kiss. As tempting as the idea was, he couldn't let himself get carried away.

"Very well. I prohibit you from kissing me again."

Prohibit? Once more, he tried to see through the darkness to read her expression, but that pretty face of hers was too shadowed. Was she serious? Surely not. She couldn't go from suggesting it one moment and then objecting to it the next. But did that mean she'd liked the kiss and wanted another?

He gave a curt shake of his head. It didn't matter. "We won't be having any physical contact during our courtship."

"Good." She seemed almost relieved by his declaration. "Hopefully you can stick to that."

"Hopefully you can too."

"I'll have no trouble."

"Neither will I." Oh aye, he would have lots of trouble keeping his hands off her, and that was precisely the problem with their pretense. But now that he'd agreed to be in a temporary relationship, he had to follow through or he would look like a coward.

She started forward down the alley. This time she didn't protest when he fell into step beside her.

He might not know exactly how to put their plan into action, but one thing was certain. He owed her an apology. "I'm sorry if I haven't been nice to you. I suppose I didn't like that you found out my . . . secret, and I've been reacting."

"That's what I figured." She turned onto a short gravel path that led to the next alley, then halted to look both ways before staying in the dark shadows.

Maybe she would have been fine returning home on her own after all.

He didn't think any of the gangs would be out stirring up

trouble tonight, especially because Shaw and several other leaders of the Farrell gang had just been arrested for instigating destruction at Kiernan's brickyard. The arrest had hopefully sent a message that the rising gang violence wouldn't be tolerated.

But just because the gangs weren't acting up didn't mean the crime in St. Louis had gone away. If anything, it was worse, mainly because the police force was lacking. Budget cuts earlier in the year had depleted the already floundering St. Louis City Guard, which was now down from forty men to only thirty.

The small force was responsible for patrolling the city twenty-four hours a day, but usually only one lieutenant and six patrolmen were out walking their beats at any given time. In a city whose population had grown by the thousands over recent years, the police were certainly outnumbered and underpaid.

As a result, the number of bank robberies had increased that year. Just back in March, the great Nisbet Robbery had occurred. William Nisbet & Company, a banking and lending institution, had been robbed of nearly thirty thousand dollars.

The outlaws had worked through most of the night with picks and hammers to smash their way through multiple brick walls, some as large as three feet thick, to reach the safe. Once there, apparently they'd hammered away at the thick sheet iron until they had a hole big enough for one of the robbers to climb through. They'd emptied the safe and gotten away undetected.

Thanks be, the police captain had been able to track down and catch the crooks two weeks later. But the robbery had triggered a string of crimes. More businesses had been targeted by safecrackers. The fire in May and then the return of the cholera shortly after that had tempered some of the crime, but it was only a matter of time before the problems escalated again.

Even so, Zaira didn't seem overly worried about the nighttime crime in St. Louis. She didn't seem to be afraid of much anymore. Not like that night long ago when Bellamy had helped her back home after she and her friends had been threatened by some ruffians. She'd been relieved to be with him, and he'd been so worried about her.

Regardless, there was no way he would let any woman walk alone this late at night, especially someone as special as Zaira.

As soon as the thought floated through his mind, he almost tripped. Zaira special? Where had that come from?

"You should know," she said, "I won't say anything about your . . . secret. And I hope you'll be kind enough to do the same for mine."

"Rightly so."

She halted abruptly and clutched his arm, cautioning him with a finger to her lips not to speak.

His muscles tightened, and his body was alert for anything. He wanted to ask what she'd noticed. Instead, he waited motionless, listening for danger.

Soft sniffles came from behind the rubbish heap that sat to the side of the alley only a few feet away.

She released him and took a step closer.

He latched on to her arm and drew her back.

"Is someone there?" she asked.

He tensed, ready to defend her if needed. He didn't carry

a gun, but he did have a knife sheathed at his side, one he'd had to pull out a time or two during fights in the pub. Only to threaten unruly drunks. Never to harm anyone.

He prayed he never would have to hurt anyone with it, not now or in the future. He wasn't the type of fellow who relished fighting, not even watching other men throwing punches. He much preferred to find peaceful, nonviolent resolutions to problems.

However, he wouldn't hesitate to use his knife to keep Zaira safe. Not even a heartbeat.

At a slight movement and a soft cry behind the rubbish, Zaira took another step forward, as though to discover whoever was there.

He held her in place while at the same time sidling in front of her. As he did so, the stench of the refuse reached him—a mixture of human waste and rotting food.

"What are you doing?" she hissed as she struggled to break free.

"What in the wee devil do you think you're doing?" he hissed back. Sometimes she was too impulsive for her own good.

At another cry—like that of a young child—they both grew motionless. Who was there?

"Hello?" Zaira said gently.

A voice came again but was quickly muffled.

Was someone hurting a child? If so, Bellamy couldn't stand back and let it happen.

He unsheathed his knife and strode to the rubbish heap, an urgency prodding him. With his knife at the ready, he stepped around the refuse. Although the darkness prevented him from seeing much, he could distinguish the outline of two children. One appeared to be slightly bigger and was holding another child on his lap.

Bellamy wasn't an expert on children's ages, but he guessed they were somewhere around the range of five and three. The older one, wearing trousers and a flatcap, had his hand over the younger child's mouth. Attired in a dress and a bonnet, she was fighting against the boy to free herself.

Before Bellamy could ask the children any questions or even ascertain if they were with anyone, Zaira brushed past him.

The little girl grew motionless, but the lad bolted into action. He shoved the lass to her feet, hopped up, and dragged the little girl forward. "Nip along, we have to go." The lad had a heavy Irish accent that told Bellamy he was a recent immigrant.

"No, Seamus," the lass whined.

"Wait." Zaira held out a hand toward the two. "I can help you."

"We're getting along." The boy didn't stop.

"But where are your parents?" Zaira persisted.

Bellamy didn't need the children to say anything to know the answer. Their parents had died from cholera and left them orphans. From what he'd heard, the orphanages were overflowing with children like this, whose parents had succumbed to the disease and who had no other family or friends to take care of them.

"My parents are just there, so." The boy, Seamus, nodded down the street. "We'll be on our way."

"I can walk with you," Zaira offered.

Before Seamus could say more, the little lass chimed in. "We're trying to find our da."

"Moya," the lad scolded, "I told you not to be saying nothing."

"But I'm hungry."

Seamus was still attempting to drag her away, but she was making his efforts difficult.

"I have food for you." Zaira crouched down to their level.

Bellamy had to give Zaira credit. She was persistent, and she was kind to care about these two orphans. But the boy was scared of them, didn't want to encounter anyone.

"Come on with you now, Moya." The lad stumbled forward down the dark alley.

She began to cry again. "I want Mama."

Zaira rose and followed them. "I don't know where your mama or da are at, but I'll do my best to help you find them if you'll let me."

Maybe their da was still alive. Maybe just their mam had died. "I'm the matchmaker," Bellamy said, hoping to convince them along with Zaira. "I'm sure I can find someone who knows about your da."

The boy paused.

Oh aye, the child believed his da was alive somewhere, and that was the hook in helping these two. "I know lots of people, so I do. If anyone's to be helping you locate your da, 'tis me."

"He's right," Zaira added, continuing to inch toward the pair. "Bellamy McKenna can do just about anything he sets his mind to."

Did she really believe that? He tucked her comment away to analyze later. For now, he had to use his persuasive powers to sway Seamus to come with them. "I know almost everyone in the Kerry Patch." Most likely the children had been staying in the Irish district of the city since new immigrants headed there because of the cheap housing.

"Do you know Seamus O'Reilly?" The hope in the boy's tone again told more of his story, that his da had come ahead of the family to St. Louis and the children with their mam hadn't connected with him. It was possible he'd already died of cholera, and they just hadn't been able to uncover that information.

"Seamus O'Reilly?" Bellamy searched through the many names of men who had come in and out of the pub over recent months. He'd met some O'Reillys, but none who went by Seamus.

"From Galway." The boy was still holding tightly to his sister, but she was no longer trying to get away.

"Seamus O'Reilly from Galway." Bellamy recognized the Connacht dialect spoken by those from County Galway, different from the dialect he'd grown up speaking in County Wicklow. "I can't recall anyone by Seamus, but I can promise that if he's in St. Louis, I can track him down."

"You can promise?"

"Oh aye."

Zaira had reached the children and now gently touched the little girl's head. The child peered up at Zaira with interest.

The lad didn't back away this time, which hopefully meant he didn't see Zaira as a threat either.

How long had the two been trying to survive on their own? Bellamy could see enough in the darkness to know they were both thin and dirty. They might have arrived in St. Louis that way. It was also possible they'd grown more ragged from living on the streets.

"Would you like to come home with me for the night?" Zaira asked. "I have a nice home—"

"No." Seamus pulled his sister away, his voice filling with a note of fear.

"How about the shed behind the pub?" Bellamy asked quickly.

The lad shook his head.

Bellamy continued before the child could turn him down too. "It has a latch on the inside of the door. You can lock it, and no one can get in unless you unlatch it."

Seamus didn't immediately speak, which was a good sign that he was considering Bellamy's offer.

"I've got some Dublin Coddle leftovers." It wouldn't be hot but would be better than anything the two had eaten in a while.

"I'll eat it," Moya said eagerly.

"Just for tonight." Seamus's voice rang with a warning to his sister.

Bellamy wasn't sure how he'd get the children to stay longer than one night. Because he would need more than a day to get information on their da. But at least they were safe for the time being. And Zaira looked relieved, even pleased, and that made him feel as though he'd accomplished something great.

11

"Hurry, Kiernan!" Zaira leaned out of the barouche that was ready and waiting on the gravel drive at the back of the Shanahan home near the coach house.

Past the balcony with its white columns that ran the width of the second-floor exterior, Kiernan was standing near one of the many open windows that allowed in the river breezes. He was kissing Alannah again.

Zaira sighed. She was happy for the newlyweds. She truly was. But she was eager to return to Oscar's Pub and check on how little Seamus and Moya had done last night. The children had walked with her and Bellamy the short distance back to the shed.

Seamus had spoken very little, but Moya had been more talkative. She'd told them their ages: They were six and three—almost four. She missed their mam, who had recently gone to heaven. They had no other family in the area except their da, but they hadn't seen him in a long time, and Moya couldn't remember what he looked like because he'd taken a ship away from home before they did.

Bellamy had whispered that it sounded like the father had come ahead of the family to America in order to find employment and housing. He also believed their mother had died of cholera—or perhaps of another disease she'd caught on the ship over. Now the two children were stuck in a strange city with no idea how to find their father.

Once they'd reached the shed, Zaira had ushered the children inside while Bellamy had gone to get them a meal. He'd returned with not only food and drink but blankets and pillows. While the children ate, Zaira had made beds on the floor.

The lantern light had revealed that both children were filthy, their clothes in tatters, and they had no shoes. They were also emaciated, so tiny and thin that she could see their bones poking through their clothing.

It was a heartbreaking situation, and Zaira had hardly been able to sleep with worry over the two, hadn't wanted them to stay in a shed like they were animals. Neither had Bellamy. He'd tried again to convince them to go inside his apartment, but Seamus had been wary about remaining there at all, even after Bellamy had shown him how to latch the door.

At least the children had been willing to eat the food Bellamy had provided. They'd devoured every morsel, and Bellamy had left more for them to have later, if they needed it. Finally, after making sure the children were content and settled in, Bellamy had walked her home. They'd talked about the children the whole way back, speculating where their father was and how to locate him.

Bellamy had assured Zaira that he would start the search just as soon as he could, that he would ask around and try to discover anything he could about Seamus O'Reilly from Galway. In the meantime, she wanted to locate temporary housing for the children. They also needed baths and new clothing and shoes.

She patted her beaded reticule where she'd tucked some of the money she'd earned so far from selling her weekly articles. The amount wasn't much, but it would be enough to purchase the items the children needed.

She was eager to get started on the busy day ahead. Not only did she have the children to tend to, but she and Bellamy also needed to make their courtship decision public. Kiernan was coming along to the pub to talk to Oscar about it before he rode out to Oakland and shared the news with Da and Mam.

Zaira had cornered him in the dining room first thing that morning to tell him of the arrangement she and Bellamy had agreed upon, and she was relieved he hadn't asked questions about when and how she and Bellamy had talked.

At first Kiernan hadn't been happy to learn she was only courting Bellamy. He'd claimed that a match would satisfy everyone much better and put an end to the rumors. However, when she'd explained that the match would be too duplicitous, Kiernan had agreed that a courtship would suffice, as long as it was done ardently enough.

Zaira hadn't wanted to ask what Kiernan's idea of *ardently* was. She hoped he didn't intend for her and Bellamy to imitate him and Alannah.

Zaira poked her head out of the carriage again and peered up at the balcony. "Please, Kiernan. Make haste!"

He was holding Alannah and whispering in her ear. She was laughing softly at something he was saying. She stood in his embrace for another moment before she stepped back, but he held on to her hand as though he couldn't bear to release it.

When he finally turned and left her, Zaira expelled a breath and sat back against the leather seat. She only had to wait another minute before Kiernan's call to the driver rang out in the morning air, and then he climbed into the conveyance and took the seat across from her.

"Ready for this?" He settled in and straightened his top hat.

"I'm ready to get it over with."

"Now, Zaira." Kiernan tugged at his cuffs. "If you're not careful, Oscar will see right through your ruse. So make sure your attitude toward Bellamy is believable."

Aye, even though she was in a hurry this morning to visit with the children, she would have to suffer through an ordeal with Oscar first. Hopefully Bellamy hadn't changed his mind about their plan since last night. He hadn't been exactly open to it. But at least he'd agreed to pretend they had a relationship.

"Bellamy and I already talked about what we need to do." As the carriage rolled down the street, she couldn't keep from watching out the window. How many more children like Seamus and Moya were wandering St. Louis streets? And was it her turn to step up and do something that went beyond just Seamus and Moya?

She'd always relegated the helping to her oldest sister, Finola, who seemed to have been born with all the compassion in the family. Finola had been providing aid to the immigrants for months because those coming over from Ireland were in terrible conditions from the famine and then the long journey to America. Finola had not only been going into the slums and dispatching food and clothing to the immigrants, but she and Riley had also been advocating for changes in the Kerry Patch that could make the living conditions better. Of course, Finola wasn't in the city anymore—not now that she was expecting a baby. Riley had moved her to his family's home in the country. He spent some of his time there but had continued to be involved in assisting the immigrants as well as his new position of leadership in fighting the cholera.

Should she seek him out? See if he'd heard of Seamus O'Reilly? Would he also have some ideas for what more she could do to help homeless children, particularly those affected by the cholera epidemic?

"Whatever your plan is with Bellamy," Kiernan said as he straightened his cravat, "please refrain from any more physical contact."

Warmth pulsed into Zaira's face that had nothing to do with the sweltering humidity of the July morning. "You don't need to worry, Kiernan. Bellamy and I are planning to show interest in each other, but we have set boundaries we don't intend to cross."

"See that you don't."

Her flush spread.

"If you carry on with him, you'll make matters worse. Then no respectable man will want you once you end the fake relationship."

"I promise not to carry on with him."

"If I hear of it, rest assured, I'll force Bellamy to turn your temporary relationship into a permanent one."

Bellamy wouldn't let that happen. He was too against

having anything long-term. He'd made that clear with his resistance to her. The only way he'd agreed to anything at all was because she'd reassured him that she didn't like him.

"I'll be fine, Kiernan."

Her brother didn't respond, almost as if he didn't entirely believe her. The rest of the way to Oscar's Pub, they talked of other matters, including the plans for her and Alannah to return to Oakland later in the week. Now that Seamus and Moya were in her life, Zaira had the feeling she wouldn't be ready to move away, not even if she and Bellamy found Mr. O'Reilly. Maybe she'd have to concoct another way to stay in the city.

As the barouche rolled to a stop in front of the pub, she was struck again, as she had been recently, with how deserted the streets were for a usually busy area of town. A few people loitered about, but the traffic was light and the pedestrians were sparse.

As Kiernan helped her down, she wanted to go directly to the alley and the shed to check on the children. But she hadn't told Kiernan about them because in doing so she would also have to explain that she'd sneaked out. He would be angry at her for going alone so late, and he'd probably ban her from leaving the house again, possibly even send her back to Oakland today.

No, she couldn't risk Kiernan's wrath. Instead, she walked into the pub behind him. At midmorning, it was still too early for the pub to be open for business. No one else was there, not even Georgie McGuire.

The clanking of dishes and the chattering of voices in the kitchen meant that someone was already at work, as did the scent of coffee along with onions and garlic.

"Wait here." Kiernan released her arm and crossed toward the bar counter and the kitchen door behind it.

She crossed to one of the landscapes on the dark-paneled wall. It was a painting of a mountainous area with vibrant green hillsides surrounding a clear blue lake and the shadows of the few clouds adding dimension.

She tried to imagine Bellamy as a boy standing on top of one of those mountains with his easel in front of him while he painted. Had he been able to paint openly there? Or had his painting always been a secret? How had he learned to paint so well? There were still so many things she didn't know about him.

Kiernan returned to the dining room a moment later. He'd taken off his hat, and his forehead was creased with frustration. "Bellamy's not here."

"He's not?"

"Apparently he left early this morning, and his sister doesn't know when he'll return."

Was he already out looking for Mr. O'Reilly? Zaira could only pray he'd find the man swiftly so the children could be reunited with their father.

Kiernan blew out a taut breath. "He was aware that we would need a meeting this morn, was he not?"

"I assumed so." They hadn't talked about specific plans, but certainly Bellamy had to know this was the next step in making their courtship official.

"I sent Jenny up to tell Oscar we're here and would like a meeting."

Zaira sighed. Leave it to Kiernan to make such demands. "We can't meet without Bellamy—"

"Thanks be to the holy mother." Oscar's booming voice

filled the pub as he stepped through from the kitchen behind the bar counter. He was hastily finishing buttoning his sleeves and his hair was disheveled, as if he hadn't yet taken the time to comb it. "I was hoping to see James Shanahan coming to make an offer for my lad, Bellamy. But I'll take Kiernan Shanahan in his stead, so I will."

She shook her head. "This isn't an offer, Mr. McKenna."

"Say no more." Oscar was smiling broadly, and his eyes danced with excitement, as if he'd just been told President Zachary Taylor was coming to dinner. "After that kiss, I figured it was just a matter of time before the Shanahans came here to make a match."

Kiernan wasn't smiling in return. "If you knew that, then why are you holding meetings with every other family in St. Louis?"

Oscar rumbled with laughter as he rounded the bar. "I always say there's nothing like a wee nudge to set the wheels of love in motion."

"Just so you know, Mr. McKenna"—she followed the man toward his corner table—"Bellamy and I aren't ready for an official match. For now, we only want to court and have the chance to get to know each other better before we decide if we're the right fit."

Oscar waved a dismissive hand and gave another short laugh. "Oh, you're a fit and rightly so. I didn't have to be here to witness the kiss, and even I know that."

"The decision is up to Bellamy and me," she persisted, relieved the pub was empty and no one else could hear Oscar's declaration.

Kiernan had followed Oscar too, and he touched her arm

and slanted her a warning look, one that told her she was being too bold.

That wasn't fair. She couldn't sit back and say nothing—not when she and Bellamy had already decided upon a course of action that would work for them.

She glanced first to the door and then to the kitchen entrance. Where was Bellamy, anyway? If he were here, he'd be able to clarify everything.

"Come on and sit with me, Kiernan." Oscar pulled out a chair and lowered himself. "Let's talk for a few minutes, and then we'll schedule a meeting with both you and your father and Bellamy where we can pluck the gander."

"Excuse me, Mr. McKenna." The panic was starting to swell inside Zaira. "Bellamy and I decided we don't want to arrange a match yet."

Oscar gave her another large, almost-affectionate smile. "I heard you the first time you told me that, darlin'."

"Bellamy doesn't want a match yet either."

"Ach, that Bellamy wouldn't know what he wants even if the right woman walked up to him and kissed him—which she did."

Inwardly Zaira groaned. Would that kiss haunt her forever?

The best thing to do at the moment was find Bellamy and get him to stop the proceedings from going any further.

As Oscar turned his attention to Kiernan and began talking to him, Zaira made her way into the kitchen.

Jenny, at the washtub scrubbing dishes, paused and stared at Zaira. Gavin was in the middle of adding something to a pot on the stove, and he halted to look at her too.

Zaira gave them both a smile. If they hadn't already overheard Oscar's pronouncement about matching her and Bel-lamy, they could probably guess why she was at the pub. "Could either of you please tell me where Bellamy went and when he'll be expected back?"

Jenny's dark brown eyes, so much like Bellamy's, were filled with curiosity as she took Zaira in. Did the young woman believe Zaira was about to join their family, perhaps even work in the kitchen alongside her?

Not that Zaira was opposed to hard work or washing dishes or peeling potatoes or whatever else people did in a kitchen. But that was one of the reasons why she longed to put off marriage for a little while—because she didn't want other things to interfere with her time to research and write her books. Someday, she would embrace managing a house and motherhood and all that came with it, but not at the present.

"He didn't tell us where he was going." Jenny's arms were submerged in murky water up to her elbows, and her apron was wet all down the front. "Only that he had to see about some things."

"Do you mind if I go out and check if he's back?" She nodded in the direction of the door.

"Feel free."

Zaira exited the kitchen, and the moment the door closed behind her, she raced across the alley to the shed. She knocked softly on the door. "Seamus? Moya?"

Only silence greeted her. Maybe they were too afraid to answer, didn't realize it was her, didn't recognize her voice.

"It's me, Zaira." She leaned in and continued to speak quietly. "The woman you met last night."

Still there was no response.

It was possible the two were asleep.

She tugged at the door, expecting it to be latched, but it swung open effortlessly. Her gaze landed on the place where she'd made the blanket beds for the two last night. Nothing was there. The blankets, pillows, bowls of food, and mugs of milk—there wasn't a trace of them or the children, almost as if they'd never even been in the shed.

She scanned the small area again, hoping for some clue as to where the children were. "Bellamy found their father already and took them to be reunited." That had to be it. She stepped outside and this time surveyed the surrounding area.

At the sight of a lean but muscular man riding down the alley in the direction the pub, she breathed out, trying to loosen the tightness in her chest. Bellamy was coming. Surely he would have answers on the whereabouts of the children, and surely he could make his father understand their desire to have a courtship and nothing more.

With the brim of his flatcap pulled low, Bellamy's face was shadowed. Even so, she could see the tension in his shoulders. As he neared the pub, he slowed his mount. Instead of turning toward the stables next to the shed, he brought his horse to a halt beside her.

"Where are Seamus and Moya?" She didn't bother with a greeting. "I'm really hoping you'll tell me they're back with their father." Not just because she loved happily-ever-afters, which she did, but also because she truly wanted what was best for the children.

He didn't bother with a greeting either. "When I came out this morning to check on them, they were gone."

12

The children had run off. Bellamy hated to be the one to deliver the news to Zaira. He'd known how disappointed she would be, especially after how invested in them she'd been last night.

"No." Zaira released the word breathlessly, almost as if the air had been knocked out of her. Was she wobbling?

He swung his leg over his mount and hopped down, reaching for her arm to steady her.

She'd turned her eyes upon him, dismay darkening the green hue to the color of the Glendalough Valley's heather-flecked hills. One of the paintings in the pub was of that very valley and the mountain ridge he'd hiked to often as a boy—one that overlooked a glacial lake below.

"Where did they go?" Her question was infused with an urgency he'd felt earlier—the urgency to go after them and bring them back.

"I've been out for the past couple of hours searching every place I could think of, asking around, and even going to the police station to see if any officers on patrol saw the two or took them to one of the orphanages."

"And . . . ?"

"And I haven't had any luck, not even a wee bit."

She closed her eyes briefly before opening them and blinking back tears. "Why did they run away? We were going to help them."

He'd already had time to think about the matter as he'd searched. "My guess is that Seamus doesn't trust any adults, probably because someone previously claiming to help him and his sister betrayed or put them in an orphanage against their will. The only thing to be doing now is pray they stay safe—"

"And we'll continue to search for them and their father." Her pretty face was filled with determination, and her mouth set with resolve.

He wanted to agree with her. But how could he allow her to roam the streets and alleys of St. Louis when he'd passed by wagons filled with the bodies of those who'd died overnight from cholera?

The new Committee of Public Health was working vigorously to keep up with carrying the deceased to cemeteries. But even the cemeteries were overflowing with bodies waiting to be buried, and grave diggers were constantly having to find more room.

The only way to alleviate Zaira's concern and to prevent her from putting herself at risk of catching cholera was to continue the search by himself. "If I promise to keep looking for the children, will you promise to nip along home and stay there?"

She sniffed, as if offended he'd even ask her such a thing.

"Of course I won't agree. I'm perfectly capable of searching too."

Her answer was exactly what he'd thought it would be. The only situation that would work was to search with her, then he'd be able to steer her away from the areas of the city most affected by cholera.

He released an exasperated sigh. "Then at least be promising me you won't go out without me."

She opened her mouth, the protest easy to see in her eyes.

He rapidly touched a finger to her lips to stop her. "At least that, Zaira. Please."

She studied his face, and some of the fight seemed to leave her expression. Could she sense his sincerity? Was she seeing that this time he wasn't being antagonistic, but that he did truly want her to be safe? He hoped so.

She didn't move. Except that her gaze dropped to his finger against her lips. She drew in a sharp breath, and the green in her eyes darkened.

His touch was affecting her. Even if she claimed she didn't like him, it was becoming more and more apparent that this attraction between them was mutual.

"Please don't go out without me," he whispered without moving his finger.

She closed her eyes but couldn't hide her desire.

Echoing desire rippled through him, but he fought against it. He had to stay in control. Because the truth was, if a brief touch could command her this way, he'd have to use it to his advantage. He didn't want to manipulate her, but he also had to find a way to keep the upper hand.

"Do you promise?" he whispered.

"Aye." She lifted her lashes, and as her gaze connected

with his again, he had an overwhelming need to bend down and replace his finger on her lips with his mouth. She was so soft and warm, and he knew she would taste as delicious as she had the last time.

But he couldn't—wouldn't—give in to physical desire. Because that's all this was between them, and all it would ever be. She was a stunningly beautiful woman, and any man would feel drawn toward her.

Oh aye, what he was feeling was ordinary and nothing to worry about.

He dragged his thumb across her bottom lip, then let his hand fall away.

She didn't move from where he'd immobilized her.

A strange sense of satisfaction sizzled through him.

"Bellamy?" Jenny's call from the back door of the pub broke the spell that had somehow been cast between them.

He didn't budge from where he stood in front of Zaira, and Zaira remained motionless, as if she hadn't heard Jenny.

Zaira was an innocent. She'd already admitted she didn't know about relationships. That's why she'd wanted to hug or kiss him, so she could expand her life experiences.

He hadn't considered the fact before, but he was her first kiss. Her only kiss.

"Bellamy?" Jenny said again. "Did you know Da's inside writing out a contract with Kiernan for your match to Zaira?"

Oscar was writing a contract for a match? The news penetrated the haze that had settled over Bellamy. He shifted to take in Jenny wiping her hands on her apron. "Zaira and I are agreeing on a courtship. That's all."

"Well, he's pretty determined to get the deal settled, so he is."

Of course he was. With a shake of his head, Bellamy stalked across the alley toward the pub. He brushed past Jenny, made his way through the kitchen, and then ducked into the dining room.

It was empty except for Oscar and Kiernan sitting at the corner table. Sure enough, Oscar was writing something down on a piece of paper he'd torn from his leather-bound matchmaker journal, where he'd kept track of the matches he made—the names and ages of the couples as well as details about their families along with any other pertinent information.

"Hold on now with you, Oscar," Bellamy called as he strode past the wall of liquor and the bar counter.

"No need." Oscar continued to write on the paper in front of him. "I've got everything figured out."

"There's nothing to be figuring out." Bellamy's footsteps echoed loudly in the quiet of the pub. He usually wasn't up and about at this time of the morning, but he'd only slept for a few hours last night after he'd returned to the apartment. Then he'd gotten up early to check on the children and discovered they were gone. He'd been awake ever since.

"Oh aye." Oscar grinned with a cunning that set Bellamy on edge. "There's a lot to be figuring out, to be sure, now that the Shanahans have finally come to visit me."

A strange wariness settled through Bellamy. Had Oscar merely been biding his time for the Shanahans to hear about the kiss? Was that why he'd been taking so long with all the other meetings he'd been having lately? Because he'd really been waiting for the Shanahans to visit?

Maybe Oscar had set up the meetings in the first place as a way to put pressure on the Shanahans to come forward. Maybe he'd also done it to put pressure on Bellamy, guessing that he would rather choose Zaira than a random stranger.

Bellamy narrowed his eyes on the older matchmaker. Holy mother. The man had outwitted him, so he had.

The front door swung open and banged against the wall with a force that reverberated through the building. James Shanahan stood in the doorway, the bright sunshine spilling past him and outlining his imposing frame. Attired as impeccably as always in a tailored suit, he was a fine-looking man. But today his face was nearly as red as his hair, and his expression was like that of an enraged bull about to charge.

He swept his gaze over the pub, and upon catching sight of Bellamy, he lurched forward, and his hands formed into fists. No doubt the fellow had finally heard what had transpired earlier in the week with the kiss and had ridden into the city first thing this morning to deal with the problem.

Bellamy straightened his shoulders, bracing for another walloping he deserved. It didn't matter that Kiernan had already punched him. Mr. Shanahan had a right to release his frustration too.

"Da?" Zaira's voice rang out behind Bellamy, and it was filled with worry. "What are you doing?"

Mr. Shanahan didn't seem to see or hear Zaira and continued to barrel forward with his glare fixed upon Bellamy.

"Da!" Zaira shouted this time. Then she did what only Zaira would do. She flung herself into the fray, held out her arms, and lifted her chin. "Leave Bellamy alone."

JODY HEDLUND

Thanks be, Mr. Shanahan pulled up short, but only just in time.

Bellamy placed his hands on Zaira's waist, intending to move her to the side and set her out of the way of any flying fists. As his fingers made contact near her hips, Mr. Shanahan's angry gaze followed the movement, and his nostrils flared.

"Take your hands off my daughter this instant." He ground out the words in a lethal tone.

Bellamy gently guided Zaira to the side and at the same time stepped in front of her to protect her. He didn't entirely release her and instead held her in place with one hand while he brought the other forward, holding it up to show Mr. Shanahan he meant no disrespect and that he also didn't intend to fight.

"Everything is worked out, Da." Kiernan had risen and was now shoving tables and chairs aside as he approached, obviously sensing that his da was mad enough to hurt Bellamy.

"No one touches or takes advantage of my daughters!" Mr. Shanahan pushed his face into Bellamy's.

"I apologize," Bellamy said quickly. "I regret I didn't take more care with Zaira."

"You ruined her!" Mr. Shanahan's spittle hit Bellamy.

"She's not ruined." Kiernan grabbed his da and pulled him away. "I've started the match process with the McKennas."

"A match?" Mr. Shanahan let Kiernan drag him back several more steps.

"We agreed to try a courtship," Zaira said as she fought to break free of Bellamy.

131

Bellamy didn't let go of her, though, and he wouldn't—not until Mr. Shanahan calmed down.

Kiernan placed both his hands on his da's shoulders. "Oscar and I have been discussing the terms of a match."

"But we want to wait." Zaira's tone held a note of vexation.

Kiernan gave Zaira a sharp look—one that warned her not to argue.

"You'll not be waiting!" Mr. Shanahan's voice rose again. "Not with the rumors I heard last night—rumors I won't be repeating."

The gossip was worsening. In fact, Bellamy had heard a tale yesterday about how he and Zaira had been secretly meeting at Dover's Pond to be with each other.

Of course, they'd done nothing inappropriate at their one meeting. But how had anyone learned of it? Had Oscar? And if so, had he stirred up more stories in order to incite Mr. Shanahan to come in and make demands of marriage?

From the corner of his eyes, Bellamy glimpsed Oscar reclining in his chair with a satisfied grin. Oh aye. Oscar had been meddling.

Bellamy gave himself a mental shake. This wasn't real. It was only pretend. Even if he and Zaira were matched instead of allowed to merely court as they'd agreed, they could still keep up a charade for a short while before dissolving their relationship.

He could feel the fight drain out of Zaira as she stopped struggling against him, as if she, too, realized there was nothing more they could do at the present to prevent an actual match. For now, they would have to go along with it.

"Doncha be worrying, James Shanahan." Oscar folded his

hands on his protruding belly. "Bellamy stands not only to inherit this pub but all the land I've bought up north of St. Louis—land that is growing in demand and price."

Bellamy knew the pub had been making a tidy profit for years, but he hadn't been aware that Oscar had purchased land north of St. Louis. When had he done so and how much?

Oscar took a drink from the Guiness he'd already poured for himself, then met Mr. Shanahan's gaze directly. "You might be looking to marry farther up for your daughter, but I was telling Kiernan that someday, Bellamy will be a wealthy man."

"The only thing I care about is Zaira." Mr. Shanahan was scanning Zaira, who'd managed to wiggle out from behind Bellamy and was standing beside him.

"I'm just fine, Da." Her face was flushed, and strands of her red hair had come loose from her bun. "You have to believe me that nothing has happened between Bellamy and myself except for the brief kiss."

"You're sure?" Mr. Shanahan's tone gentled.

If Mr. Shanahan truly cared about Zaira's feelings in the matter, then Bellamy had to give the wealthy man credit. He'd come a long way over the past year in his view of finding matches for his children. Perhaps in seeing the happy love matches his three older children had found, he was softening and realizing what was truly important in a marriage.

"Bellamy is a good man, and none of this is his fault." Zaira lowered her gaze, but not before Bellamy saw the guilt in her eyes. "I'm the one to blame—"

"I take full responsibility." He wasn't about to let Zaira reveal that she'd felt the need to hug or kiss him in order to research her novel. She'd kept her published life a secret from her family for a reason, likely because her da wouldn't support her endeavor and would make her stop. And Bellamy didn't want her to have to stop.

She deserved to be encouraged in her talents, and he couldn't stand by and watch while her fledgling writing career was taken from her by her well-meaning but strict father.

"No, Bellamy." Her eyes were filled with questions.

"I should have been more careful, and there's no arguing that." He leaned down and gently placed a kiss on her head. He wasn't sure why he did, only that it felt right to do so in the moment.

She inhaled, then closed her slightly parted lips. Her gaze was still upon him, but it now held gratefulness.

The anger and redness in Mr. Shanahan's face began to fade, and his attention shifted back and forth between Bellamy and Zaira, as if he was trying to discover what was really going on between them.

"There you have it!" Oscar's voice rang with enthusiasm. "Zaira and Bellamy are meant to be. Don't tell me you can't see it too, James."

Mr. Shanahan studied Zaira's face more closely. "I think I'm seeing it."

What exactly were the two men *seeing*? As far as Bellamy was concerned, his interactions with Zaira had been platonic, except for maybe the kiss on the head. But even that had been more brotherly than romantic.

Oscar scooted out the chair beside him. "Come on and sit down, James. We may as well pluck the gander right now and make this whole thing official."

Mr. Shanahan hesitated only a moment longer before he and Kiernan made their way toward the corner table.

"You too, Bellamy." Oscar waved him over. "You need to be part of the discussion."

Bellamy released Zaira's arm, took a step, then halted. "You'll wait for me to search for the children?" He kept his voice to a whisper. He hated to think how angry James Shanahan would become if he discovered even more of Zaira's indiscretions.

She nodded, seeming to realize the same.

"Good." He could feel her watching him as he walked to the table, and something inside him liked her attention, reveled in it.

Even so, he couldn't forget how unlucky in love the matchmakers in his family were. He didn't want a messy marriage for himself. And the very last thing he wanted was to drag Zaira into such a mess.

13

Through the haze of small bonfires, the encampment of refugees along the river was more deplorable than Zaira had imagined it would be. She had to breathe through her mouth in order not to gag from the reek of rubbish as well as human waste. The Mississippi River, under the hot July sun, was sluggish and contained a stench all its own.

Some of the immigrants had canvas tents held up by ropes. Others had constructed makeshift shacks out of boards and crates and scraps of material. Still others seemed to be living out in the open without any shelter.

Zaira was trying to wait patiently on the edge of the camp as Bellamy had instructed her, but she'd steadily crept closer and now swatted at the flies and gnats swarming the air and feasting on the refuse littering the ground.

She'd heard a toddler crying—one too young to be Moya. Zaira had also heard shouts of children playing, but the group that had passed by had been mostly older boys, and she hadn't seen anyone who looked like Seamus. However, from the lead Bellamy had gotten a short while ago, a boy and a girl who fit the ages of Seamus and Moya had been spotted among the river camps.

Bellamy hadn't wanted Zaira to come to this part of the city at all, the area worst affected by the cholera. Apparently, two wagonloads of dead had been carted away from the river camps just that morning.

Already she'd seen a man lying face down in the long grass close to one of the tents, and he hadn't moved since she'd noticed him. His clothing was worn and stained, and if he was sick, no one seemed to be taking care of him. Maybe he'd lost his family already. He could be Seamus and Moya's father, or someone very much like him.

Zaira might not be able to help that particular man, but she had to help the children, at least until their father was found.

She stood on her tiptoes and scanned the camp again for Bellamy. With his tall, lean body and dark hair, he was easy to spot. He was talking with a woman sitting against a rock, a babe in her arms, and the woman was pointing upriver. Bellamy responded, then reached into his pocket and handed the woman something.

As he moved away, the woman lifted the item, and Zaira recognized one of the biscuits Gavin had made for the noon meal. Bellamy must have stuffed extras in his pockets, having anticipated handing them out. Or perhaps he'd brought them along for Seamus and Moya.

He was a kind man to give one to the woman. Over the past couple of days, Zaira was glimpsing a side of Bellamy McKenna she hadn't seen often, and she liked it. A lot. Not that she hadn't already liked many things about him, because she had. She'd always known he was kind and giving and friendly. But this compassion showed that he cared more deeply about things than he'd let on.

He'd been really sweet during the confrontation with her da earlier in the day too. Surprisingly so. Had he even kissed her on the head? Or had she merely dreamed it? Either way, he'd been noble to take the blame upon himself for the kiss in the pub, especially because Da had been so angry about it.

She'd been afraid that she'd lose her position as the sweet and easy daughter who didn't cause any problems. If only she really was as sweet as they believed. But of her brothers and sisters, she was probably the least perfect, and she was the most duplicitous—with her writing, with her recent publications in the newspaper, with her research that included a lot of sneaking around, and now with her pretend match with Bellamy.

She knew God could see all her lying and deceiving and rebellion, and she certainly didn't have His favor. Once her parents learned about all her lying and deceiving and rebellious ways, she wouldn't have their favor anymore either.

For now, though, she'd averted another crisis. Her da had accepted Bellamy's apology and had been open to forming the match. Of course, she'd been flustered that the men had moved forward with a match instead of the courtship she and Bellamy had privately agreed upon. But she hadn't been able to stop the process.

During the ride home after plucking the gander with Oscar and Bellamy, Da had been in a congenial mood. Was *congenial* the right word to describe him? Maybe relieved? Reassured? Allayed?

Aye. *Allayed.* She liked that word the best. It was a good, strong description. Da's worries had all been allayed.

At some point in the future, whenever it seemed best to both her and Bellamy, they would have to let their families know they were parting ways. Perhaps they could stage a big fight or a disagreement to make the dissolution of their match believable.

In the meantime, the rumors that she was marrying the matchmaker would spread around St. Louis, and soon people would forget all about the inappropriate kiss she'd shared with Bellamy. She would become the envy of every single girl in the city, but that was just fine with her. She would enjoy her claim to Bellamy while it lasted. Secretly, of course. She couldn't chance him discovering that she was pretending to dislike him.

As he made his way toward her, his eyes narrowed in a way she was learning meant he wasn't pleased with her. "The devil, Zaira. I told you to stay on the edge of the encampment," he said when he got close enough.

"If you can traipse through the camp, why am I not allowed to stand here, where I'm mostly still on the edge?"

"Because I don't want you to catch the cholera."

"And what?" She lifted her brow at him. "Are you invincible?"

"Oh aye. I've been around people over the past few months with cholera, and I haven't been afflicted with it yet, so I haven't."

Bellamy had been there for her brother-in-law Riley when he'd battled cholera. He hadn't caught it then, so maybe he would be okay.

They returned to their horses and a well-worn path that bordered the river. It wound through shrubs and tall grass, with insects flying up in the air as they led the horses on foot.

During the past hours of searching, she and Bellamy had already discussed the growing problems with the city not being able to keep up with the swelling number of immigrants who came north by steamboat every day.

Many of them had come from Ireland because of the blight that had destroyed potato crops over recent years. Bellamy claimed that most had become reliant upon the potato for daily sustenance. The problem was that after an unusually wet and cool year in 1845, much of the potato crop had rotted in the fields, leaving people without food. The blight had persisted for the past few years, continuing to ruin potato crops.

The prime minister had imported corn to provide relief and avert starvation. But when the poor—many of whom were tenant farmers and laborers—couldn't keep up with paying rent, they were evicted from their homes, adding homelessness to the problem.

Charities and soup kitchens were helping, and the government had tried to provide employment for men in building roads and other public projects. But Bellamy believed the assistance to be grudging and ineffective, and he had expounded on how much more could be done to alleviate the problems.

Bellamy had been more knowledgeable about the issue than she'd expected. Clearly he soaked up a great deal of information in his line of work from the diverse people who came in and out of the pub. And he was bright and articulate in addition to being compassionate.

All more to like about him, which was proving to be a problem, because she didn't need to like him any more than she already did.

Bellamy halted and scanned the sloping riverbank that spread out in the clearing. It was less populated with only a few tents, and it looked cleaner and didn't have quite the stench as the other area.

"I'll head down and inquire." Bellamy moved off the trail while pinning her with a censuring look. "Please stay with the horses."

"It's not fair that you have different standards for men and women."

He cocked his head and studied her for a moment longer than necessary in that unique way of his that said he was seeing more than most people.

"What?" she asked.

"Just so we're clear, I don't have a different standard, which is why I believe you as a woman have every right to keep writing and publishing."

"But . . . ?"

"No *buts*. You also have a right to go into the immigrant camps, but I'd like to selfishly keep you safe."

Selfishly keep her safe? What exactly did he mean by that? Whatever the insinuation, warmth wafted through her—warmth she didn't want to feel and didn't want to acknowledge. She had to force herself to ignore it.

"Bell-amy," she dragged out his name with a teasing voice. "Are you implying that you care about me?"

He shook his head and returned to his descent. "Only to the extent that I'd like to avoid having your da kill me if anything happens to you."

"Blame it on my da," she called after him. "But I know the truth now."

He snorted.

She smiled. She'd done it. She'd kept herself from having a lovesick moment over him. This game of feigning not to like him was complicated, but she could do it.

Her gaze snagged on a movement in the brush ahead. Someone or something ducked out of sight into the tall grass behind a dogwood. Had it been a rabbit or a squirrel? Or a person?

"Hush now," said a child—a boy. It was followed by whining—decidedly from a girl, both resembling Seamus's and Moya's voices from the previous night.

Zaira's heart thudded an extra beat.

Bellamy was already down the hill and making his way toward a tent. She wanted to yell out to him that she'd found the children, but she also didn't want to scare Seamus into running away again.

She quickly secured the lead lines. Then, holding her breath, Zaira crept as quietly as possible toward the dogwood. She strained to hear anything more. But she couldn't distinguish any sounds past the unique *chik-ewww* of the Mississippi kite with its slender gray body soaring nearby above the grassland, hunting the grasshoppers buzzing loudly in the heat of the day.

As she reached the dogwood, she didn't hesitate. She pushed aside the low branches and was rewarded by the sight of two little faces, the sunshine bathing them and making them squint.

"Seamus and Moya." Relief filled her. "I've been worried sick about the two of you all day."

Seamus was holding a hand over Moya's mouth. She said something, but his hand muffled the sound.

"We don't need your help," Seamus stated in a huff.

In the daylight, Zaira could see that both of them had

brown hair—or perhaps their hair was brown because of the filth. Their faces were thin and smudged with dirt, making the blue-gray of their eyes all the brighter. Lines streaked through the dirt on Moya's cheeks, probably from tears.

"It's me, Zaira, from last night." She held up both hands so they could see they had nothing to worry about. "Bellamy and I have been searching for you."

Moya broke free of Seamus's hold, and she scrambled forward before he could grab her back. In the next instant, she was flinging herself upon Zaira. The lass wrapped her arms around Zaira's skirt and buried her face in the folds of satiny material.

"You're just fine," Zaira crooned. "Everything will be all right."

"I want my mama." Moya's heartbroken cry was garbled in Zaira's skirt, but it was still clear enough.

Seamus slid out of the brush and tugged on his sister. "Come with you now, Moya."

She resisted her brother and clung to Zaira more tightly.

"Why won't you let us help you, Seamus?"

The lad glared up at her. "You helped us last night, and now we're moving on."

"We can give you a place to stay until we locate your da."

"We'll not be going to an orphanage."

"What if I told you that you don't have to go to an orphanage?" Zaira stroked Moya's head. "What if I told you that you could stay at my house with me?"

"I'll go." Moya raised her face and peered up at Zaira eagerly.

Seamus shook his head. "That's what the last man told us, but then he took us right to the orphanage."

Bellamy had been right. Seamus was afraid of being captured and placed in another orphanage. How was it that Bellamy was able to read situations and people so well? The quality certainly could help him be a good matchmaker. But it also meant that he would be able to read her well too. Perhaps enough to see past her playacting to how she really felt. She would have to be extra careful around him.

"I wanna go to your house." Moya dug her fingers into Zaira's skirt. "Please."

Her da had indicated they would be leaving the city tomorrow morn to return to Oakland. Even though she'd pleaded with him to stay longer—and had made it seem like she wanted to be near Bellamy—Da and Kiernan had both been adamant about getting away from the cholera and back to the fresh air of the country.

In fact, neither Da nor Kiernan knew she'd left the house for the afternoon to search with Bellamy. They thought she was resting in her room during the heat of the day.

How would she ever explain the presence of the children without having to reveal her sneaking around? Who would care for them when she was at Oakland? Would there be a way to bring them with her to the country?

She sighed. She could hardly get Seamus to come with her to Bellamy's shed, much less leave the city. The child was determined to find his father and wouldn't be satisfied until they were reunited.

She didn't blame him. She could only imagine how overwhelming and frightening this new land was. It was probably vastly different from Ireland, so locating his father was his lone hope of having anything familiar or stable.

"See?" Seamus's tone was tinged with accusation. "You can't really take care of us."

"No, that's not it." Except he was right. She didn't know what she would be able to do for the two. But maybe Bellamy would have an idea. Could they stay with his family? She glanced over her shoulder, hoping he'd come sooner rather than later, before Seamus could take Moya and run away again.

The grassy trail was empty, with no sign of him.

Could she defy her da and stay in town with the children? She'd never disobeyed him openly before. Instead, she'd always at least made a show of being submissive while secretly doing what she needed to.

How could she stand up to him now? Not when he just wanted her to stay safe in the same way she wanted Seamus and Moya to stay safe.

No, the best option was to find a way to take care of the children without him knowing.

"Listen, Seamus." She crouched down so she was eye level with both. "I'm leaving the city tomorrow. But what if I try to find a nice family you can stay with? Someone who knows you're only there temporarily until you can be reunited with your father?"

Seamus seemed to ponder the matter, then he shook his head in protest.

"You need to do what's best for Moya." Zaira brushed the little girl's tangled hair back to reveal her pitiful, dirty, but expectant face. "Do you think all this running around and hiding is good for her? That your parents would want you to do this?"

"They would want me to take care of her."

"This isn't taking care of her." Zaira leveled a stern look at the boy. "Moya is tired and hungry and dirty. And you're constantly exposing her to cholera."

Seamus opened his mouth to respond but just as quickly closed it as remorse flashed in his eyes.

Zaira was being hard on the boy, but since he cared about his sister, she prayed the remorse would prod him to finally accept help. "*You* might be able to survive out here." Even that was questionable. "But you can't expect Moya to last much longer. You need to give her a secure home for now. And I'll help you find one."

If Bellamy's family couldn't take in these children, surely with all his connections, he would be able to locate someone who was kind and compassionate and willing to help.

Moya leaned into Zaira again, this time laying her head against Zaira's shoulder. "I wanna go home."

Seamus was watching his sister, his eyes too sad and too mature for a boy of six. After several long seconds, he nodded. "Okay."

Zaira released an inner sigh.

"But if you try to separate us," Seamus interjected, "we'll leave again, and you'll never find us."

Had someone at the orphanage threatened to separate him from Moya? Was that why he was so afraid? "I promise you and Moya will get to stay together." Zaira wasn't sure how she'd keep that promise, but she intended to do so one way or another.

146

14

$\mathscr{B}$ellamy followed Zaira through the back door of the pub, with Moya in his arms and Seamus on his heels.

Jenny, mixing batter in a large bowl at the worktable, and Gavin, slicing bread across from her, abruptly halted their supper preparations to stare.

As the back door closed and enveloped Bellamy in the heat of the kitchen along with the strong odor of fried fish, he could hear Moya's stomach growl. She'd fallen asleep during the ride back to the pub, and now she lifted a sleepy head and sniffed the air.

"Jenny and Gavin, this is Moya." Bellamy nodded at the lass then the lad. "And that is Seamus."

"Pleased to meet you both." Jenny wiped her hands on her apron. If she was surprised by their filthy condition, she didn't let it show. Instead, her eyes held questions.

"We were wondering"—Zaira flashed a bright smile filled with enthusiasm that was hard to resist—"if you might consider letting Seamus and Moya stay in the apartment until we can locate their father."

Jenny's eyes widened, the request clearly taking her by surprise.

On the way home from the encampments along the river, Zaira had brought up the possibility of the children staying with his family. Bellamy had agreed it was the best solution since having the children live at Zaira's house would tempt her to remain in the city instead of getting away from the cholera.

"Their mam has gone to heaven," Zaira continued, "and so they currently don't have a place to live."

"I see," Jenny said kindly as she glanced again from Moya to Seamus. "I'm sorry to hear of the loss."

Seamus studied her in return.

Bellamy had already explained to the children that he was taking them back to the pub. At first Seamus assumed he and Moya would have to sleep in the shed. But Bellamy had indicated that if Jenny and her husband were agreeable, the children would stay in the apartment above the pub.

"We do have plenty of room, so we do." Jenny shared a look with Gavin.

He nodded.

Jenny smiled at Seamus. "We'd be happy to have you for as long as you need."

"I'd be happy too." Moya was now looking at Jenny, her eyes filled with hope.

Seamus didn't smile back, but the stiffness fell from his shoulders.

Bellamy allowed himself a full breath. He hadn't necessarily been worried, but a part of him had wondered if having the orphans might be too much for Jenny—a glaring reminder of the children she'd never been able to have for herself.

"Do you have work for me?" Seamus peered around the kitchen, which was as untidy as usual.

Zaira tsked. "Of course not—"

"I'll not be staying nowhere for nothing." Seamus straightened to his full height, which wasn't much taller than Bellamy's waist. "I'm used to working hard and can do a lot more than you'd expect."

"Oh aye," Bellamy spoke before Zaira could turn down the boy's offer. "Naturally, we'll have work for you."

"Bell-amy." Zaira shot him a narrowed look. "We're not placing conditions on him."

"No, of course not," Jenny added, speaking directly to Seamus. "God's blessed us with a good home and plenty of food, and we can do nothing less than share our bounty."

Zaira started to nod.

"But," Jenny continued, "we'll not be turning down the help if you've a mind to offer it."

"I've a mind." Seamus spoke seriously, as though a miniature man lived inside his body.

Zaira's nose scrunched up with the beginning of more protest. Obviously, she didn't know what it was like to be poor and to also try to cling to one's honor. Sometimes honor was the only thing the poor had left, and if Seamus felt better working for his keep, then they needed to let him.

Bellamy crossed to Jenny and held out Moya.

Jenny hesitated for only a heartbeat, then gathered the little girl in her arms. Moya didn't resist Jenny and instead leaned into her.

"I'll be back shortly." Bellamy crossed toward the door. "After I take Zaira home."

Zaira said her good-byes to the children and promised she'd check in on them from time to time when she could. But she didn't linger much longer. He guessed she was needing to get back home before anyone realized she was gone and came looking for her.

When she'd shown up at the pub in the early afternoon inquiring if he was ready to go search, he'd already been making plans to head to the river and check among the camps. He should have told her to stay back at the pub.

But when it came to Zaira, he couldn't say no very easily. Not only was she persuasive in getting what she wanted, but he found himself giving in to her whims so he could make her happy.

When they exited the kitchen, she stopped him with a touch to his arm, which always turned up the degree of heat in his body more than he wanted to admit.

"I walked over here by myself, Bellamy, and I'll be just fine going home alone."

"I'll accompany you." He broke away from her light hold and started toward the horses. "I'm sure your da will be expecting me to escort you home."

She didn't say anything and didn't move from the shade of the building. Even flushed and damp with perspiration, she was prettier than any woman he'd ever met.

When he reached his horse and gathered the reins, he glanced back at her with a raised brow. He was putting her in an awkward situation where she would have to explain that she'd gone behind her da's back this afternoon. But Bellamy wanted her to know that he knew the truth.

She met his gaze, a glimmer of guilt in her eyes. "He doesn't know I'm with you."

"Is that a fact?" He'd left the horses near the watering trough, and now they swished their tails and flicked their ears to ward off flies. "So he won't be happy to see me, then?"

"Bell-amy," she softly chided.

He liked the way she said his name, although he wasn't sure why. "I'll still ride with you home."

"I don't mind the walk."

"And I don't mind the ride."

She sighed with exasperation. "The truth is, Da doesn't even know I left the house, and I'll need to sneak back up the trellis."

Bellamy stuck his foot in the stirrup and hauled himself into the saddle before giving her a pointed look. "That wasn't so hard, was it?"

She was watching him, her head cocked. "What wasn't hard?"

"Telling me the truth."

She flushed even more and ducked her head.

"Seems to me you're not only a grand actor, but you're the expert at lying."

Her head snapped up, and her eyes suddenly blazed. "How dare you!"

"How dare I confront you about all your lying?"

"That's swell coming from someone who's an expert at it too."

Was he an expert at it too? He hadn't considered himself a liar. But he supposed it looked like that to her since he had a pseudonym for his painting and had just agreed to be in a fake match with her. Both were big deceptions.

He'd thought he was justified in making the choices he had. But maybe lying was never justified. Maybe he'd been wrong on both scores, especially in God's eyes.

Whatever the case, he'd come too far with the deception to change courses now, hadn't he?

He gave a curt nod toward the other horse. "Let's go. I'll ride with you most of the way and then you can walk the last block home by yourself."

He nudged his horse several steps forward, waiting for her. A moment later he could hear her climbing into the saddle.

For the duration of the ride, they avoided talking about themselves and instead spoke about Moya and Seamus and all the other children like them. They decided the best plan was to ask Riley if he had any ideas for how to do more to help the cholera orphans.

When they neared Third Street, Bellamy reined in. She dismounted, handed him the lead line for her horse, and gave him a nod before turning and walking away.

He watched her until she rounded the corner. Even then he nudged his horse forward and lingered at the end of her street. She paused at the edge of the Shanahan property, glanced back at him, and gave him a small wave. Then she disappeared into the brush.

As he made his way back to the pub, his thoughts kept circling back to the lying, and all the lying Oscar had done with Mam. There had always been so much deception between the two, especially Oscar pretending to care about Mam but never loving her enough to accept her for all her quirks and creativity and spontaneity.

How many times had Bellamy heard them arguing? And how many times had he heard Oscar come up with excuses about how she was needed in the pub kitchen or dining room in order to keep her from painting?

Not that Mam hadn't lied too. But most of her dishonesty had been in response to Oscar's attempts to control her. She'd taken to sneaking around and leaving the house at odd hours. She'd started associating with questionable people because they understood and accepted her better. In those last years of her life, she'd begun drinking and had to lie about it to Oscar so he wouldn't get angry with her.

Oh aye, Bellamy knew a lot about lying. It wasn't a path he wanted to take with his life, but it seemed he'd headed that direction anyway with a woman who was quite proficient at it herself.

All the more reason to make sure to end things with Zaira just as soon as it was viable. She wasn't the right woman for him, and he wasn't the right man for her—not when any connection to him would only lead to unhappiness. He couldn't do that to Zaira.

15

"An autumn wedding would be perfect." Mam's declaration to her friends nearby rose above the chatter of the circle of young ladies surrounding Zaira.

The forty or so guests mingled about Oakland's sprawling yard where the tables and chairs were placed in the shade of the oak trees and covered in the finest linens, china dishes, and crystal goblets. Freshly picked bouquets of flowers in vases adorned each table.

Zaira tried to keep smiling and listening to the guests, but her heart was weighing more heavily with every passing moment of the supposed celebration: the eating of the gander, the meal to announce her match with Bellamy.

Across the yard, Bellamy stood with her brothers— Kiernan, Madigan, Quinlan, and Riley—along with neighbors who'd been invited to the party. Bellamy was more handsome than usual, which was a nearly impossible feat since he was always so striking. But something about his wearing a dark suit with a long tailcoat instead of his more casual day wear added to his appeal.

She, of course, was attired in one of her fanciest dresses, a blue floral silk with a lace bertha trimming the low neckline. Mam had wanted Zaira to have a new gown tailored for the occasion, and Zaira had hoped the dress fittings would allow her to make frequent trips into the city to the seamstress.

Over the past three days since she'd left St. Louis with Da and Kiernan and Alannah, Zaira had wanted to check on how Moya and Seamus were doing with the McKennas. However, since the men had given them only a few days to plan, there hadn't been time for a new gown, and she hadn't been able to concoct any other excuses to go to town.

She'd been relieved to learn from Bellamy when he'd first arrived with Oscar a short while ago that the children were still staying with them and seemed to be adjusting. Although she hadn't talked with Bellamy for long, he'd informed her that both Seamus and Moya had taken baths and accepted the new clothing Jenny had purchased for them. They were also eating well, and Seamus had been helping in the kitchen with fetching water and other simple chores that kept him busy. Bellamy had continued to put out the word regarding the children's father, but he hadn't found any information on the man's whereabouts.

Even with mostly good news regarding the children, Zaira was anxious to see them again. She needed to go into the city soon to turn in the next chapter of her story to the newspaper. She wasn't sure what justification she'd find for escaping from Oakland, but she would figure out something. She always did.

"Maybe by autumn the cholera will be gone," said one of Mam's friends as she pumped her face with a fan, the lace and ruffles of her gown rustling in the breeze.

Another friend nodded, fanning her face too. "My husband said that the highest recorded daily deaths of one hundred twenty-four was on July 10, and that each day since has shown a marked decrease."

"Thanks be." Mam made the sign of the cross.

Thanks be, Zaira inwardly echoed. Even so, the slowing of the disease didn't take care of the problem of homeless children like Seamus and Moya. How many more were wandering the streets, hungry and confused, wondering where their parents had gone?

"You're so lucky, Zaira," said Emilie Conway, grasping Zaira's arm and pulling her back into the conversation with the young ladies, all of whom were also attired in their prettiest gowns. "You managed to win the handsomest man in all of St. Louis. How did you do it?"

Dottie Buckley made a swooning sound. "Remember last All Hallows' Eve when Zaira peeled the whole apple skin without breaking it? When she threw it over her shoulder, it landed in the shape of a *W* for *William Bellamy McKenna.*"

Zaira forced a smile. The old tradition of casting an unbroken apple peel over the shoulder was nothing more than a superstition. It couldn't really predict a future spouse, and she and her friends had only done so to be silly.

"I've been sprinkling salt on the four corners of my bed every night." Emilie dropped her voice to a conspiratorial whisper. "And I've been dreaming about a man with pale hair, wearing a gray suit."

The salt sprinkling was another Irish tradition, one that claimed if a woman put salt on her bed, then in her first hour of sleep she would see the man she would marry—or at least glimpse his hair color and the clothes he would wear on their wedding day.

There were other such customs, like putting a piece of somebody else's wedding cake under a pillow to make a woman dream about the man she would marry. Or dropping hair and nail clippings into a fire to create a dream about the future spouse.

Zaira had always had fun with the traditions with her friends. But the W in the apple peeling didn't stand for *William Bellamy McKenna*. Their relationship was only a farce. He didn't like her. And she could tell he was still angry with her for all her lying because he'd only spoken to her about the children since he'd arrived, and he'd hardly looked her way.

Dottie made eyes at one of the young men standing near Bellamy and then giggled. "I'm considering having a love potion made to help me find my true love."

Was there such a thing as true love?

Zaira wanted to believe that was possible—had always believed she'd eventually find a man who loved her passionately and whom she loved passionately in return. But what if she never found a man who could love her for who she really was? A man who knew about her secrets and flaws and still accepted her and loved her regardless? Maybe such a man only existed in fiction.

After all, she had to pretend to be someone else in order to keep her mam and dad happy with her. They had such traditional views of what a woman should be like that they would never understand she wanted more—needed more, needed freedom, needed to create. Why would that change in a husband?

Regardless, she was here now, and she had to make the best

of the situation—her fake engagement to her fake fiancé. She felt terrible that her mam had gone to so much trouble for the party.

Zaira had tried to object to such a big celebration, had even suggested waiting because of the cholera in hopes of deterring Mam's plans. But Mam had pushed forward anyway, stating that they were all safe in the countryside, that she missed the gatherings with her friends, and that eating the gander would be the perfect occasion to have company.

Da and Kiernan had also decided it would be a way to show the community that the Shanahans weren't cowering away after Kiernan's marriage to Alannah and that the past was behind them.

Emilie nudged her arm and leaned in. "Look who's coming our way."

Bellamy was crossing toward them, and Emilie was boldly staring at him as though he was a dessert she wanted to gobble up.

Strange prickles formed inside Zaira. Emilie shouldn't be looking at her fake fiancé that way. Her friend didn't know the relationship wasn't real. And it was rude to make eyes at a man who was taken.

It didn't matter that Zaira understood her friend's attraction to Bellamy. His freshly shaven face showed off his angular jaw and high cheekbones. His dark hair was parted neatly on one side and slicked back. And his eyes were just as dark and almost brooding tonight, as if he wasn't happy with the party.

Well, the party wasn't her fault, if that's what he was thinking. She wasn't happy about it either. But she would try to enjoy the evening. After all, she never wasted a single moment of anything that happened in her life. It was all fuel to ignite her writing inspiration. Surely some day she could write all about the fake engagement party in one of her novels.

As he neared, the conversations from the clusters of women around her tapered to silence. Everyone was watching her and Bellamy. Everyone wanted to see them interact. And everyone would be judging their relationship.

She couldn't give people anything more to gossip about. Instead, she had to pretend she was interested in Bellamy and make the guests believe the match was a good one. That's what her parents would expect of her tonight, and she couldn't let them down or disappoint them, especially so publicly.

No, she had to use her best acting skills with Bellamy and put on a show.

She curved her lips into what she hoped was a welcoming smile.

As he stopped, he didn't smile in return.

"I've been wondering when I would get to spend some time with you." She widened her smile and made sure to sound cheerful.

Bellamy held out his elbow. "I've been told it's time for us to take our spot together at the table so the meal can begin."

She slipped her hand into the crook of his arm and allowed him to guide her toward the center table. As they moved out of hearing range from the other guests, she leaned in and whispered, "You've made it clear you detest me. But remember, you have to at least pretend to like me."

He leaned in toward her ear. "I don't detest you."

"You could have fooled me and everyone else here."

"I'm sorry, so I am." His arm brushed against her shoulder. "I just wish we could have avoided all of this."

"Me too." She sighed. "But since we're here, we have to at least be cordial to each other, or people will start to wonder what's going on."

"Rightly so." He released a tense breath too. "I'll try to be doing better."

"We can at least be friends, Bellamy. That's not too hard, is it?"

He hesitated.

It was long enough to send a shiver of apprehension through her. Did he dislike her so much that he didn't even want to be friends?

"Never mind." She couldn't keep the stiffness from her tone. "Just see that you're somewhat affectionate, and let's hope that's convincing enough for everyone."

As they reached their table, he halted, pulled out her chair, and helped her get situated like any good gentleman would before taking his own seat. With all eyes upon them, the moment was awkward. But this would probably be the first of many awkward moments she would have to endure while matched to a man who didn't want or like her.

Nevertheless, she forced herself to continue with the charade no matter how hurt she felt. Because ultimately her hurt was irrational. She'd known from the beginning of concocting this plan that a relationship with Bellamy could never amount to anything, and she couldn't allow herself false hope.

With Oscar at their table entertaining everyone with stories from the matches he'd made over the years, the laughter flowed easily, and she soon relaxed again, doing her best to ignore Bellamy beside her.

He was hard to overlook, though, because he exuded a

magnetism that had always drawn her attention. Watching his strong fingers cutting meat on his plate sent a shiver through her. Catching sight of a vein throbbing in his neck above his cravat made her stomach tumble. Even just a twitch in his hard jaw caused her heart to thump an extra beat.

It wasn't fair that he had so much of a pull on her, and she had none on him.

When they were nearly finished with the meal, his knee brushed against her leg under the table, and she was conscious all over again of his body beside hers, his manliness and how well his suit fit him.

She slid a glance at him sideways only to find that he'd glanced at her too. Their gazes connected, and something in his eyes reached across the distance and lit a flame low in her stomach. What was in his eyes? Heat? Attraction? Desire?

It couldn't be.

She dropped her gaze, the intensity in his eyes too much to understand. But in the next instant, she couldn't keep from looking back up, needing more, needing the connection, needing to feel the heat again.

He'd glanced away too, but as if he sensed her looking at him again, he returned his attention, watching her more fully. Reflecting the cloudless blue evening sky overhead, his brown eyes turned the color of dark whiskey, and this time the interest was obvious.

Her heart fluttered with warm desire—the desire to like him openly and not in secret, the desire to show him and everyone that she cared about him, the desire to lean in and trace his strong jawline.

She couldn't do any of that, but she could touch his hand,

couldn't she? It wouldn't be inappropriate, not when they were trying to convince everyone they were truly a match.

With her hand fiddling with her spoon and his resting on the table only inches away, she released her hold of the spoon and shifted her fingers—still smudged with ink, even though she'd tried hard to remove it for the occasion—until her pinky brushed his.

For a second, he didn't move, then his pinky shifted and wrapped over hers.

The flutters inside her chest pumped faster. What did this mean? Was it a peace offering of some sort? Or was it merely for show?

His pinky held hers for a moment, and then he moved it, caressing her finger.

At the deliciousness, she stopped breathing altogether. She loved his touch. It was better than anything else she'd ever known.

A clinking of a utensil against a goblet started up nearby. She wanted to ignore it, but it was too persistent, and she finally broke her connection with Bellamy at the same time he broke his with hers to find that Oscar was tapping his spoon against his goblet, now drained of the wine.

He was beaming at them and so was everyone else. Her da's eyes were tender upon her, and Mam's seemed to be filled with knowing. Riley and Finola were smiling and exchanged a loving look. Alannah nodded, as though she'd been proven right about something, and Kiernan's eyes held surprise. Clearly he hadn't anticipated Bellamy's affection to be so obvious.

Well, that made two of them. Zaira hadn't expected it either.

The guests at the other tables had grown silent, and all eyes were upon Oscar. He nodded at Bellamy, encouraging him to do something.

Bellamy pushed his chair back from the table, fumbling in his coat pocket as he did so. He stood and reached out a hand to her.

She wasn't sure what he was planning, but she was always ready for any level of drama. So she willingly and happily placed her hand in his and allowed him to help her to her feet.

He didn't release her hand. Instead, his gaze found hers. This time it was filled with uncertainty, as if he wasn't sure he was doing the right thing. As he began to lower himself in front of her, she suddenly knew why. He was giving her a ring, the symbol of their pledge to be married.

No doubt, he'd been instructed by Oscar to do so tonight at the feast. It wasn't a requirement by any means. Plenty of couples got married without the fellow giving a ring to his bride-to-be. But it was a sweet tradition, and certainly the matchmaker himself would adhere to it.

On one knee before her, Bellamy situated a ring in his fingers before looking up at her. "Zaira, would you accept my ring as a token of my desire to marry you?" Earnestness filled his expression, almost as if he was being sincere about the offer.

The ring was simple but elegant—an Irish claddagh band comprised of two hands holding a heart that had a crown upon it. The two hands represented friendship, the heart signified love, and the crown stood for loyalty.

It was beautiful and perfect and romantic—everything she'd ever dreamed of when it came to her engagement. Except the union wasn't real.

She pushed that thought from her mind. For tonight, she could pretend she really was getting engaged to Bellamy. She could pretend the ring meant something. And she could pretend they would live happily ever after.

She allowed herself a smile and breathed out the one word required of her. "Aye."

Bellamy slipped the ring on her finger with ease, no fumbling or shaking, as if he'd done it already a dozen times. He probably had seen dozens of engagements in his lifetime as he'd accompanied Oscar to matches. What was he thinking of theirs? That he was sorry his special moment had to be just an act? Was he wondering how he'd gotten mixed up with her like this? Or was he trying to make the best of the evening too?

He finished settling the ring on her finger and then offered her a small smile that seemed to tell her not to worry. His smiles were always so heart-melting, though. This one was no exception. Her heart turned to warm liquid in her chest.

As he rose, everyone began to clap. He didn't release her hand right away. Instead, he continued to face her, likely waiting for the clapping to stop and for the moment to be officially over.

"Kiss!" someone shouted from another table.

Bellamy didn't move, and his expression didn't change, almost as if he hadn't heard the suggestion.

"Oh aye!" This came from Oscar with a laugh. "Give her a kiss, Bellamy, and show everyone how it's done."

Oh, sweet saints. She could feel a blush blooming in her cheeks.

Someone else echoed Oscar, and Bellamy tossed the fellow a grin.

With more calls of "kiss" rising in the air, Bellamy glanced down at her mouth. Then he met her gaze, and his eyes contained an apology.

She knew as well as he did they had no choice but to kiss. If they refused, they would look petty and raise all kinds of questions. Besides, if she was honest with herself, she didn't want to turn down the opportunity to kiss Bellamy. For as rocky as her relationship with him was, she couldn't deny she'd enjoyed kissing him and had dreamed about it often enough that she wanted to kiss him again.

"Kiss her!" Oscar's voice boomed above all the other guests calling for the same thing.

Bellamy bent in, and without another moment of hesitation, he touched his lips to hers.

As he did so, the world around her disappeared, and she was swept away to paradise where kissing him was the only thing that mattered. His lips were firm and commanding, just as they'd been last time, but more so. And her lips meshed with his, like they'd been made to fit there.

He was still holding her hand, and he slid his fingers through hers, languidly intertwining them and bringing each of her fingers into contact with each of his. The intimacy of the touch sent shivers of delight skittering along her arms. At the same time, his mouth covered hers more thoroughly, as if he needed more of her because what he had wasn't enough.

Something in his craving stirred a deliciousness inside her—a desire to keep kissing him, to make it her life's mission to have this pleasure with him every single day. Was this what it was like for Finola and Riley, Enya and Sullivan, and Kiernan and Alannah? Was this why she caught them kissing so much?

More clapping rang out around them as well as cheers.

Bellamy broke the kiss just as suddenly as he'd started it. He took a rapid step away from her, releasing her hand in the process. But he grinned widely at the guests, as if he'd won a bet and was pleased with himself.

Had he liked the kiss as much as she had?

With a flourish, he pulled out her chair and helped her sit back down. Then he took his place beside her while accepting the congratulations from friends and family goodnaturedly. When the chatter and conversations at the tables began again, he leaned in.

"How am I doing?" he whispered with a charming grin that didn't reach his eyes.

What did he mean?

"With my acting?" he clarified, as if he'd seen the question in her eyes. "Was I affectionate enough?"

So everything had been just an act? He'd been pretending it all?

A strange disappointment settled in her heart. His touch, his looks, his kiss had felt authentic. But she should have known it wouldn't be real to him, that he'd just been following her instructions to do a better job at feigning to like her.

Well, he'd done it. In fact, he'd almost fooled her. As he turned away to joke with someone, she could only sit beside him, breathless and aching and longing for more—more from their relationship and more from him than this acting.

16

*S*o you'll be cutting off our supply of beer entirely now?" came a frustrated call from the crowd of tavern owners and shopkeepers who had assembled for the meeting.

Bellamy stood among them on Charles Street in the afternoon drizzle that was only cooling off the city a little, not enough to clear out the foul vapors and humid air.

"Hopefully just until the end of the month," Riley replied. "Perhaps mid-August at the latest." Riley Rafferty, also known as Saint Riley of the Kerry Patch, was at the center of the meeting with several other members from his Committee of Public Health. A fine black hat covered his blond hair, and he wore a dark suit that turned him into a fine gentleman, befitting his role as a leader. Even so, his muscular form and weathered skin gave away the fact that he was a laborer and wagonmaker.

Since the beginning of the month with the decision to cut back on drinks made with malt, the supply of beer had dwindled. Now with the committee's decision, no one could serve any beer. Doing so would bring stiff fines. Regardless of the bad news, most members of their community respected Riley for his efforts in trying to fight the cholera.

Not only were the tavern owners affected but so were the breweries. In fact, the ordinance would likely hurt the breweries, like the Meiers', even worse since at least the taverns could continue serving food and other drinks that weren't made from malt.

Bellamy hadn't seen Zach Meier since that day the Whitcombs had left by steamer for Iowa. Perhaps the news today of the banning of beer would be the excuse Bellamy needed to pay the Meiers a visit and in doing so find a way to encourage Zach not to give up on Deirdre.

Whatever the case, the newest regulation would be hard on all of them. But the truth was, the men at the impromptu street meeting today were willing to make sacrifices in order to put an end to the cholera epidemic. They were all desperate to keep themselves and their loved ones safe, so even if they didn't like having to stop selling beer, they would do it.

"The death toll is decreasing every day." Riley's voice rang out above the crowd, his presence as commanding and energetic as always. "That means the measures we've implemented are working."

The Committee of Public Health had been laboring tirelessly to clean the city, carting away accumulated trash and waste and sending around street inspectors to fine those who didn't comply with new cleanliness regulations.

The committee had also ordered the burning of purification fires to fill the air with smoke and fumes. They believed doing so would help kill the miasma of the disease that might linger in the air. They were also trying to provide pure water for residents and had opened up more water hydrants.

Riley and his committee had made a great deal of progress in a short amount of time, including providing more hospital beds and getting the ill the care they needed. They'd even started Quarantine Island to the south of St. Louis where all incoming steamboats had to stop, be inspected, and deposit their sick in the hastily built quarantine wards before being allowed to dock in St. Louis. Since cholera was raging in Europe as well, the hope was to prevent infected immigrants arriving via New Orleans directly from Europe from spreading the illness.

Riley was right that the numbers of those dying from cholera were finally decreasing. If they could just continue their efforts to stop the spread, maybe they would be able to bring the living nightmare to an end and no longer have to worry if each day would be the last with the people they loved.

People they loved.

Zaira's face flashed to the front of Bellamy's mind as it had dozens of times since the party at Oakland two evenings ago—her heart-shaped face after he'd kissed her, with her cheeks flushed, her eyes bright.

She'd been the most beautiful woman there. Not only had her gown molded to her exquisite body, but the blue had also made her red hair striking and her green eyes vibrant. From the moment he'd arrived, he'd been attuned to her every move, almost to her every breath. He'd tried to ignore her while talking with the fellows, but even then, he'd been drawn to her, wanted to stare at her, and admired everything about her.

Sitting down to dinner had been even more difficult. He'd been so near to her and yet tried to keep from being obsessed with her. At the close of the meal when her hand had brushed against his, he hadn't stopped to think, had simply reacted by grazing her finger with his. He was fairly certain she'd felt the same attraction to him he'd been battling with her—the attraction that he'd been working hard to contain ever since meeting her.

As he'd gotten down on his knee and slipped the ring on her finger, that attraction had flared up again between them. He'd felt it. So when the calls had started up for them to kiss, he'd done so all too willingly. She'd kissed him in return with a fervor that told him she hadn't been pretending—at least in that moment.

That realization had scared him, and he'd pulled back and put their relationship into its proper place as a fake relationship that couldn't have a future. The rest of the evening, he'd kept busy talking and mingling with everyone but her, and she'd seemed to want to stay away from him too. At the end of the evening, her good-bye had even been somewhat cold, which hadn't bothered him, at least not much.

It was all too easy to let his desires for a woman like Zaira flood him so that he wasn't thinking rationally. Maybe that had been the problem with the men in his family, letting themselves get carried away with the physical attraction to a woman instead of ensuring they were compatible in the ways that truly mattered. Maybe that's why the matchmakers had always made massive mistakes with their own matches. After all, it was a universally known fact that it was easy to spot the problems of others at a distance but fail to see the problems right under your own nose.

The truth was, even if his desire for Zaira was growing, he wasn't about to throw away all caution and embrace a real relationship based on his physical desires. No, he had to stay in control of himself, and he couldn't forget they would only be together for a short while before going their separate ways. Then Zaira could find a man who would give her a happy and fulfilling marriage.

A hand clamping on his shoulder brought Bellamy back to the street and to the meeting that was adjourning. Riley stood before him, grinning.

"So, what is it you needed to talk to me about privately?" Riley asked. "Are you wanting my help in plotting how to get Zaira to the church so you can marry her right away?"

The young man was obviously referring to the way Bellamy had finagled Finola into going to the church for their wedding. Bellamy had indeed worked magic—or at least it had felt a wee bit that way—to bring the two together after having them walk away from each other and their relationship on multiple occasions.

"I saw the way you were looking at her," Riley teased. "And I'm guessing a wedding sooner rather than later is in order."

Bellamy's insides tightened at the direction of the conversation. He wanted to blame the tautness on frustration, but he couldn't deny that just the thought of having a wedding to Zaira, then a wedding night afterward, was more than a little appealing.

"In fact," Riley continued, "everyone is putting bets on how long the two of you will hold out before having the wedding."

Bellamy had heard a few comments about the betting, but he hadn't known the gossip was so widespread. He offered Riley a smirk, knowing he had to play along rather than burst out in denial. "I'll not be telling you and have you winning the bet."

"Why not?" Riley's grin widened. "I've got money on a week. Just tell me this, will it be less than that?"

Did people really think he was that enamored with Zaira that he couldn't wait more than a week to marry her? He almost sighed, but he kept his smirk in place. "You'll have to wait and find out just like everyone else."

"You're not holding the new ordinance against me, are you?"

"We all have to do our part."

"Thank you for understanding." All humor dissipated from Riley's face as he glanced to the few lingering men from the meeting.

"That's actually why I wanted to talk to you." Bellamy leaned against the outer wall of the pub and tried to ease the tension that had come from talking about Zaira. "You know we've taken in two orphans?"

Riley nodded. "Zaira told us about it at the party."

"I'm sure you're also aware there are many more children who've lost both parents to cholera and are now roaming the streets."

"Aye, Zaira expressed the same concern." Riley's expression turned grave. "Since talking with her, I've had one of the inspectors go to the orphanages and have discovered there aren't enough beds for all the children, but we've instructed the nuns to at least feed the children even if they can't provide shelter."

"What if we can do more for them than that?" Bellamy could admit their apartment was more crowded now that Seamus and Moya were staying with them. He'd started sleeping on the floor and had let the children bed down on the sofa—one on each end.

But the two were doing well considering all they'd gone through in their short lives. Seamus was trying hard not to be a bother and to make himself useful. All his initial resistance to staying was gone, and he'd hinted a time or two that he was worried about having to leave and live on the streets again.

Jenny had also been good for them. She was a natural mother and had won them over from the first moment she'd met them. She seemed happy to have them there, so much so that last night he'd warned her against getting too attached since he was still looking for their father. She'd assured him that she would take care of the children as long as they needed, but that they would be better off with their father when he was found.

"What do you have in mind?" Riley leaned in, giving Bellamy his full attention.

An idea had been formulating in Bellamy's mind over the past couple of days. "Naturally I have a lot of connections and know a lot of people."

"That you do."

"With my knowledge, I believe I can be helping to find families for some of the homeless children."

Riley nodded slowly. "Go on. Tell me more."

"Many people are eager to do something. They just don't know what."

"And you think more families might be willing to house children?"

"After hearing about our taking in Seamus and Moya, I know some who already want to do the same. I'll put out word of the need, if you're agreeable."

"I like the idea, and I do think we can make it work, but first I need to discuss with the committee rules to protect the children."

Bellamy liked how Riley operated. He was open-minded but also smart.

"In the meantime, why don't you put together a list of families who would be willing to take children in."

"I can do that."

"Good." Riley stuck out his hand for a shake. "I'll be back tomorrow, and hopefully we can start taking immediate steps to get orphans off the streets and into homes."

Bellamy shook Riley's hand before they parted ways. As Bellamy returned to the pub, he made quick work of hauling the beer to the shed, where it would have to remain until they were notified that they could start selling it again. Without the beer, they would have even fewer customers. But if they only suffered a loss in profit when the cholera was over, they would consider themselves lucky when so many had suffered the loss of loved ones.

As he rolled the last keg across the alley, laughter wafted through the open window of the upstairs apartment. It belonged to only one woman. Zaira.

Against his wishes, his pulse spurted faster. He'd been telling himself he didn't miss her and didn't want to see her. But now that she was here, he needed just one glimpse of her beautiful face, just one smile, just one word.

He finished storing the keg, then he headed up to the apartment.

Jenny was sitting on the sofa with Moya on her lap, and Seamus sat beside Zaira on the floor, demonstrating how to tie a shoelace, something Jenny had taught him when she'd given him boots, the first pair he'd ever owned with laces.

Seamus had already proudly shown Bellamy his new feat. Now he beamed as he tied the laces for Zaira. She was chattering with Seamus and Moya, sparing Bellamy only the barest of glances and ignoring him almost completely.

He didn't care. He leaned against the doorframe and watched her as openly as he wanted, not holding himself back from admiring the graceful curve of her neck, the few curls dangling loose by her ears, the slope of her cheeks, the slight dimple in her chin.

He didn't paint many portraits, but she had the kind of beauty he would relish recreating. Every time he was with her, he saw something more in her that he wanted to capture on canvas, and today it was the relaxed, comfortable way she interacted with the children.

Would Zaira be a good mother?

He suspected she would be. She was compassionate and nurturing and soft-spoken, unlike his own mam, who'd been busy and distracted when Oscar hadn't been fighting with her.

When Seamus finished tying his shoe, Zaira asked both children all about the past few days, and they excitedly told her about the food they'd eaten, their bed on the sofa, the chores they'd done, and more.

Zaira surprised the children by handing a book to them, an illustrated book of *Aesop's Fables*. Although Jenny had already reluctantly returned to the kitchen to help Gavin with the supper preparations, Bellamy wasn't in a rush and took a seat at the table while Zaira proceeded to read one of the fables to the children.

When she finished, she closed the book with a tender smile. "I wish I could stay and read another story, but I really need to go."

She'd probably come to town to turn in her weekly chapter to the *Daily Republican*. It was about the time of week she usually did so. Although she hadn't told him she was using the name K. S. Flanders, he'd guessed that was her column since it was new, and the story sounded like something she'd write—dramatic and intriguing.

And the kiss in segment two? Had she been describing the first kiss they'd shared in the pub? It had been romantic and passionate, and it had only made him want to kiss her again.

Moya held on to Zaira's hand tightly. "Can you come tomorrow and read another story?"

Zaira brushed a hand over the little girl's cheek. "I wish I could, but I'm afraid my parents don't like me being in the city."

Did they know she was here now? Or had she lied to them about where she was going?

His silent questions must have radiated across the short distance because she glanced over at him before focusing more intently upon the children and answering their questions about her family's country estate.

"Bellamy?" Jenny's voice rang up the stairway. "A man is here wanting to talk to you about taking in children."

"Is that a fact?" Bellamy rose.

"Oh aye."

Maybe word was already spreading that he was looking for families to house orphan children. If so, he hoped he would have a good list compiled before Riley returned tomorrow.

"Tell him I'll be right down." Bellamy was due back in the pub soon anyway. If only he could have had a few minutes more with Zaira, maybe even a wee bit of time without the children. But what would he have said to her? What would he have done?

He certainly wouldn't have kissed her again. He'd only done so at the party because everyone had been calling for it and he'd felt pressured into it.

She rose, and the children did too, all three of them watching him expectantly. "Do you think the visitor has word about Mr. O'Reilly?" she asked.

"Maybe." He didn't want to disappoint anyone, but so far, all the information he'd uncovered about Seamus and Moya's da had only led him to the wrong man. O'Reilly was a common Irish name, and Bellamy was surprised at how many Seamus O'Reillys there were in the city and surrounding area.

He made his way downstairs and out into the pub, where a young man was waiting to relay the news that a Seamus O'Reilly was living in the Carondelet district to the south of St. Louis, doing construction. The young man didn't know if this particular Seamus O'Reilly was from Galway or if he had a wife and two children. But Bellamy could do nothing less than head down to Carondelet and find out if this was the Seamus they were searching for.

As soon as he returned to the kitchen, Zaira was waiting, her expression animated with anticipation. "Well?"

"It's too late in the afternoon to go. I'll wait until the morning."

Seamus and Moya were less excited, probably because they'd already had their hopes dashed with each of his failed inquiries so far.

Moya held up her arms to Jenny, who scooped the little lass up and hugged her tightly, whispering reassurances that everything would be all right. Moya wrapped her arms around Jenny's neck, and Jenny pressed a kiss onto the child's forehead and then caressed her hair.

The two were growing really attached. What would happen to both if Mr. O'Reilly finally came to collect his children? Maybe it would be better to reunite them with their da soon, before they settled into life at the pub even more.

"On second thought," Bellamy said, "maybe I should nip along now." Carondelet was only a five-mile ride. He could ride there and back before darkness settled.

"The pub won't be busy tonight, not with the ban on beer," Gavin spoke up from the stove. He regarded Jenny with a worried look, probably because he realized that Jenny already loved the children and that she'd only be hurt when they left.

All the more reason to find the children's da.

"I'll take care of pouring drinks," Gavin continued, "until you get back." Tonight there wouldn't be much pouring, maybe some whiskey or brandy or a few of their other hard liquors.

Bellamy shared a look with his brother-in-law—one in which they both silently agreed they needed to protect Jenny as best they could from heartache.

"Then I guess I'll be running on." Bellamy made it outside into the alley when the kitchen door opened, then closed with a bang.

"I'm going with you," Zaira called, her determined footsteps thudding behind him.

17

Zaira needed another adventure. She was tired of being cooped up at Oakland, and going with Bellamy to look for Seamus and Moya's father would be exciting.

She hurried after Bellamy, hoping he would let her come along.

He halted abruptly and spun.

In the next instant, she found herself stumbling and bumping against his chest. He steadied her with both hands, but she rapidly backed away from his touch, needing to keep the distance and barriers in place so she didn't make a fool of herself the way she had at the eating-of-the-gander party.

She'd allowed herself to get carried away with her feelings for Bellamy that night. As a result, his rejection had stung harder than she'd anticipated. Over the past couple of days of moping, she'd decided that to survive their pretend match, she had to be much more careful.

"What will your da and mam say when you don't show up for supper tonight?" Bellamy's tone taunted her, letting her know once again that he knew she'd lied to her parents about her whereabouts.

"I told them I was coming into the city to visit you."

Bellamy cocked an eyebrow at her, as though he didn't believe her.

She hadn't necessarily lied about coming to see Bellamy. A part of her had wanted just a tiny glimpse of him—well, maybe more than tiny.

She'd also wanted to see Moya and Seamus. More importantly, however, the deadline for her chapter was today. She should have delivered it yesterday, but her revisions had taken longer because the words hadn't flowed well, and she'd kept getting distracted by her thoughts of Bellamy and the children.

The cloudy afternoon was no longer misting, but the threat of rain still lingered. It was getting late in the afternoon, and she needed to deliver her chapter to Mr. Knapp before the newspaper office closed for the day. Maybe it wasn't a good idea to go with Bellamy after all.

"Alannah needed to gather a few items from home that she'd left there, so Mam let us come together." Technically, Alannah hadn't really needed anything but had agreed to come with Zaira so she could drop off her manuscript. "She's waiting at the house. I can send her word that I'll be late."

Bellamy crossed his arms, and whenever he did so, he looked overly confident, almost arrogant, but still much too handsome. She could sense that he was going to say no, and maybe she should just gracefully leave before he rejected her again.

On the other hand, a little ride into the countryside down to Carondelet wouldn't harm anyone. "You can use my help."

She crossed to the trough where she'd left her horse. "After all, I was the one who found Seamus and Moya, wasn't I?"

Bellamy watched her a moment, then shrugged. "If you're wanting to spend time with me so badly, just say so."

"I don't."

He smirked but didn't say anything more as he quickly saddled his horse and mounted. As they started off, he patted a pouch under his suit coat. "I'll be needing to make a deposit at the bank first."

"Then you won't mind if we swing by the *Daily Republican* after that, will you?" She slapped the pannier bag near the saddle, where she'd stowed her manuscript.

"What are Frannie and Albert up to this week?" Bellamy slanted a look her way. "Is she going to leave with him? Or will she stay with her family and try to protect them?"

Zaira pulled up short and couldn't hold back a smile. "Why, Bellamy McKenna. You've been reading my story."

"I don't have much choice." He kept riding, forcing her to prod her mount into a trot to catch up to him. "One of the regulars at the bar reads the stories in the newspapers aloud each week."

"Sure, Bellamy. Blame it on a customer. But I know you can't wait to see what happens next."

Bellamy snorted as he turned his mount into the alley that ran behind First Bank.

A part of her was thrilled he was reading her story, although another part of her warned that she shouldn't care. All that truly mattered was pleasing her new readers, and last week when she'd dropped off her chapter, Mr. Knapp had told her they'd gotten a great number of positive remarks and interest in the story.

"So what do you think?" The question slipped out. Maybe she cared about his opinion on her story more than she wanted to admit. After all, besides Alannah, he was the only other person who knew about her secret writing life.

He was silent, narrowing his eyes on something ahead. It was an area of the city that hadn't been affected by the fire, and the buildings were some of the oldest in the city with fine architecture.

"You don't think I have talent, do you? To you, it's all drivel and worthless and—"

"Hold up," he whispered, drawing his horse to a halt while reaching for her reins and doing the same for her horse.

"What's wrong—?"

"Shhh." He pressed a finger to his lips. His gaze was fixed intently on two men carrying large bags over their shoulders and who seemed to be sneaking down a back stairwell of a large building.

Bellamy nudged his horse back a step into the shadows of the alley, motioning her to do the same.

She moved next to him and waited. What were those men doing? Something nefarious?

Bellamy dismounted and draped the reins of his horse over an iron stair rail. "I'm going to get a little closer," he whispered, "and try to see what's going on. Wait here."

He crept around a barrel, then ducked behind another one.

Not wanting to be left behind, she slid down from her horse, then hurried to catch up with Bellamy.

When she reached him, he was already creeping down the same back stairway the men had traversed only moments ago. As he approached the lower entrance door, he tried the handle, and it opened easily.

His frown deepened. "How in the blazes?"

He peeked inside, then entered.

She caught the door before it closed and slipped in after him.

He drew up short and scowled at her. "I asked you to wait for me."

"No, you didn't."

"Aye, I did."

"You didn't *ask*. You *ordered* it."

Their whispers echoed in the dark hallway, which was lit only by scant light filtering in through the glass window in the door at the opposite end. The dim lighting allowed them to see that no one else was there, that whoever Bellamy had followed had disappeared.

"Zaira." His voice was firm. "I wanted you to be staying with the horses, so I did."

She waved a hand of dismissal. "Where are we, and what are we doing here?"

"This is the lower level of the bank."

"The bank?" She glanced at the door they'd just entered. "Why would the bank leave their back door open like that?"

"That's what I'm trying to figure out." He scanned the hallway. "The two men who entered didn't look like bank workers."

A chill raced up her spine. "If they weren't bank workers, who were they?"

"Men who probably shouldn't be here."

She dropped her voice to an even lower whisper. "Do you think they're hiding in a room and waiting to leave after the

bank closes?" Everyone in St. Louis knew about the robberies that had happened in the spring. While there hadn't
been any recently, maybe the criminals were getting back to
their thieving now that the cholera was starting to decrease
in intensity.

Bellamy crossed to the closest door and turned the handle,
and the door opened. He glanced at her and hesitated, as
if he was calculating the danger. What if the men he'd seen
enter were hiding behind one of the doors and had weapons?

At approaching voices from the opposite side of the inner
door with the glass window, Bellamy's eyes widened. With
his knife unsheathed and in hand, he pushed open the door
of the room beside them, surveyed the inside, then reached
for her. "Come on."

She didn't hesitate even a second. She hurried after him,
and he quickly closed the door behind her, darkness envel-
oping them.

A second later, the door down the hallway squealed open,
and the voices grew louder. "I unlocked the first room on
the left," came a harsh whisper. "I told you to wait there."

The first room on the left? Was that where she and Bellamy were?

She bumped up against a tall chest of drawers, and her
hand brushed a stack of papers on top. A damp mustiness
filled the air, as though the room was seldom used, perhaps
to store bank archives—old documents, papers, and files.

Beside her, Bellamy grasped her arm to steady her.

Footsteps shuffled down the hallway. Who was out there?
The two men Bellamy had noticed entering the back door?
And perhaps someone who worked at the bank who'd left
the door unlocked to allow the men in?

As the footsteps and whispers drew closer, Bellamy's hand on her arm tensed. Although the room was dark and she couldn't see anything, she could feel him lean into the door, probably to keep anyone from entering.

A second later, the door handle rattled, and someone shoved against the door.

Bellamy seemed to be pressing his full weight to keep it closed.

The man on the other side grunted with the effort of opening it. A moment later, a key jiggled in the lock. The man tried again to open the door.

At a distant noise, the man swore. "It won't unlock." He stepped away, the keys jangling again. "I guess you'll have to stay in the maintenance closet."

"How long should we wait before coming out?" came another voice.

"At least two hours in here," said the first man with the keys.

A door opened nearby—perhaps the door across the hallway.

"Will that give us enough time to cut through the wall and the safe?" another voice chimed in. "We need as much time as we can get."

Zaira almost gasped but instead cupped a hand over her mouth. The men were bank robbers. And she and Bellamy had discovered them.

A thrill of excitement wound through her. The men didn't realize she and Bellamy were here thanks to Bellamy's quick thinking and determination in holding the door closed. Just as soon as the way was clear, she and Bellamy could tiptoe out and alert the police about the plan.

She could see everything unfolding. The robbers would be hammering away at the safe, and the police would race in with their guns at the ready and catch the thieves in the act. She and Bellamy would be credited for saving the bank. In fact, they would be heroes for the daring deed.

Beside her, Bellamy was motionless, still leaning against the door to hold it closed. She wanted to say something to him about her ideas, but with the commotion and voices only feet away, she kept her hand over her mouth so she didn't give away their location.

From what she could tell, the man with the keys was opening a different door and ushering the others inside. "We'll be finished and locking up within the hour. You have to wait until well after that to make sure everyone is gone."

Was the fellow a bank teller? Maybe a manager? Or even a custodian who took care of the property?

Whatever his role, he was obviously aiding the robbers, perhaps intending to take a percentage of what was stolen.

With a final word of caution, the man with the keys closed the door on the robbers, then made his way back down the hallway.

As soon as the far door squealed open and then closed, she could feel Bellamy finally release his tight hold on their door. He didn't move away completely, almost as if he was afraid of someone still coming in and discovering them here. But at the very least, for now, they'd escaped detection.

They wouldn't be able to go until the robbers across the hall left in an hour or so. Until then, they were stuck waiting in the cramped room. If they could see where they were and what was around them, maybe they could move a little and find a place to sit down. As it was, they probably needed to remain motionless so they didn't accidentally bump into anything and make noise that would give them away.

After long minutes, Bellamy's hand circled her arm. He tugged her toward the door and positioned her until she had her back against it. Then he drew her down to the floor so they were both sitting with their backs against it.

Her shoulder and arm were pressed against his, and even though she wasn't scared, she drew some comfort from the fact that he was here beside her. She rested her head back against the door, and from the position of his body, she could tell that he was doing the same.

The minutes ticked slowly by. She was going to be even later getting home than she'd stated in the message she'd had delivered to Alannah.

The biggest problem was that she wouldn't be able to turn in her next story segment by the deadline. By the time she and Bellamy left in an hour or so, the newspaper office would be closed, and Mr. Knapp would be gone.

Maybe she could give it to Bellamy, though, and ask him to deliver it first thing in the morning. Surely he would be willing to since he'd offered to deliver it in the past.

Whatever the case, being late in delivering the manuscript was worth this adventure and this opportunity to catch thieves in the process of robbing a bank.

Finally, when her backside was starting to get sore from sitting in one place for so long, the door of the room across the hallway clanked open.

"Mr. Wright said it would be better to wait two hours," came a loud, high-pitched whisper from one of the robbers.

Mr. Wright. At least she and Bellamy had the name of one of the men—possibly the bank worker—involved in the plot.

Even if all Mr. Wright did was unlock the back door and let the two men in, he was still an accomplice and would need to be held accountable.

"We've waited long enough," said a rougher and lower voice. "We've got to get started now so we can get as far away as possible before morning and the bank opens."

Zaira almost smiled. The two wouldn't be going anywhere except the calaboose, as the city jail was called.

The whispered arguing continued down the hallway, then the door squealed as it opened and shut. Once silence settled over the hallway, Zaira started to scramble to her feet.

"Ach, hold on with you now, lass." Bellamy was on his feet, too, and positioned himself in front of the door. "I'll be the one checking to see if we're clear to go, not you."

His whisper seemed loud in the silence. And his warm breath was beside her face, which meant his face was also near.

She had the urge to stroke his cheek and reassure him that everything would be alright, but in the next instant he was fumbling for the door handle. He tried turning it and pulling, but nothing happened.

"What's wrong?" she whispered.

He tugged again. Still the door didn't budge.

"We're locked in, aren't we?"

"Oh aye, that we are." This time Bellamy heaved hard, shoving the door with his shoulder. He did so several times, but the door was solid wood and seemed to fit in the frame snugly. "When Mr. Wright tried to unlock the door, he actually locked it instead."

"Probably so." Did that mean they were trapped?

The possibility didn't necessarily disappoint her. Surely

they'd find a way out. They were both smart people, and they could put their minds together to figure out something. Even if they couldn't discover a means to free themselves, she was getting the adventure she'd been longing for.

The only frustrating thing was they wouldn't be able to rush to the police right away and alert them to the burglary in process.

Bellamy slammed into the door again. This time it seemed to rattle the walls.

She grabbed on to his arm. "If they hear the noise, they'll come back and look for us."

He stopped himself short, his breathing labored.

"Besides, maybe it's time to admit you're not as strong as you think you are."

"You're probably the one who thinks I'm strong."

She released a soft snort. "Aye, that's why I agreed to the match. Because of the size of your muscles."

"I thought so." He seemed to draw in a steadying breath. "You can't get enough of my muscles."

"You know me so well."

"So I do, enough to also realize how enamored you are with my blarney."

"I do love your blarney." She spoke the words sarcastically, but truer words had never been spoken. She loved his charm and his humor and even his sarcasm.

If she had to pick one person to be stuck with, it was Bellamy McKenna. In fact, she would relish every moment.

18

What had he gotten them into?

Bellamy jammed his fingers into his hair, his frustration mounting more with every passing second.

"Let's see if we can find another way out." Zaira started moving away from him but bumped into something that fell to the floor with a clatter.

He reached out a hand blindly for her but grasped only air. "Someone wise once told me if they hear the noise, they'll come back and look for us."

She released a scoffing laugh. "We can't just sit. If we do, they'll escape with the money."

He liked that she wasn't afraid or upset at their circumstances. She never seemed to let a situation bother her. And she was daring—another admirable trait.

"We have to get out and alert the police," she insisted.

In the blackness of the basement room, he couldn't see even his hand in front of his face. But he shifted to the door and this time swept his hand along the doorframe, checking for any way at all that he might be able to pry the door open.

His fingers skated over the smooth wood, then over the handle. The lock was on the outside . . . because the bank obviously wanted to prevent random people—like them—from browsing the rooms filled with private documents.

Maybe Zaira was right, though. Maybe he should make an effort to find another way out or an item he could use to break open the door.

For a short while, they bumped and felt their way around the room. But it didn't take long to discover that the walls were lined with tall drawers, and each drawer contained only papers. Aside from a tin wastebasket Zaira had knocked over, they found papers, folders, and a few random pens, but nothing else except a vent high up in one wall. He managed to take it off, but the space was too small for either of them to fit into.

At some point—after at least an hour of attempting to wiggle the door handle and hinges loose—he resigned himself to the fact that he and Zaira would be stuck in the storage room for the night. Zaira seemed to resign herself, too, and sat down with him against the door.

Bellamy didn't know exactly where the safe was. But from the echo of hammers and chisels, he guessed it was on the opposite side of the door at the end of the hallway. The echo wasn't loud, but he could feel the reverberations once in a while against his back.

Of course Zaira proved to be an easy conversationalist, and they talked about many topics—Seamus and Moya, the struggle with homelessness, the problems of the new immigrants, and the plan to connect children to families who could temporarily house them.

At some point they started talking more about their

families, and though he didn't like going into specifics regarding his relationship with Oscar and all that had happened with his mam and their marriage, he didn't mind talking about Jenny and Gavin. He shared with Zaira about their last year in Ireland before immigrating and about the adjustments once they arrived. She asked him about Jenny not having any children and what that had been like.

Zaira shared equally about her family and what her life had been like growing up in such a large, affluent family. Although she didn't say so directly, he got the sense that she'd been somewhat overlooked as the middle child and that she'd done her best to keep the peace amidst all the other turmoil her family experienced.

Late into the night, after hours of talking—even about her writing and his painting—Zaira began yawning more frequently, and her whispers grew softer until they tapered off. Her even breathing told him she'd fallen asleep. When her head drooped to one side and came to rest against his shoulder, he didn't move away, even though a warning went off inside him, especially because he couldn't deny how many things he liked about Zaira Shanahan.

Had he ever talked with a woman as openly as he did her? He couldn't remember anyone who interested him as much. He'd actually enjoyed the time with her and liked getting to know more about her. Underneath her sassiness, she had a tender and sweet heart.

Even so, he couldn't let the attraction interfere with putting an end to their fake relationship. Just because he liked her didn't mean he wanted to marry her, especially because their whole relationship had started on a lie. That didn't bode well for the future.

At some point, he dozed too, even with the distant thudding of a hammer or chisel or both. When he startled awake, the grogginess of sleep had him utterly at sea for only a moment before he remembered where he was and what had happened.

The first thing he noticed was the silence. The hammering and chiseling seemed to have stopped. Had the robbers broken into the safe, stolen the money, and run off?

He wished he could gauge what time it was and if morn was at hand. But without a window or the ability to see his pocket watch, he didn't know how many hours were left before the bank workers arrived for the day.

Once people were here, he and Zaira would have to find a way to alert them to their presence inside the storage room. He could only pray that someone from his family or hers had been worried about them last night when they didn't return and had started looking for them. But it was possible everyone assumed they'd gotten delayed in Carondelet during their search for Mr. O'Reilly.

Whatever the case, he hoped they didn't have to wait much longer. From his spot reclining against the storage room door, his back ached and his legs were stiff. Zaira was still resting her head against his shoulder and had also laid a hand on his arm.

From the steadiness of her breathing, he could tell she hadn't awoken, and he didn't want to bother her yet, not until he had to. One of them might as well get a wee bit of sleep.

Stifling a yawn, he shifted a little to take some of the pressure off his tailbone.

At his movement, she began to stir. Although he couldn't

see her, he could feel her lift her arm away from him and then stretch it above her head. When she brought it back down, she seemed to attempt to place her hand back on his arm, but instead it landed upon his chest right next to his heart.

After the past hours of talking and being so close, to listening to her breathing, to feeling her warmth, to having her hair tickle his jaw, he was much too keenly aware of her presence.

She yawned, then snuggled her head against his arm while at the same time flattening her fingers and gently patting him.

She'd patted him. Like he was a cat.

A strange protest swelled in him. Clearly she wasn't affected by him the same way he was by her.

She released a soft sigh, as if she was settling in again to go back to sleep.

Before he could stop himself, he slid his arm around behind her, drawing her closer so that now she was leaning against his body with her head on his chest.

She seemed to hesitate, as if she wasn't quite sure what to think of the new position.

She was even softer than he'd remembered, and her body fit so well against him. With her head tucked beneath his chin, more of her hair brushed his skin, and the silkiness of it brought an aching need to his chest.

He knew he shouldn't, but he lifted his free hand and stroked the loose strands. After the long, restless night, her hair had fallen free of the usual knot. His fingers followed the trail of the hair downward, combing it gently.

Holy mother. Had he ever touched anything as exquisite as her hair? He honestly couldn't think of anything that compared, and he had the overwhelming need to bury his fingers there, this time more deeply.

With it flowing over her shoulders, it was practically begging to be touched, so he delved his fingers in again, winding them until he had a fistful. Only when he brought the fistful of it to his mouth and nose and breathed her in did he realize she'd grown absolutely still and her body tense.

He pinched his eyes closed. What in the devil was he doing? Why was he giving in to this desire for her? Out of respect for her and to their pretend relationship, he had to put an end to any physical contact immediately.

"I'm sorry," he started.

Before he could finish, she lifted her hand from where it was still resting on his chest and placed it against his lips, cutting off his apology. She held her fingers there with a gentle pressure that shifted his mind from her hair to her fingertips.

He wanted to kiss them. Rather than denying himself, he brushed a kiss against her fingers.

She sucked in a sharp breath but didn't move away.

Should he issue another apology? He didn't want to. Instead, he wanted to kiss her fingers, this time lingering on each one before moving to her palm or her wrist. Did he dare do it?

The thudding in his chest beat hard, demanding more.

Before he could gather his resolve, one of her fingers skimmed his lower lip. The touch was delicate, like a flower petal. She traced along the curve and then moved to his top lip, where she softly drew a line all the way across to the other side.

She was feeling whatever was building between them too. That was obvious.

As she began to lower her hand, he scooped it up and this time brought it to his lips. He kissed the tip of one finger, then the next, and the next until he reached the end.

With each kiss, she drew in a breath, as if each of his kisses surprised her—or delighted her.

What was he doing? He couldn't kiss her, not even her fingers. It was too much.

He started to release her, but before he could, she drew his hand to her lips and began to kiss each of his fingertips the same way he'd just done to hers. Her lips skimmed each one, softly, gently, but lingering long enough that he felt the imprint of her mouth. It seared through his skin and branded him, marking him as hers.

Could he really be hers? Was that a possibility? Or was it only a dream?

As she reached his last finger and placed the kiss there, he didn't want her to stop, wanted her to go on kissing him, not on his fingers, but on his lips.

Somehow during the finger kissing, she'd twisted around so she was facing him and almost sitting on him. Instead of lowering his hand, she placed it against her cheek, giving him permission to touch her face.

While he couldn't see her beauty, he had no trouble imagining the lovely shape of her face as he cradled her cheek and rubbed his thumb over her jawline.

In the next instant, she brought her hand to his face, palming his cheek, letting her fingers explore the crinkles beside his eye, his eyebrow, then his forehead. She circled back around to his chin before her fingers once again grazed his lips.

The desire to kiss her fingers again pulsed rapidly. He

started to reach for her hand but before he could, she guided his face forward so that her lips collided with his. The impact was forceful and thorough, leaving him no doubt that she wanted the kiss.

He had no doubt he wanted it too. He angled in and welcomed the kiss she was offering, giving back to her the forcefulness and thoroughness in turn.

Passion flared up almost instantaneously, like flames crackling between them and around them, consuming them with a heat. She was on fire, and everywhere she touched him or everywhere he touched her ignited more flames. But he didn't incinerate. Instead, he only wanted more, needed more, burned for more.

This kiss wasn't like the other two they'd already shared—the one in the pub and the one at the engagement party. No, this kiss was unlike anything he'd ever known, one filled with a longing he suspected wouldn't be sated by anyone else but her. Oh aye, this kiss had unlocked something inside him, something he feared he wouldn't be able to cage up again. It wasn't just passion toward Zaira. It was something deeper, something more encompassing, something more life-altering.

Was it love?

A swell of panic rose inside him. No, it couldn't be love.

He gave a shake of his head, breaking their connection and pulling away. He was on his feet in the next instant and took a step back.

He didn't want to be swept up into the feelings of being in love, didn't want his heart to dictate his actions, didn't want to be so passionate about her that he couldn't think rationally about whether they were right for each other or not.

He'd already determined that passion would only cause him to rush into a marriage, perhaps with the wrong woman. Because how could he know that Zaira was right for him? That he was right for her? That they wouldn't despise each other in a few years?

Oscar had always said those who were most passionate about each other often had the most beautiful highs but also the most tragic lows. No doubt he'd been speaking from personal experience.

She hadn't moved from her spot on the floor. But her confusion hung in the air, and their heavy breathing filled the silence.

He needed to say something. But what could he? How could he possibly explain the complexity of relationships the McKenna matchmakers had? And that he had to be extra careful when it came to his own match?

If all the matchmakers had been blinded by their emotions, then maybe he couldn't allow himself to have a marriage with any feelings—at least initially. Maybe it was better if he entered into a relationship that was cordial and agreeable. Something platonic. More like a business exchange. Not this burning passion he felt with Zaira, a passion that made him lose his mind and all self-control.

Aye, that was it. In order to succeed where all the other matchmakers in his family had failed, he had to take an opposite strategy. He needed to be clearheaded and form a match based on logic—a logic that would put solid character qualities over feelings like the ones he was having with Zaira.

No matter how difficult such a strategy might be, especially with Zaira, he had to do it.

19

What had happened between her and Bellamy? One minute he was kissing her like he could never get enough of her. And the next moment, he was cold and distant.

She wanted to say something, ask him what was wrong. But a part of her was afraid of what he would say, that he would reject her again.

She pushed up from the floor, needing to stretch after sitting for so long. The quietness in the bank basement was eerie, and she guessed the robbers had finished cracking the safe open and already made their getaway.

So much for being the heroine and saving the day. Instead, she was an utter failure in this adventure she found herself in. Not only hadn't she discovered a way to free herself and outwit the crooks, but now she'd made a fool of herself with Bellamy. Again.

She hadn't misread him, had she? His touch, his kisses on her fingers, even his putting his arm around her, had all made her feel as though he truly cared about her. No one could kiss with so much emotion behind it the way he just had and then pretend like it didn't mean anything. No one else was present for them to impress like at the party, and he couldn't tell her he was just acting.

"Bellamy?" She couldn't let it go. It just wasn't in her nature to do so.

She could almost feel him stiffen.

"What's going on?" The question tumbled out. "For a pretend relationship, our kisses aren't very pretend."

He exhaled a long sigh. "I'm sorry—"

"Please don't apologize." Her chest squeezed. "Instead, give me the explanation I deserve."

"'Tis a long story." His voice was laced with frustration.

"We have plenty of time for a long story." They had nothing *but* time at this point.

"Oh aye, so we do."

She waited for him to keep going, to reveal that perhaps he already had a secret relationship with another woman, or that he wanted to wait until he was famous with his painting before he allowed himself to get serious, or that he had a terminal illness that would prevent him from a long-term relationship.

Okay, so maybe the last reason was something that belonged in a fictional story. But the other two reasons were possibilities. "Do you care about another woman? Is that it?"

"Ach, the devil. Do you really think me capable of cheating, Zaira?"

"I don't know. Then is it your art? You want to get established or famous as a painter before you get married, don't you?"

He blew out another tense breath. "No, that's not it."

Her muscles had tightened with each of his answers. "Then what, Bellamy? Why are you avoiding whatever this is that is happening between us?"

There, she'd said it. She'd admitted their relationship was more than playacting. Thankfully he couldn't run away from her, was trapped in the same room, and had to say something.

He was silent for another long moment. Then he spoke in a low, raw voice. "You should know something about the McKenna matchmakers. They're unlucky in love."

She nearly scoffed but then voiced her response as calmly as she could. "How so?"

"Matchmakers in my family, for as far back as anyone can recall, always end up in bad marriages. They're lucky in finding love for others but unlucky for themselves."

"What exactly does that mean?"

"They fall in love, but the love ends up being a disaster, so it does."

She tried to take in what he was saying so she could respond thoughtfully. "I'm sure matchmakers aren't the only ones whose marriages start out with luster but then fall into disrepair."

"But the matchmakers' marriages *always* fail."

"So you want yours to be different?"

"Aye."

She could admire his desire to have a good marriage. That was noble of him, since some men didn't consider whether a marriage was good or bad, only that it was ordained by God and for the procreation of children. On the other hand, he couldn't let fear stop him from getting married. "Did you ever consider that unlucky streaks are always made to be broken?"

"It hasn't been broken yet."

"Maybe we can't sit back and wait for luck to decide the future of our marriages. Maybe we have to decide the future of our relationships ourselves."

"Sounds like something Oscar would say."

"Or you."

He shrugged. "The matchmakers have advice on relationships for everyone else, but they can never make the advice work for themselves."

"I think I've also heard Oscar say that happiness in a marriage doesn't happen by chance, that happiness is a matter of choice."

"He didn't choose it, that's for certain." The bitterness in Bellamy's tone took her by surprise.

She knew Bellamy's mam had died before the McKennas immigrated, but he hadn't spoken much about her, even last night during their conversations about their families. "You may not want to talk about this, Bellamy. But if you've a notion to, I'd like to hear about your mam and Oscar."

Bellamy hesitated, then shifted, as though he was leaning against a wall. "My mam told me that Oscar was her knight in shining armor, that he rescued her from a terrible home and took her away so they could have their fairy-tale life."

She smiled. "It's hard to picture Oscar as a knight in shining armor."

"He always loved the *craic*, the grand times, the late nights."

"Now, that doesn't surprise me because he still does."

"Oh, aye. If there's a party to be had, Oscar Fingal Mc-Kenna is sure to be present."

"Your mam was the same?"

"If truth be told, she liked the craic more than Oscar."

"Then they must have made quite the pair."

"Everyone said they were a perfect love match, and never did a fellow adore a woman as Oscar adored her." Bellamy's tone suddenly turned sad.

"What went wrong?"

"She loved to paint and would spend hours and hours at it. And he never supported her in it, even tried to get her to quit."

"Oh, that's terrible." Zaira knew that was a possibility with her writing, that her future husband might not support it, especially once she had children and was busy with her family. "I'm sure it's difficult for any mother to find the balance between her family and what she loves doing."

"I admit, Mam wasn't always good with that balance. She was gone a lot—gaining inspiration for the painting, or so she'd said. And when she was home, she spent nearly all her time painting."

"Then you painted to be with her?"

"Aye. 'Twas the only time she noticed me." His admission was soft. "In my childish mind, I thought that if I was good enough at painting, maybe she'd want to be with me more."

"So you tried harder?"

"I practiced all the time."

"But it didn't keep her attention?"

"She loved showing me all her techniques and helping me with my paintings. But it never lasted long." He fell silent, and the hurt of the past seemed to rise like a living phantom.

"She must have been really talented."

"She was amazing."

"So are you, you know. You take after her."

"Thank you."

Zaira could only imagine how much he'd wanted his mam's attention and approval. Maybe that's why Oscar hadn't supported her painting. "Do you think Oscar got frustrated with her because he wanted her to be a better mother to you and your sister?"

"'Tis possible. But whatever the issue, he could have been a more encouraging husband."

She waited for Bellamy to say more about it, but he lapsed into silence. Her mind turned over and over with everything he'd revealed, and she tried to fit together all the pieces. Seeing his parents' marriage fall apart had confirmed his belief that matchmakers were unlucky in love. Now that it was his turn to get married, he was afraid of having a bad marriage for himself.

But he wasn't destined to have a failed marriage, especially because he was aware of the unlucky streak and the need to change it. Armed with such knowledge, wouldn't he be one step ahead of his da and the others who had come before him? Bellamy could enter his own marriage ready to work hard. He wouldn't be leaving things to chance, would instead make the choice to have a good marriage.

Somehow she had to convince him to give marriage—maybe even give their relationship—a chance. "You can be a better husband than Oscar."

"Rightly so. That's why I'm needing to be careful who I choose." His voice held a determination she hadn't expected. "Which is why I'm taking my time and not rushing into anything."

"Here I've been thinking that you just didn't want me." She tried to lighten her tone so she didn't sound like she was pushing him to admit his feelings for her. Because she wasn't, was she?

He didn't respond.

Maybe he didn't want her. Then why had he kissed her the way he had? "I'm confused, Bellamy. I felt something when we kissed. You can't deny that you did too."

Several more heartbeats passed before he spoke. "I'm not choosing a wife based on my feelings alone. When the time comes, I'll choose based on solid qualities."

"And what *solid qualities* are you looking for in a wife?"

"We're not meant to be together, Zaira. We may have some attraction, but it's not enough."

"So you're telling me you're physically attracted to me, but you don't like me as a person?"

"You're a great woman and will make some man a fine wife. I'm just looking for someone different."

"What solid qualities am I missing?" she asked again.

He sighed with exasperation.

"What?" she persisted.

"For one thing, honesty."

He'd already made it clear he didn't like all the lying and the deception. And she could admit she'd easily allowed herself to become more and more deceptive, especially since she'd started trying to get published. She'd had to make up excuses and hide what she was doing from her family. Once she'd started being deceptive in one area, it had been all too easy to do so in others.

But she'd been honest with him about who she was, more so than with any other person, even Alannah. Regardless, he still found her lacking and was rejecting her. Wasn't that ultimately what she was afraid of? Wasn't that why she'd kept her writing a secret from her parents? Because she didn't want to lose their approval?

She'd always felt that the ties to her family were tenuous, maybe because she was so often taken for granted or she'd had affirmation for who they *wanted* her to be and not who she *really* was.

If they knew about the daring and impassioned writer she was, they wouldn't think she was so sweet anymore. What if they found her lacking and rejected her too?

"I know I've got an issue with honesty too, Zaira, and I've had a role in our deception." His voice held regret. "Deception was a big part of my parents' marriage, and it only tore them apart."

"It's not too late to work at being honest." She wasn't sure why she was trying so hard to convince him to fight for them. But a part of her couldn't let go of the possibility yet.

"Ach, but that's just it. The lying and deception are already right at the front of our relationship."

"So, you don't believe in fixing what's wrong?"

"Since I'm fated to face so many challenges in my marriage, I'd like to start out on solid ground."

"Oh, I see." She couldn't keep her frustration from swelling. "You're looking for a perfect relationship with a perfect woman so you can hopefully have a perfect marriage."

He didn't offer a word of protest.

She huffed. "Good luck finding the perfect wife, Bellamy."

"I won't find a perfect wife. I know no one is perfect, least of all me. But if I can arrange perfect matches for others, then I can strive to find one for myself too."

"Is there really such a thing as a perfect match?" Her romantic heart liked to think so. But when two imperfect humans came together, weren't there bound to be issues and problems? "No one is immune from adversity. Maybe a perfect match has to do with how well a couple displays humility and perseverance and the willingness to forgive."

A shout of alarm came from the area beyond the hallway. She sat up, and she could hear Bellamy move as well.

Someone had finally arrived at the bank. Had they discovered the robbery?

20

*B*ellamy banged against the door of the storage room. "In here!" he shouted. Beside him, Zaira banged on the door too. He wasn't sure how much time had passed since they'd heard voices in another part of the bank. It felt like an eternity but had likely only been five minutes.

He was fairly certain it was morning and that the first tellers or manager were starting a new day of work and had discovered something amiss in the main area of the bank.

"Help!" Zaira called.

He closed his eyes and rested his forehead against the door. What had he been thinking to kiss her so passionately? The trouble was, he hadn't been thinking. Now he'd just stirred up more emotion between them that hadn't needed stirring.

She'd obviously experienced a connection to him the same way he had to her, and she hadn't been bashful in bringing up her questions about what was next for them.

Whether or not they had more feelings for each other, they'd agreed upon a temporary relationship. That was all he was capable of giving her. Besides, she deserved better than to be strung along by a man like him who was cursed when it came to love.

He never should have agreed to her plan in the first place. Because he'd always been attracted to her and had just been in denial about it. He'd thought she was the most beautiful girl in the world from the moment he'd first set eyes on her years ago when he'd been twelve and she'd been only nine.

He'd only been in St. Louis for a week after moving from Ireland and had been at mass with Jenny and Gavin. The Shanahan family had already been in the front pew. He'd spotted her right away. With her pretty red curls, she'd been difficult to miss. She'd shifted to watch him when he'd entered the pew with his family, and her beautiful green eyes had captivated him. He'd been admiring her when she'd stuck her tongue out at him. Of course, she'd followed with a big smile, one that had melted him.

Maybe his heart had always had that soft spot for her— not only her beauty but her sweetness and sassiness.

Aye, she was beautiful and talented and amazing in so many ways, and she would make some fine fellow really happy.

That fine fellow just wouldn't be him.

But who? Who would be good enough for Zaira?

His mind raced with the faces of different men he knew and respected. But he threw out the prospect of each one, his gut hardening at the image of her with another man. Would she kiss someone else the way she had him? As if she wanted more of him and couldn't get enough?

Scowling, he shook his head. He didn't want to think

about her kissing anyone. He could hardly stomach the idea of any fellow laying a finger upon her, much less holding her tight and ravishing her lips.

The truth was, he wanted to be the *only* man who ever touched her. If he couldn't have her, he didn't want anyone else to have her either. But the other truth was that someday he would likely be the one who had to find her a match, and he wasn't sure he would be able to do it.

More loud voices shouted from somewhere in the building.

Were the bank workers coming down to the lower level to check on the vault?

He banged on the door again. "Hello! We're trapped in the storage room! Can you let us out?"

Zaira pounded against the door too. "Help!"

Amidst their pounding came the distinct squeal of the interior door at the end of the hallway.

"Do you think the robbers got trapped?" someone asked from the other side of the doorway.

"Hello!" Zaira shouted. "We're not the robbers. But we got trapped down here last night!"

"Someone is in one of the rooms," another person called.

"I don't know how." The second man's voice was vaguely familiar. "I made sure the doors were all locked last night."

Bellamy stiffened. It was the voice of the bank worker, Mr. Wright, who'd been in the hallway yesterday with the keys, who'd locked them in the storage room unintentionally and then told the robbers where to hide.

Although Bellamy had seen Mr. Wright on occasion when he'd come to the bank, the middle-aged fellow with a balding head, long nose, and solemn expression had never struck him as particularly dangerous. But if the man had been working with the robbers, then he was more menacing than anyone had suspected.

"I'll go check if anyone is there," Mr. Wright spoke again. Beside him, Zaira knocked on the door. "We're here—"

Bellamy cut her off, cupping his hand over her mouth and grabbing her arm to keep her from making any more noise. If Mr. Wright suspected they'd been present when he'd been plotting with the robbers, there was no telling what he might try. Maybe it was best if they didn't let him find them and waited for someone else to come along.

Yet now that Mr. Wright had heard their voices, he probably wouldn't stop searching until he located them and tried to decipher how much they'd overheard or witnessed regarding his role in the bank robbery.

The best thing to do was pretend they had no idea there had been a bank robbery. They could make up a story about how as a newly engaged couple, they'd wanted time alone, found the bank door open, and slipped inside but had been too enamored with each other to hear anything else.

Would Mr. Wright believe them?

Bellamy leaned into Zaira to whisper the plan but hesitated. With such a tale, the gossip would spread about him and Zaira again. Even without a lurid story, people would eventually find out he'd spent the night with Zaira in the bank storage room.

No one would ever believe the only thing they'd done was talk. Of course, they would be right because it wasn't the only thing they'd done. They'd had the best kiss of all time. But most people would assume they'd shared more than kisses, especially because they were engaged.

The hallway door closed with a thud. Then footsteps tapped toward them. Only one set. Mr. Wright's. That meant he would be alone and would be able to do whatever he wanted, make up whatever story he wanted, or eliminate them however he wanted.

Bellamy tensed. Maybe he should spring out as soon as the door opened and take the fellow by surprise. He could probably wrestle Mr. Wright to the ground, especially with as thin and wiry as he was.

On the other hand, Bellamy didn't want to chance putting Zaira into any more danger than she already was. So until he could ascertain the level of peril, they needed to proceed with caution.

He leaned in toward her ear, could feel her lips and warm breath against the hand still covering her mouth. "We have to pretend we're ignorant of hearing him with the robbers."

"How?" she mumbled.

"Follow my lead."

A key rattled in the lock. In the next instant, the door opened slowly, inch by inch.

Bellamy dropped his hand from Zaira's mouth and instead wrapped his arm around her waist, drawing her near. Then he brushed aside the loose hair from near her ear and bent in. "We have to act like lovers."

"What?" she said louder than she should have. "No."

"Aye. Trust me." He pressed his lips to her bare neck, drawing a quick gasp from her.

The door opened even wider to reveal the dark hallway with only the faint light from the far window to illuminate anything. Even though Bellamy kissed Zaira's neck one more time farther up and closer to her jaw, he glimpsed Mr.

Wright's profile. Was that a revolver he was holding and pointing at them? Mostly at Zaira?

Bellamy slid his hand to his waist and the knife underneath his coat. He pretended to be startled, jumping back and using the motion to unsheathe the weapon while still concealing it in the folds of his clothing. "No need to fear. 'Tis Bellamy McKenna the matchmaker and my betrothed."

Mr. Wright swung the gun toward Bellamy.

Bellamy breathed in his relief. He would much rather have the fellow pointing it at him than at Zaira.

"What are you doing here?" Mr. Wright's tone was laced with accusation.

"We got carried away last night." Bellamy hated that he had to lie again but knew there was no other way at the moment. "And somehow we got locked in the room."

"How did you get in there in the first place?" The bank teller kept his voice low, but the suspicion was all too clear.

"I came to make a deposit for the pub and noticed the back door open. We stepped inside to, well, to have a wee bit of privacy . . ." He tried to sound embarrassed. "And somehow we got locked in."

Mr. Wright's gun didn't waver. "So you were here last evening?"

"We were busy," Zaira chimed in as she laid her head against him and rubbed his arm.

"Ach, you can be putting away the gun." Bellamy nodded toward the weapon. "We didn't take anything, if that's what you were thinking."

Mr. Wright seemed to be considering whether to believe them.

"We got stuck," Bellamy repeated, "and now we'd like to be on our way."

Zaira wiggled slightly. "Aye, I'd like to use the privy as soon as possible." She was playing along well, although she probably really did need to use the privy.

Mr. Wright narrowed his gaze upon them. "Our bank was broken into last night. What can you tell me about it?"

"Nothing—" Bellamy started.

"We did hear some noise," she said at the same time.

Why did she admit that? Maybe their story would be more believable if they didn't deny everything. After all, anyone trapped in the storage room would have at least heard some noise rather than none at all.

"Oh aye," Bellamy quickly amended. "There was some hammering, but we weren't paying heed to that."

"So you know nothing about the bank robbery?" Mr. Wright persisted.

"Should we?" Bellamy wrapped his fingers more securely around the hilt of his knife.

"Of course we would like to find out who was behind the safecracking. So if you have information, we will pass it along to the police."

"No." Bellamy shook his head. "We didn't see anyone, not until just now."

Mr. Wright still didn't budge.

Bellamy didn't like the way the conversation was going. Something told him the fellow didn't entirely believe their story.

"The two of you know more than you're admitting." Mr. Wright readjusted his grip on the gun. Although the darkness of the hallway shrouded him, it was clear he had no intention of letting them off easily.

"In fact, I think you were involved."

Zaira huffed. "How could we be when we were locked up all night?"

Mr. Wright waved the gun back and forth. "You probably were finishing with the break-in when you heard people arriving."

Bellamy tried to guide Zaira behind him, but she clung to his arm.

"You stashed the money," Mr. Wright continued. "Then you hid in here hoping you would be able to sneak out later."

"That doesn't make sense." Zaira didn't seem to be in the least afraid or disturbed that someone was holding them at gunpoint. "We can't lock ourselves in."

"The door wasn't locked when I came down." Mr. Wright's voice dropped again. "And when I had to shoot, it was in self-defense because you were trying to escape, and I needed to stop you."

"That still doesn't make sense." Zaira spoke as if she were having a conversation about the plot of her book, probably not comprehending the full danger they were in.

But in one quick second, Bellamy realized what Mr. Wright was doing. He didn't want to chance that they'd overheard his instructions to the robbers last night, so he was brainstorming aloud the excuses he could give to everyone else for why he shot and killed them.

As Mr. Wright fixed the gun on Bellamy, another thought flashed through his mind. The man would eliminate him first so he wouldn't be alive to interfere with Zaira's murder. Except Bellamy couldn't fathom letting Mr. Wright or anyone harm a single hair on Zaira's head.

As the fellow straightened his arm and began to pull the

trigger, Bellamy shoved Zaira behind him, using a force he didn't realize he had. With his other hand, he lunged toward Mr. Wright with his knife.

The gunshot cracked the air with a deafening blast.

From behind him, Zaira screamed, but he knew she was only surprised and not hurt.

Pain radiated through Bellamy's shoulder. He'd been hit by the bullet. But even with the burning, he lunged at Mr. Wright, plunging the blade into the man's arm.

Zaira screamed, "Bellamy! Be careful!"

He wasn't in a position to be careful, not when he had to keep Mr. Wright from taking another shot. He stabbed his knife again, this time aiming for Mr. Wright's torso.

Bellamy had picked up tips on knife fighting at the pub, had listened to others talk about self-defense. So he wasn't a novice. Nevertheless, he didn't want to hurt Mr. Wright more than necessary. He certainly didn't want to kill him. Yet if that's what it took to keep Zaira safe, he'd do anything.

As his knife sliced into Mr. Wright's chest, the man released a pained cry. His hand wavered, and he lowered his gun, staggering backward.

Even though Bellamy's shoulder was throbbing and blood was running down his outstretched arm, he shoved Mr. Wright with enough force that the fellow tumbled against the opposite wall of the hallway.

Bellamy sprang after him, grabbed the arm holding the gun, then slammed the fellow's hand hard against the cement wall while at the same time putting pressure on the chest wound.

Mr. Wright writhed and cried out again with agony, but he still clung to the gun.

Bellamy banged the man's hand against the wall again, and this time the revolver fell from his grip to the floor with a clatter.

Before Bellamy could bend down and swipe it up, Zaira was beside him and kicked the gun down the hallway out of reach.

Mr. Wright no longer seemed to be paying attention to the gun and was holding his chest, the blood from the slash there seeping through his fingers.

Blood flowed onto Bellamy's hand and dripped onto the floor. Was it his own blood or Mr. Wright's?

"Don't move, Mr. Wright!" Zaira called.

Bellamy wavered, a strange dizziness hitting him. He grabbed a fistful of Mr. Wright's shirt, his knife still at the ready but the blood on his hand making his skin slick.

From the corner of his eye, he could see Zaira pick up the gun and aim it at Mr. Wright.

The door down the hallway opened, and voices called out in alarm—probably other people coming to discover what the commotion was about.

Pain again raced through Bellamy's shoulder and this time down his arm. He clenched his jaw to force back a moan, and he tried to focus on his knife. He couldn't let it fall and chance Mr. Wright grabbing it.

In fact, with Zaira holding the gun, maybe it was best if he moved away so if she needed to take a shot, he wouldn't be in her way.

He released his grip of Mr. Wright, took one step, then had a strange sense he was floating. His knees hit the hard floor, the hallway disappeared, and he fell into oblivion.

21

"Bellamy!" Zaira screamed. She wanted to rush to Bellamy's side and help him, but she couldn't shift her aim from Mr. Wright. Even though he was wounded, she had to make sure he didn't get away.

He had to pay for all his crimes.

Several more people raced toward them, including a distinguished gentleman she recognized as a friend of her da's, the bank owner, Mr. Conway. The Conways shared the same social circles as the Shanahans. In fact, the Conways—including Emilie, one of her closest friends—had been at the eating-of-the-gander party out at Oakland earlier in the week.

Surely Mr. Conway would realize she hadn't been a part of plotting the bank robbery as Mr. Wright had suggested. No doubt the fellow had been accusing her and Bellamy to take the blame away from himself. But they'd heard him talking with the robbers last night, had heard him admit to unlocking the doors. If their testimony wasn't enough to implicate him, surely they could find other proof that he'd been involved.

"Mr. Conway," she called, "it's me, Zaira Shanahan. And I've caught the mastermind behind the robbery, Mr. Wright."

Mr. Conway halted beside her. "Zaira Shanahan. My word, child. What are you doing down here?"

Thankfully, a police constable was one of the other men striding down the hallway. He'd probably been nearby, patrolling the streets when the bank workers discovered the robbery. Zaira was never more relieved than at that moment to have him arrest Mr. Wright.

"Mr. Wright not only orchestrated the robbery," Zaira said as she handed over the gun to the constable, "but he tried to kill Bellamy."

Without waiting to find out what Mr. Conway and the police did with Mr. Wright, Zaira rushed over to where Bellamy had fallen. Her heart pounding, she lowered herself to his side. "Bellamy. Talk to me."

He lay face down and didn't move.

"Bellamy!" She began to tremble but somehow got her hands to work to roll him over. Blood was everywhere. It was pooled on the floor, saturated his shirt, and even smeared across his face.

"Bellamy needs a doctor!" she called out as she ran her hand over his chest, searching for an injury, frantic to stop the bleeding.

She suspected he'd been hit by the first gunshot, but he hadn't acted as though he'd been in pain. Instead, he'd charged toward Mr. Wright, then had stabbed the fellow and disarmed him in no time.

Mr. Conway crouched on the other side of Bellamy and

spoke curtly to a worker down the hallway. "Send someone for the physician." As he turned back to Zaira, thankfully he didn't ask her again why she and Bellamy were there at the early morning hour.

Hopefully, no one else heard what she and Bellamy had told Mr. Wright about spending the night in the bank storage room. Hopefully, instead, they would be able to assure everyone that their stay had been accidental, that they'd simply been in the wrong place at the wrong time—or the right place at the right time, if one wanted to solve a crime, which she did.

No matter the excuses, she wouldn't be able to hide the fact she'd spent an entire night alone with Bellamy Mc-Kenna. People would hear of it.

Perhaps the gossipers would be more forgiving since she was engaged to him. Perhaps the scandal wouldn't tarnish the Shanahan name. Perhaps she'd find a way to avoid disappointing her parents.

Whatever the case, she and Bellamy wouldn't be able to put an end to their match. Not anymore. After all that had happened, she wouldn't be surprised if her da and mam pushed her to get married sooner.

If Bellamy lived . . .

She again skimmed her fingers over him, peeling back his coat and vest and finding a bloody hole in his shirt at his shoulder. From what she could tell, the bullet hadn't gone all the way through his body, but blood was still bubbling out of the wound.

She wasted no time lifting her petticoat, pressing it to the bullet hole, and attempting to stanch the flow of blood.

She wasn't sure how long she sat on the basement floor

beside Bellamy, holding his wound tightly, but Mr. Conway stood and spoke with the constable and Mr. Wright, who was sitting against the wall a dozen paces away, moaning from his knife wounds.

At some point, the older physician who usually looked after her family hurried down the hallway and knelt beside her with his leather satchel. Someone else had already lit a lantern and now moved it closer at the physician's command.

As the light splayed across Bellamy's face and revealed the pallor of his skin and his shallow breathing, tears pricked Zaira's eyes. She didn't want Bellamy to die. Even if she could never gain his approval or love, she would still always care about him.

The tears spilled over. She was pathetic to care about a man so much when he didn't reciprocate and had basically told her she wasn't the woman for him. Aye, she was very pathetic. She needed to build a few walls around her heart to protect it from being broken. But she couldn't keep herself from liking him, maybe even being in love with him.

Was she in love with Bellamy McKenna?

She'd never been in love before, not even close. Probably because she'd always been so taken with Bellamy and never had eyes for any other man.

The physician worked swiftly to remove the bullet from Bellamy's shoulder. Then he carefully cleaned and sutured the spot. Throughout it all, Bellamy remained unconscious and at times hardly seemed to be breathing. Zaira hardly seemed to breathe either. But the doctor assured her Bellamy would live, even with all the blood loss. He would be weak and tired and have a great deal of pain, but he'd been fortunate the bullet hadn't caused much damage.

221

"Zaira!"

At the call of her name, Zaira glanced up to find Alannah and Kiernan hurrying toward her down the hallway. At the sight of the concern creasing both of their faces, tears welled up again.

"There you are." Kiernan's tone contained frustration.

"We've been so worried about you." Alannah stopped and held out a hand to Zaira. "Kiernan found your horses wandering around an alley near Front Street, but there was no sign of either you or Bellamy."

"We've been here all night." Zaira wiped her hands on her skirt, then allowed Alannah to help her to her feet. "We got trapped in the bank storage room."

"We know that now." Kiernan cocked his head toward Mr. Conway, who was down the hallway on the other side of the doorway where a couple of constables were now leading away Mr. Wright.

Mr. Conway must have not only sent for the doctor but had likely also had a message delivered to her family's house to alert Kiernan of her whereabouts.

Alannah started to draw her into a hug.

Zaira stepped back, not wanting to stain Alannah's clothing.

"Are you injured too?" Kiernan was scanning her, likely seeing all the blood that covered her gown.

"No, this is just Bellamy's blood."

Kiernan took in Bellamy. "We thought the two of you were captured by the Farrell gang in retaliation for Shaw's imprisonment."

"No, thanks be."

"Oh aye, thanks be." Alannah's voice contained relief.

"With how close the horses were to the river, we'd also considered the possibility that you'd both fallen in and ended up downstream."

"We left our horses in the alley behind the bank." Since they hadn't planned to be gone long, they'd neglected to secure them tightly, so it was possible the horses had wandered off.

Kiernan lifted his hat and combed through his auburn hair, which was as mussed as his suit. "We had search parties out for half the night, combing the streets and riverbanks." Exhaustion lined his face. No doubt he hadn't gotten much sleep.

"I'm sorry, Kiernan. I didn't mean to cause a fuss."

Kiernan replaced his hat. "You made a big fuss, and now the whole city knows that the matchmaker and his fiancée are missing. They'll also soon know that the matchmaker and his fiancée spent the night together in a basement room at the bank."

Zaira released a sigh. "Is there any way to stop the spread of the rumors?"

"No. Which is why you'll marry Bellamy just as soon as he's awake." Kiernan's voice held a finality that confirmed everything Zaira had already known was coming.

However, she didn't have the energy to argue with her brother at the moment. "Do Mam and Da know I was missing with Bellamy?"

"Oh aye, they do." Kiernan leveled a hard look at her that made her heart quiver. "When you didn't return last night, Winston rode out to Oakland to alert us. Da and I came back to the city right away."

Alannah tucked Zaira's hand through her arm. "I was worried about you, so I was."

"You did the right thing."

Alannah's pretty eyes were filled with concern as she tugged Zaira toward the back door that led to the alley. "I'm sure Zaira is needing some fresh air and a chance to take care of personal needs."

"I won't stop you." Kiernan waved them forward.

Zaira didn't want to leave Bellamy behind, but the doctor was mostly done, had only the wrapping of the bandage left.

Bellamy would likely require much tending over the coming days, and she wanted to be the one to do so. Jenny was already busy enough with her duties at the pub and now caring for Moya and Seamus, and she wouldn't need the extra work with Bellamy.

As Zaira exited the building and started up the short flight of steps that led to the alley, she blinked against the brightness of the morning sunshine penetrating the hazy coal smoke that was a permanent shroud over St. Louis.

Riding down the alley toward the bank were about a dozen men. Was this one of the search parties?

She spotted her da among the riders. Even with his hat on, his bright red hair was easy to see. His brawny body and broad shoulders made him stand out in the crowd too. Like Kiernan, he had a commanding presence wherever he went.

At the sight of her, a warm smile lit up his face. "Ach, here she is, my Zaira. We just received news that you and Bellamy got trapped at the bank while trying to stop bank robbers."

She smiled wearily in return. "We hoped to prevent the robbery but were unsuccessful."

He reined in beside her, hopped down, and scanned her,

his brow furrowing, likely because of all of Bellamy's blood. "Are you hurt?"

"No, but Bellamy was shot in the shoulder."

The other men were halting and dismounting now too, listening to their conversation as she recounted the details of the previous night and then the encounter with Mr. Wright this morning.

"The doctor says Bellamy will recover just fine," she said as she finished her tale.

Some of the worry eased from Da's face. "We've been looking for you for hours."

Her heart gave an extra thud at the prospect that she'd caused him the trouble. "I'm sorry, Da. I didn't mean for all this to happen."

"Since you're sorry, lass, you know what to do." He turned his cheek toward her and pointed at it.

She lifted up onto her toes and planted a kiss there. Then she smiled at him again, and he tweaked her nose, as he usually did. But this time, he didn't smile in return. Instead, his eyes seemed sadder, burdened, and she'd been the cause of it.

Kiernan had exited the bank after them and now stepped beside her with his arm around Alannah's back. He shared a look with Da, then spoke in a low tone so none of the other men could hear. "After she spent the night with him locked in a storage room, we'll need to move up the wedding."

"Oh aye," Da said solemnly and in a hushed voice. "That we will. Right away, as soon as Bellamy is able."

Dismay settled inside Zaira as Kiernan and Da continued to converse in whispers about this newest development between her and Bellamy.

The issue was that Bellamy didn't want to marry her *at all* and would be even less inclined to marry her *early*. The whole situation was bound to cause everyone only more distress. Guilt pricked her. Kiernan knew about her pretend relationship with Bellamy, so he would understand Bellamy's objection to a hurried wedding, but her da would be surprised when Bellamy protested.

What if Bellamy decided to go through with marrying her because he felt obligated to preserve her reputation? As a man of honor and integrity, he wouldn't want her to suffer and would sacrifice his own desires to do the right thing by her.

The truth was, she didn't want Bellamy to marry her because he *had to* but only if he *wanted* her. However, he'd already made it clear she wasn't the woman for him. That meant she couldn't marry him, not when he would always regret their imperfect relationship.

But what could she do to get out of marrying Bellamy, especially without earning more of her da's disappointment? Was there anything at all? Could she come up with a believable excuse?

Bellamy's words from earlier lingered at the back of her mind. He'd told her that one of the qualities she was missing was honesty, and he was right. Somehow she'd turned into a downright deceptive person.

She hadn't always been so dishonest. So why had lying become the first thing she considered doing whenever she was faced with a dilemma?

Was it because she cared more about what people thought of her and pleasing them than doing what was right and pleasing God?

"Miss Shanahan," said a man breaking free from the others. It was Mr. Knapp, the owner of the *Daily Republican*. Had he been a part of the search parties too, or had he gathered with the men while on his way to work because he'd been curious about what was going on?

With spectacles perched on his nose, he approached with a kindly smile. "Kiernan found the manuscript in your saddlebag last night. I told him you were probably on your way to deliver it to me when you were delayed." Mr. Knapp held it up and gave it a loving pat.

Da's gaze shuffled back and forth between her and Mr. Knapp. "I'm still confused about this manuscript. Mr. Knapp told us that a K. S. Flanders is writing a weekly column for the newspaper but that you deliver the segments for the fellow."

Zaira stared at the bundle of paper wrapped up in twine with Mr. Knapp's name boldly on the cover page. She was glad Mr. Knapp had it and hopefully still had time to print it for this week's episode. But how could she possibly explain all this to Da?

Should she make up a story about how she was friends with K. S. Flanders?

The trouble was, her da knew most important people in St. Louis. If he investigated the matter further, he would discover Mr. Flanders didn't exist. Should she tell him Mr. Flanders lived in another town? That he wanted his true identity to remain a secret?

It's not too late to work at being honest. Those were the words she'd told Bellamy earlier. She'd just lectured him about how imperfect couples had to work on fixing things, but had she ever considered that she needed to fix herself first? That perhaps she was overdue in repenting for using dishonesty?

Zaira expelled a tight breath. Being truthful was the right path, even if it was harder. She knew that from all the lessons she'd been taught over the years from her parents and from the nuns at school.

But was she ready to face the disappointment from her da and mam? She'd tried to avoid it for so long, but maybe she had to finally stop trying to make them happy with her choices, stop living in fear of their disapproval, and stop worrying about embarrassing her family.

Instead, she had to accept herself and who she really was. Maybe if she did that, her parents would eventually learn to accept her for who she really was too.

Could she do this? Could she be honest about her secret writing life? But what other choice did she have except for making up even more elaborate lies and causing the situation to be even worse?

She met Alannah's gaze.

The dear woman's eyes were filled with compassion, and she reached over and took Zaira's hand in hers and squeezed it.

Alannah had kept the writing a secret, clearly hadn't even told Kiernan—although from the way he was studying her, he was likely figuring it out.

Even now, something in Alannah's expression conveyed that the secret was still safe, that she wouldn't be the one to expose it.

"Da, Mr. Knapp." Zaira's throat grew suddenly tight. "I have something to tell you."

Mr. Knapp's eyes were kind behind his spectacles. Did he already suspect the truth?

Da's brows, on the other hand, only furrowed more deeply. "You should know." Zaira cleared her throat. "I am K. S. Flanders."

Everyone and everything seemed to go as silent as if she'd just shouted the news from the rooftop. Both Da and Kiernan stared at her with unblinking eyes. Mr. Knapp glanced between her da and her, perhaps waiting to see what Da's reaction would be before making a comment.

She'd finally done it. She'd brought more scandal to the Shanahan name than all her other siblings combined. Everything within her wanted to shrivel up and disappear into the gravel of the alley.

Alannah, still holding her hand, pressed it gently. Her pretty features were tight with earnestness, encouraging her to say everything that needed to be said.

Zaira swallowed the fear threatening to suffocate her. She'd started down this difficult path of telling the truth, and she couldn't stop now. She could only hope and pray that Da and Kiernan would be as understanding as Alannah, even as understanding as Bellamy.

She straightened her shoulders, then pushed forward with the rest of what she needed to say. "I've been writing and publishing weekly stories with the *Daily Republican* under a pseudonym: K. S. Flanders."

Again, no one spoke. But the growing disappointment on Da's face was easy to read.

She turned to Mr. Knapp. "I'm sorry for not being honest with you about my real identity."

He just offered a small smile. "I have worked with other authors who've done the same."

"Thank you." She faced her da and brother. "I'm sorry—"

"Not now, Zaira." Kiernan looked around at all the other men who were watching their family drama unfold. "We'll discuss the matter later when we're home."

Da extended a hand toward Mr. Knapp. "I'll take the manuscript."

Mr. Knapp's eyes seemed to ask what she wanted him to do.

She wished she could blurt out that her da couldn't stop her, that she was old enough to make her own decisions. As much as she longed to be bolder and not worry about Da's reaction, she couldn't make herself protest.

Da reached for the manuscript and practically wrenched it from Mr. Knapp's hands. Then he walked to the rubbish container beside the rear bank door, tossed the bundle of papers inside, and glared at her. "You'll have some explaining to do, lass."

She could only stare at the container. She'd suspected Da would be displeased with her unladylike pursuit and her sneaking around. But she hadn't expected he would disregard her writing that rapidly and with such finality. Were all her dreams and hopes and plans just garbage to him?

A pulse of anger shot through her. If he could toss away something this important to her, then why had she cared about pleasing him for so long? Why not just walk over, pull out the manuscript, and hand it right back to Mr. Knapp?

Her fingers twitched with the desire to do so.

The rear door of the bank swung open, and one of the bank workers poked his head out and glanced around until he spotted her. "Miss Shanahan, Bellamy has regained consciousness, and he's asking for you."

The interruption was the perfect timing to avoid saying

anything else to her da, especially something she might regret later.

She didn't waste another moment and made her way toward the rear entrance. Even if Bellamy didn't want her for a wife, he was still asking for her. That had to count for something, didn't it?

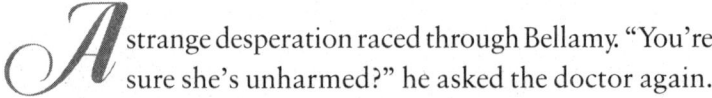

22

A strange desperation raced through Bellamy. "You're sure she's unharmed?" he asked the doctor again.

The silver-haired man was packing the leather satchel beside him. "I didn't personally examine her, but she claimed to be fine."

Bellamy pushed up with his uninjured arm, making it to his elbow.

"Careful now." The doctor eased Bellamy back to the hallway floor of the bank basement. "We're getting ready to transport you soon."

Bellamy tried to sit up even more. He needed to find Zaira to see if she was okay. But as soon as he elevated himself again, both pain and dizziness slammed into him so that he felt he might be sick to his stomach.

"Bellamy?" Her voice echoed from a distance.

He shifted to watch her slip through the outer door and start running toward him, her hair unbound and flowing about her in long, flaming waves.

As she drew nearer, the doctor stood and moved aside. The lantern light fell over Zaira, highlighting her beauty—the delicate lines in her face, her wide eyes, the elegant curves of her body. She had such a determined stride, such a confident way of holding herself, such a spark of life.

He loved every part of her, and he suddenly wanted to pull out a blank canvas and spend the day painting her. He had the feeling that even if he painted her portrait every day for the rest of her life, he still wouldn't be able to capture everything about her. She was an endless source of beauty and inspiration.

In the next instant, she was kneeling beside him. "How are you feeling?" She grasped his hand and held it tightly.

"I'll survive." He tried to assess her, but she was leaning over him and had cupped one of his cheeks.

Her face hovered above his, her eyes worried. "Are you in a great deal of pain?"

He shook his head. Even though the doctor had given him some laudanum, his shoulder still throbbed. But that didn't matter. All he cared about was that she was unharmed. "Did he hurt you?" He managed to get the question out even though each word felt heavy.

"I'll survive." Her words were soft and teasing and followed by a slow smile, one he wanted to kiss.

If only he had the strength to do so. But he was weaker than he'd realized, and his head thudded back to the floor and his lashes fell closed again.

Oh aye, he loved every part of her. Every single part. He didn't know why he'd resisted her for so long, why he'd been opposed to having a relationship with her, why he'd fought against his feelings for her. Why had he, when all he wanted to do was pull her into his arms and have her for the rest of his life?

Somewhere in his jumble of thoughts, he knew there was a reason why they couldn't be together, why he'd worked so hard to keep his distance from her. But he couldn't think of one thing about her he didn't like.

The truth was so obvious. He loved her, and he couldn't imagine ever loving any other woman the way he did her.

"Bellamy," came the stern voice of James Shanahan from behind Zaira.

Bellamy pried open his eyes to find Zaira's worried face still above his.

"Bellamy, son," Mr. Shanahan called again.

Bellamy tried to find the red-haired man, but his vision blurred, and his consciousness began to fade.

"Prepare yourself for a wedding." Mr. Shanahan spoke loudly. "You'll be marrying Zaira just as soon as it can be arranged."

He thought he heard Zaira's protest, but blackness claimed him, taking him to a land where there was nothing but emptiness.

❖ ❖ ❖ ❖ ❖ ❖ ❖

Bellamy stirred, and as he did so, he could feel the firmness of a mattress beneath him. The silkiness of sheets surrounded him, and a feather-stuffed pillow cushioned his head. The quality was too fine to belong to his family, which meant only one thing. He was at the Shanahans'.

"I'm sorry for deceiving you both." Zaira's voice came from beside him, and he guessed she was sitting in a bedside chair. A decidedly feminine scent wafted in the air and in the linens, and he guessed he was probably in Zaira's room.

"Your apology won't fix the mistake." Kiernan's voice dropped low and was edged with frustration.

"But we can put an end to that right now." The harshly spoken statement came from James Shanahan.

Bellamy tried to pry open an eye, but he felt groggy and his body heavy.

"Da, please," Zaira responded. "Try to understand—"

"No, you need to understand," Mr. Shanahan spoke forcefully. "This sort of behavior is inappropriate for a young woman, and you'll be stopping this immediately."

What was Mr. Shanahan referring to? Were they discussing the inappropriateness of two young unmarried people staying the night together? Surely the two knew by now that he and Zaira hadn't done so intentionally and that their time together had been innocent—except for one long and excellent kiss.

Obviously no one knew about the kiss, and even if Mr. Shanahan or Kiernan had discovered it, how could they condemn one kiss? Especially because he and Zaira were engaged?

"What if I don't want to stop?" Zaira's question held a note of boldness that Bellamy hadn't heard her use with her da before. What was she saying, that she didn't want to stop being with him? Was she growing to care about him too?

His mind spun back to the few minutes of being with her in the hallway before he lost consciousness again. What had her da said?

"As soon as you're married," Mr. Shanahan continued, "you'll understand the need to focus on your husband and home."

Zaira released an audible sigh. "That's why I want to wait."

"When is the priest coming?" Mr. Shanahan asked impatiently.

"Any moment," Kiernan answered.

"He should be here by now."

"We also need to wait for Bellamy to awaken."

He tried to stir to let them know he was gaining consciousness, but he couldn't get his eyelids to lift or his lips to open. He suspected the doctor might have given him more pain medicine for the ride to the Shanahan mansion, and that now he was too weak and tired to participate in the conversation.

"Da, Kiernan." Zaira spoke again, the boldness still in her tone. "It doesn't matter if the priest comes or not. I'm not marrying Bellamy."

"You have no choice." Mr. Shanahan's statement was curt.

She was silent for several long heartbeats. "Our relationship is only pretend."

"Pretend?"

"Aye, ask Kiernan. He knows that Bellamy and I agreed be together for a short while to help each other out, and that we never intended to go through with the marriage."

A strange protest welled up inside Bellamy. She was right. Even last night, he'd pushed her away after their kiss when she'd been questioning what their relationship meant. He hadn't wanted to explore what might develop between them, hadn't given a future with her any consideration.

Oh aye, his family had a terrible history with relationships. And he'd always been scared of repeating the same mistakes. But in attempting to avoid the mistakes and searching for a perfect match, was he making things even worse?

No man or woman was ever perfect. He wouldn't be a good matchmaker if he didn't acknowledge that fact.

Zaira's accusation pressed at his consciousness. *"Maybe a perfect match has to do with how well a couple displays humility and perseverance and the willingness to forgive."*

Was she right? If a husband and wife were so busy looking for perfection from one another, would they overlook the need for humility, perseverance, and a willingness to forgive? Those attributes that would really make a difference in having a happy and lasting marriage?

"What's all this about a pretend relationship?" Mr. Shanahan asked.

Kiernan cleared his throat. "It was a way to protect Zaira after her first kiss with Bellamy."

"And?"

"I assumed once they were together, they would soon realize they're already in love with each other."

"We're not in love." Zaira's response was quick and angry. "We don't even like each other."

Kiernan snorted. "Everyone could see at the eating-the-gander party that you're both crazy about each other."

"We drive each other crazy, but that's all."

"It doesn't matter now," Kiernan continued. "After you spent last night together, there will be no breaking off your relationship now."

"Oh aye, I'll be breaking it off." Zaira's chair bumped against the bedside table as she rose.

Bellamy blinked, finally opening his eyes to morning

sunshine pouring in through an open window. She was facing her da and brother, who were both standing just inside the door of a room that was definitely Zaira's. With white furniture and yellow everywhere, it was feminine and bright and whimsical, just like Zaira.

Kiernan was scowling at her. "You'll marry him, and that's all there is to it."

Her back stiffened. "Bellamy will never agree to it either."

He wanted to tell her she was wrong, but the words stuck inside him. Was he really ready to throw away all the caution he'd previously used and jump into a marriage with Zaira? He didn't want to go from one extreme to the other, using restraint to using none at all.

"Bellamy won't have a choice," Kiernan said. "He'll understand that your reputation is severely compromised, and he'll do the right thing."

"Aye," Bellamy managed to croak. "So I will."

Zaira spun and nearly tripped over her chair in her haste. Kiernan and Mr. Shanahan both straightened and riveted their gazes upon him, their eyes filled with accusation.

"I won't need convincing to do the right thing." This time Bellamy's voice came out stronger. Although he felt weak, the doctor had assured him the wound would heal and that he'd be fine within a week or two. In the meantime, he would have to rest since he'd lost so much blood.

Mr. Shanahan nodded curtly. "I knew Bellamy was a man of honor."

Zaira narrowed her eyes on Bellamy as though she was thinking of everything they'd talked about after their kiss. "I refuse to trap a man into marriage so he can save my honor."

"You won't be trapping me—"

"You told me I wasn't the woman for you. So what else would a marriage to me be?"

He'd been a fool, that's what. He'd been fighting his attraction to her after kissing her because deep down he'd known he was falling harder for her. And he'd tried to put something between them to keep himself from reaching for her and promising her forever.

"No," Zaira said more adamantly. "I refuse to marry a man who is only doing so because he has no other choice. When I get married, I want to marry someone who is doing so because I'm his first choice."

"You are his first choice." Kiernan pinned Bellamy with a look that told him he'd better agree. "Like I said, everyone can see that you belong together."

"Everyone?" She released a scoffing laugh.

"Ach, Zaira." Bellamy tried to push up from the mattress, but his body ached too much to cooperate. "We'll get married, and we'll make the best of it, so we will."

"Make the best of it?"

His proposal was likely the most unromantic ever spoken, and he wanted to slap himself in the head once the words were out, especially when her lips pinched into a thin, straight line. He needed to say something else, something sweet, something worthy of the romance she loved so much. But his brain was hazy and wasn't working as quickly as it normally did.

"I've made up my mind." Zaira situated the bedside chair against the wall. "I'm not getting married. Instead, I'd like to focus on my writing for a while."

Her writing? Had she told her da and Kiernan about her newspaper column? If so, why?

"No, Zaira." Mr. Shanahan crossed his arms and pinned her with a severe look. "It's time to put that nonsense behind you."

"Nonsense?" Her voice rose in pitch.

Was Mr. Shanahan calling Zaira's writing *nonsense*? If so, that was very insensitive.

"Aye. You're a grown woman, and it's time to put childish ways behind you."

Bellamy's muscles were tightening more with each word the man spoke. "Zaira's writing isn't nonsense or childish. She has great talent, and readers love her stories." He hoped she knew he was referring to the question she'd asked him last night about her story but that he hadn't made time to answer.

All three turned to look at him again. He wished he could sit up and present himself as capable, calm, and confident as always. But he could hardly move without a wave of dizziness hitting him.

Kiernan raised a brow at him. "So, you've known about her writing for the newspaper?"

"Naturally."

"And that's why you don't want to marry her." Kiernan's question came out a statement.

"The opposite. I believe she has the right to keep writing and deserves a husband who will support it." He caught Zaira's gaze, hoping she would understand how sincere he was, hoping she would realize he'd never be unsupportive like Oscar was to his mam.

Zaira regarded him warily.

Kiernan waved a dismissive hand. "All the more reason for

240

the two of you to get married, since you'll support Zaira's writing."

Zaira spun and began to cross the room. "It isn't enough reason for us to get married, and I won't do it."

"Oh aye, lass." Mr. Shanahan's face was turning red. "You'll be doing it today when the priest arrives, and that's all there is to it."

Zaira didn't stop until she reached the door. Then she gave her da a sad but resigned look. "I've never wanted to cause problems when you already had so many. I always wanted to please you. But why was I trying so hard to make you happy when you obviously haven't cared about my happiness?"

With that, she stepped into the hallway and shut the door behind her.

Mr. Shanahan opened his mouth to respond, but no words came out.

Exhaustion fell over Bellamy, and he couldn't keep his eyes open any longer. Even though his mind was fuzzy, one thing was becoming all too clear: The more Zaira pushed him away, the more he wanted her. Of course, as a matchmaker he knew the *heart-wants-what-it-cannot-have* was one tactic for bringing a couple together. Was that what he was experiencing with Zaira?

Or was it another tactic? Resistance changing into *fear-of-losing-the-loved-one*?

Maybe it was both.

Maybe it was also the realization that she'd told the truth about everything. She'd been honest about their relationship. She'd been honest about her writing for the newspaper. She'd been honest about her objection to a hasty marriage. She'd even admitted to a publishing venture even though she had so much to lose, especially the respect of her family.

Admiration welled up inside him. Zaira had displayed an enormous amount of courage to speak the truth.

What about him? What had he done to display even a wee amount of courage?

Nothing. He'd lectured Zaira about the need for honesty, and he'd disparaged having a relationship with her because of the lack of honesty. In doing so, all he'd accomplished was showing himself to be nothing but a hypocrite.

If he really wanted to have a different marriage than Oscar and his granda and all his ancestors, then maybe he had to be willing to change himself instead of trying to change Zaira.

23

The deep ache inside Zaira was too much to bear. She swiped at the tears running down her cheeks, but they flowed anyway. She hugged her arms around her chest to ward off the pain in her heart, but it throbbed regardless.

"Zaira." A soft voice from the balcony door sounded behind her.

She didn't have to turn to know it was Alannah. After the discussion in the bedroom earlier, Kiernan had probably gone straight to Alannah and told her everything, including Zaira's refusal to marry Bellamy. Kiernan had likely sent his wife to work at convincing Zaira to go through with the wedding.

"I can't do it." Zaira sniffed back the tears. "So you may as well go tell Kiernan I won't change my mind."

The pad of footsteps crossed the second-floor balcony at the back of the house until they stopped beside Zaira, where she sat in one of the elegant iron chairs that overlooked the gravel driveway, carriage house, and other small outbuildings. A few trees and neatly trimmed shrubs bordered both sides of the property, and clusters of asters and irises grew in the couple of raised flower beds that lined the house.

She'd come out hoping the view would give her some solace, but it hadn't worked. Deep inside, she knew that admitting to the truth about everything had been the right thing to do. If only the turmoil had gone away instead of raging harder.

Alannah dragged a chair closer to Zaira's and then sat, fluffing out the silky skirt that had once belonged to Zaira but that she'd gladly and willingly donated to Alannah.

"Please, Alannah." Zaira wiped at the wetness on her cheeks again. "Please tell Kiernan I can't marry Bellamy . . . at least not today."

"That's not why I came out here." Alannah tucked a handkerchief into Zaira's hand. "Kiernan knows I won't be pressuring you to do something you're not ready for, so I won't."

At the kind words, more tears began to flow. Zaira dabbed the handkerchief against her eyes. "Thank you, Alannah. You're a true and good friend. The very best."

"You're a true and good friend too."

Zaira swallowed another wave of emotion that threatened to bring more tears and maybe even sobs. "I refuse to marry a man who doesn't love me in return. I'd rather live with my ruined reputation than subject Bellamy to a life he doesn't want."

"How do you know he's not just scared? That maybe he really does want it?"

"He told me last night we weren't meant to be together, that even if we have some attraction, it's not enough."

"I don't believe him."

"He also said I'd make another fellow a fine wife, but that he's looking for someone different than me for himself."

Alannah released a sigh. "Why is Bellamy so good at see-ing the dynamics in everyone else's relationships but unable to see what's going on in his own?"

"That's just it. We don't have a relationship. It's all just pretend." Well, maybe not *all* pretend. Their attraction was very real and had only grown the longer they were together.

"Zaira," Alannah said gently, "I can see you have feelings for him."

Was it that obvious? If Alannah had noticed, what if Bel-lamy had been able to all along? And what if that had driven him away?

Zaira leaned forward and buried her face in her hands. "It doesn't matter how I feel. What matters is that he has been insistent from the start of our fake relationship that he doesn't want to marry me."

"It's obvious he has feelings for you too."

In the bedroom, Kiernan had said she and Bellamy were both already in love with each other and would soon realize it. As much as she wished her brother was right, he wasn't. Bellamy had shut down any hope of a future together.

"The fact is, feelings or not, Bellamy isn't ready to get married."

She appreciated that he wanted to protect her reputation and was a man of honor. But after all he'd revealed about his mam, it was clear he still had too many issues to work through before he would be ready to consider marriage to her or anyone else. Maybe he already knew that, and maybe that was one of the reasons why he'd wanted to postpone Oscar's matchmaking.

Whatever the case, she needed to get away from everyone. Even though she wanted to be the one to take care of Bellamy while he was injured and recovering, she was afraid that if she stayed, Kiernan and Da and even Bellamy would eventually pressure her into the wedding.

The other sad truth was that she didn't want to be around Da, not after he'd called her writing nonsense and childish. Oh aye, she'd disappointed him, probably more than any of her other siblings.

But he'd disappointed her, too, with his unwillingness to consider that writing was important to her. Instead of listening and giving some credence to her pursuit, he'd dismissed it, and that hurt maybe even more than his stern insistence that she marry Bellamy whether she wanted to or not.

Oh aye, she needed to escape the weight of the damage she'd brought to her family and seclude herself at Oakland. She wouldn't be able to hide from her mam there. But at least she'd be out of the city and away from Bellamy and all the reminders of her mistakes.

"I need to go back to Oakland," she whispered.

"Are you sure?" Alannah whispered in return.

She nodded. "Will you stay and take care of Bellamy in my stead? I just can't do it. I'm afraid I'll give in too easily and marry him, and then we'll both be miserable."

Alannah squeezed her hand. "I'll see to him, so I will."

More tears welled in Zaira's eyes. "Thank you."

Alannah was silent for a few long seconds before speaking again quietly. "You should know, you're one of the bravest women I know. God gave you a gift with your writing. It took valor to push forward and get published."

"I lied to make it happen."

"I'll not be saying that dishonesty was the right choice. But it's also not right that in the climb to the same peak, women have to take a path that is more winding and twice as long as a man's straight hike."

Zaira liked Alannah's analogy. If anyone could understand the difficulties for women in getting work, Alannah could because she'd had a hard time obtaining employment as an editor even though she excelled at it.

"But you climbed the impossible trail to publication," Alannah continued, "and I believe you'll find a way to keep doing it, this time without having to hide it."

Would she, though? Zaira hadn't given thought to what she would do next with her novel and the weekly newspaper column. She supposed in a way she'd given up and tossed her dreams into the rubbish bin when Da had thrown her manuscript there. Maybe she'd thought of allowing her da to have his way, that he'd forgive her and she'd regain his approval.

But the same question as before echoed in her mind: Why should she worry about making him happy when he didn't consider her well-being and what she wanted—needed—in her life?

A flame of indignation flared back to life inside her, the same indignation that had flared there when she'd walked away from the men in her bedroom a short while ago. Alannah was right. God *had* given her a gift with her writing. She loved it, she was good at it, and she couldn't just cast it aside because her da thought it was nonsense and childish.

No, she needed to keep pushing forward with publication for herself and for all the other women who wanted to use their God-given gifts too. Maybe if she persevered, she'd eventually make the way easier for women authors who would come after her.

She stood, resolution stiffening her backbone. She knew what she needed to do on her way out of the city. She needed to stop by the rubbish bin behind the bank, pull out the chapter Da had thrown away, and then drop it off at the *Daily Republican*. She'd explain herself to Mr. Knapp and this time be completely honest with him.

She could only hope he'd give her a second chance.

24

*B*ellamy released a frustrated sigh. What was he doing hiding in his shed painting in the dark of night when he should be standing out in the open with his easel and his paints and capturing a landscape?

He rolled his injured shoulder, then pressed a glob of white oil paint from the tube onto the palette before fishing the paintbrush from behind his ear and dabbing it in the white. As he lifted the brush to the canvas, he made a mental image of Dover's Pond and the glassy surface with all the lily pads.

He'd been to Dover's Pond several times over recent months. He should be able to recreate the landscape with no trouble at all. But even as he added the white to the water to help with the shimmering reflection, the vision of Zaira as she'd looked that day when he'd gone out to visit with her about Deirdre Whitcomb's match took up most of the space in his head.

Who was he kidding? Zaira took up *all* the space in his head. And she always had regardless of how hard he'd tried to prevent it. Even while avoiding his feelings for her, he'd been slightly obsessed with thinking about her.

He tucked the paintbrush back behind his ear and stared unseeingly at the canvas, the lantern hanging from the ceiling illuminating the painting he'd been working on since his return from the Shanahans' two days ago.

He'd only stayed in bed there for one day and one night, not nearly long enough to recover. But the next day, he'd forced himself to get to his feet after the doctor had fashioned a sling for him to use to immobilize his shoulder. That had been all he'd needed to give himself permission to stop lying around.

Besides, he hadn't wanted to impose on the Shanahans any longer, especially Alannah, who'd been the one tending to his needs since Zaira had returned to Oakland.

She'd left without saying good-bye.

The truth was, he hadn't given her a reason to see him again. In fact, since the start of their relationship, he'd done just about everything he could to push her away. And it had worked. She'd been gone from the house before the priest had arrived to marry them, much to Mr. Shanahan's dismay. The gentleman had stormed about and finally said he would ride after her and demand that she return.

Bellamy had sensed there would be no making Zaira change her mind, so he'd asked Mr. Shanahan to wait, to give him time to plot a different way to encourage the union without force. Bellamy had assured Mr. Shanahan he'd use his matchmaker skills to finalize the match with Zaira.

So far, Bellamy hadn't been able to come up with a plan. Why was he so cunning and intuitive for everyone else, but he couldn't form a coherent thought when it came to Zaira?

Bellamy reached for the tube of yellow oil paint, un-screwed the lid, then lifted it above the palette. But as he started to squirt out a dollop, he halted. There was already enough yellow there to paint the entire canvas.

Was yellow on his mind because of all the yellow in Zaira's room? Or because she reminded him of yellow and sunshine and wildflowers and golden beauty?

He managed to secure the lid back on the yellow tube, then tossed it on the tall worktable beside him.

Her accusation had been rolling around his mind for the past few days—that he was looking for a perfect relationship with a perfect woman so he could have a perfect marriage.

Had he been looking for perfection so he could break his family's curse? In himself and in a woman?

Although he knew that such perfection was unattainable with humans, that only God was perfect, the fears still lin-gered in his heart. He worried that somehow, no matter what he did, he would fail in his marriage, especially that he'd fail Zaira and make her terribly unhappy.

At a firm rap against the door, Bellamy froze. The knock-ing didn't belong to Jenny. Hers was usually soft and hesi-tant, as though she didn't want to disturb him. This was the kind of knocking that belonged to a man.

"Bellamy?" It was Oscar.

Surprise rippled through Bellamy. What was Oscar doing up in the middle of the night? And why was he at the shed? He never came out when Bellamy was painting. Never. As if by ignoring the painting he could pretend it didn't exist.

The door rattled, the inside latch keeping Oscar out. "Can I come in?" Oscar asked none too quietly. If he got any louder—which could easily happen—they'd risk waking up the rest of the neighborhood, including Moya and Seamus, who were still living with Jenny and Gavin and seemed to be content with the arrangements.

Gavin had been the one to ride down to Carondelet to check out the lead for Mr. O'Reilly. Seamus had wanted to ride with, and Gavin had allowed the lad to share a horse and had taught him some horsemanship during the morning together. While they hadn't located the children's father, Seamus had come home excited about being atop a horse.

Oscar knocked again more forcefully.

Swallowing an irritated sigh, Bellamy crossed to the door, unlatched it, and swung it open.

In the glow of the lantern light coming out of the shed, Oscar stood hatless, his shirt untucked, and one of his suspenders hanging down. He dug his fingers through his thick gray hair, combing back unruly strands.

With his heart picking up tempo, Bellamy waited for Oscar to speak. Was something wrong with Zaira? Or were the Shanahans in a bit of a bother? Was that why Oscar had come out in the middle of the night?

At a dog bark from down the alley, Oscar glanced over his shoulder into the darkness before peering past Bellamy to the interior of the shed. "Can I come in?"

Bellamy wanted to tell Oscar no, that the shed was private, that he wasn't welcome there. On the other hand, from the creases in Oscar's brow, Bellamy he stepped aside and waved him inside.

Oscar, smelling heavily of whiskey, lumbered past him.

With the ban on beer still in place, they'd been serving more hard liquor. Even so, more customers had dropped away. Now they had only a dozen of the regulars who came out at night to the pub.

Truthfully, Bellamy was grateful for the lull in business over the past days, since he'd been unable to help as much as he usually did.

Still, he would be happy along with the rest of St. Louis when the cholera was officially done. Today they'd gotten news that the death count from yesterday had been the lowest it had been since back in early June. They'd almost allowed themselves to hope that with the coming of August just around the corner, the end of the epidemic was finally in sight.

That didn't solve the issue with homeless children, though. Saint Riley had stopped by the pub earlier and picked up the list of families willing to serve as temporary parents for children left orphans by the disease.

Bellamy had hoped to have a longer list, but with his injury and the lack of customers in the pub, he'd had a difficult time getting the word out about the need to house the orphans. He'd found himself wishing for Zaira's help in raising the awareness, knowing she would have loved being a part of the recruiting.

As it was, however, he hadn't seen her since the morning when he'd regained consciousness in her bedroom.

While Oscar crossed directly to the easel and canvas, Bellamy closed the door and then leaned against it, trying to maintain a casual air even though Oscar's presence in his sanctuary was creating a tempest inside him.

Oscar was quiet as he took in the half-finished painting of Dover's Pond. Not that the landscape was recognizable yet as Dover's Pond. And if it had been, Bellamy doubted Oscar could identify the place. Probably had never been there.

For long seconds—almost agonizingly long—Oscar studied the work in progress. He cocked his head one way and spoke softly. "The contrast with the lighting is good, Bellamy."

Bellamy looked at the painting now too. What did Oscar know about contrasting colors and lighting?

Oscar examined the painting for another moment before he turned around and met Bellamy's gaze. "You're a better artist than she was."

The compliment was so unexpected Bellamy couldn't think of a response. Oscar never talked about his painting, much less offered a compliment about it. He'd never even spoken the word *painting*, only called it *you-know-what*. So why now? Why tonight?

Bellamy shook his head. No, Oscar couldn't come in here like this and pretend he cared either about Mam's art or his.

"Wait, Bellamy." Oscar held out a hand as though he could sense the storm escalating within Bellamy and wanted to prevent it from unleashing.

But it was too late. Bellamy had been waiting for years to say something—anything—about Mam and all that had happened. Now was his chance, and he planned to take it. "She might have been a better artist if you'd supported her and her painting instead of trying to keep her from it."

"Is that what you think?" Oscar's eyes widened, revealing a despair so profound that it almost took Bellamy's breath away. "That I didn't support her painting?"

"You were always trying to keep her from going away to paint. And when she was home painting, you complained about it all the time."

Oscar sighed, his shoulders sagging, probably under the weight of guilt.

"I'll never do that to Zaira with her writing." Bellamy wasn't sure why he felt the need to tell Oscar his resolution. But the truth was, ever since Mr. Shanahan had called her writing "nonsense" and "childish," Bellamy had privately vowed to support her writing no matter what it took.

"I know you'll be a better husband than me, Bellamy." Oscar's voice was laced with sadness and regret. "But you should know, I never tried to keep your mam from her painting."

"I heard all the arguments. And Mam told me how much you disliked that she painted."

"I loved her paintings. And I loved her—" Oscar's voice caught, and his eyes turned glassy. He quickly turned away and drew in a deep breath. "What I didn't like was her using opium and cannabis to help her with her inspiration."

Bellamy had known his mam had turned to alcohol to drown out her problems, but he hadn't realized she'd also been using drugs.

"I tried to get her to stop," Oscar continued in a low voice filled with heartache. "And she did stop for a while after we got married and had Jenny."

"She used drugs before you met her?"

"She came from a hard life, and I thought I could give her a better one."

Bellamy nodded. Mam had always thought her marriage to Oscar would give her a better life too. But maybe she'd been the one to ruin her chances by falling back into using drugs.

"I was naïve," Oscar admitted. "I hoped I would be

enough, that Jenny would be enough, that having another babe—you—would give her reason to be sober."

Bellamy had always known he wasn't enough for Mam, that she didn't really care about him the way other mothers did for their children. And now he understood why. Her erratic behavior, moodiness, distance—it all made more sense.

"All I wanted was for us to be together." Oscar still was halfway turned away and was pressing his thumbs into his eyes. "But she could never resist using drugs for very long. They were always more important than anything else."

In those last years, she'd started being gone for longer periods too. Bellamy had always assumed Oscar's lack of support and love had driven her from home. But had the drugs drawn her away? Where had she gone? Who had she stayed with?

Bellamy felt sick to his stomach just thinking about the possible answers.

"I knew painting made her happy," Oscar said quietly. "And I wanted her to be happy. More than anything. But the drugs destroyed her."

Bellamy didn't know what to say. He'd carried around resentment for years toward Oscar. Maybe if he'd known the truth about Mam, his relationship with Oscar would have been different. "Whyever didn't you tell me?"

Oscar sighed. "I wanted you to have happy memories of your mam and of those times you had painting together with her."

"But all of these years I've believed you didn't support her painting . . . or mine."

"I know you've been selling your paintings at a local gallery, and I know people are buying them and rightly so."

Bellamy hadn't realized Oscar knew all that, although he supposed it wasn't too hard to figure out.

"I haven't revealed my identity yet." But maybe it was finally time to do so. Even if he lost customers who didn't want to buy from him because he was Irish, at least he wouldn't be hiding a huge part of himself any longer.

"I'm sorry." Oscar's whisper was choked. "Your painting reminded me too much of her and all the pain of losing her."

Bellamy's throat grew tight again. He could only imagine how difficult it had been for Oscar to see the paintings and be reminded of his wife and all he'd lost.

Oscar cleared his throat and wiped his eyes again. "I've been trying to figure out why you let Zaira leave the city and didn't fight to get her back. Tonight I realized one important thing."

Of course, Bellamy had been contemplating ways to convince Zaira to marry him. But Oscar was right. Bellamy had let her leave and hadn't fought for her.

"I realized," Oscar continued, "that you're afraid of letting yourself love a woman because you don't want to have a failed marriage like mine or Granda's."

"Oh aye. Rightly so."

Oscar pivoted and faced Bellamy squarely, looking him in the eyes. "I've always said that love doesn't follow the usual mathematical equations."

Aye, he'd heard Oscar say that before many a time. Bellamy couldn't deny that Oscar was intuitive when it came to relationships. He could see things others couldn't and was wiser than most in the ways of love.

"You and Zaira are not the sum of your parents. You

start at one plus one equals two, and you keep the rest of the family out of the equation."

"But we're influenced by our families—"

"*Influenced*, yes, but you are not *destined* to have a relationship like me and your mam. And Zaira isn't destined to have a relationship like her da and mam. Instead, the two of you can choose to have the exact kind of relationship you want and make it as different as you want."

"I understand that, but the McKenna matchmakers have always been unlucky in love."

Oscar snorted. "That's what people speculate, but it's not true. My granda might not have had a happy second marriage, but his first marriage was one of the happiest ever known."

"Really?" How had Bellamy not heard that?

"It was a short marriage, to be sure. It lasted only two years, and she died giving birth to a stillborn babe. But 'twas said there'd never been a couple who loved each other more than those two."

Bellamy had only ever seen his granda as discontent, but maybe he'd been so of his own making, had always been comparing his second wife to his first.

"Ach, Bellamy. There's no such thing as being unlucky in love. Love is what we make of it."

Bellamy expelled a breath, feeling suddenly lighter than he had in a long time.

Oscar slipped a handkerchief out of his pocket and wiped his nose and then his eyes. "You want to know the secret of the best marriages I've ever witnessed?"

"What?" Maybe Oscar had told him the secret at some point, but it obviously bore repeating in the moment.

"If you both are growing in the qualities that God sets

out in Scripture, in things like patience, kindness, gentleness, self-control, love, and forgiveness, then you'll bring that maturity to solving your problems and weathering difficulties."

Oscar's advice was similar to what Zaira had mentioned about a perfect marriage being more about those inner qualities than anything else.

Bellamy wasn't naïve to think that even with growth of character that he'd avoid problems. But he and Zaira didn't have to make the same mistakes as their parents. They would be starting a new life, and they could build it on the foundation of all those godly qualities that made a person stronger and better.

Aye, he and Zaira could do that. He wanted to do that. As soon as possible. Now. He glanced at the door. Was it too late tonight to go see her?

"So, what do you think?" This time Oscar grinned, as though he could see Bellamy's resolve.

After dismissing her and not treating her the way she deserved, Bellamy would have a lot of work to do to win her. But he wanted to show her how serious he was about their relationship and about his love for her. And hopefully he could convince her to give them another chance and maybe even to love him in return.

"I think I'll need the help of the matchmaker." Bellamy let a grin of his own make an appearance. "A wily one with ideas on how to win the woman I love."

"I have an idea or two, so I do. But it will take you a few days and plenty of determination."

When Oscar finished laying out the plan, Bellamy nodded. "It's solid, even brilliant."

Oscar released what sounded like a relieved laugh. "I am the best."

"Aye, so you are." Bellamy meant the words. In the past, he'd been critical of Oscar's methods of matchmaking. But through the whole experience with Zaira, Bellamy was learning he still had a long way to go until he was an expert in the ways of love. Maybe he would never reach that goal, but he was sure willing to try.

25

Zaira held out her hand and examined the gold bracelet she'd clasped around her wrist. At the center of the bracelet, four garnet jewels formed a flower around a center diamond with turquoise enamel.

The gift from Bellamy had been delivered yesterday afternoon by a messenger to Oakland. And it had been the third gift Bellamy had sent. Three gifts in three days.

She unclasped the bracelet and set it back on the bureau in her bedroom next to the matching brooch and necklace, each of which contained garnet florets and diamonds with the turquoise embellishment.

They were exquisitely beautiful and exactly the sort of colorful jewelry she would love to wear. Except that she couldn't wear them, couldn't accept the gifts. In fact, she'd taken off the claddagh ring, too, and placed it next to the jewelry she planned to give back to him.

Tomorrow. She was going into town tomorrow to deliver her next segment to Mr. Knapp, the next chapter in her novel that she'd worked on rewriting for the past few days since returning to her family's country home.

She hadn't told her da or mam yet that she hadn't quit writing the way they'd assumed. She also hadn't told them she'd pulled the manuscript from the rubbish bin by the bank and taken it to Mr. Knapp. And she hadn't told them Mr. Knapp had only been too happy to continue publishing her work because of the growing interest in the story.

She'd asked Mr. Knapp not to say anything to her da so she could find a way to inform him she was continuing her writing with the newspaper. Since Da had been staying in the city, she hadn't had an opportunity to talk to him more about it.

As much as she balked at the thought of having to face him, she knew she had to. Now that she'd started down the hard path of honesty, she wanted to keep going, no matter how difficult it would be.

The next step was *telling* Da her plans—not *asking* for permission. She wanted his approval, but she didn't need it.

Da wouldn't be happy with her decision to keep writing. In fact, he would be irate that she was defying him. He would probably lose his temper and be even more disappointed in her than ever. But he wouldn't cast her out of the family, would he?

She swept her gaze over her lovely bedroom, her heart pinching at the prospect of giving it up. The ivy-patterned wallpaper was accented by potted plants situated around the room, making her feel as though she were in a garden. The bed canopy was created from wispy white tulle and the comforter patterned in white and green stripes and decorated with lacy white throw pillows.

Whatever might happen, she had to press forward in doing what she knew was right. She needed to stop hiding and learn to live her life more openly, then pray that Da—and the people she cared about—could accept her for who she was and not who they expected her to be.

It was still terrifying to think she'd been so bold, that she was still being so forthright, especially after concealing her true self. Regardless, she'd poured her heartache and frustration into the rewrites of the chapter, and she believed it was her best writing so far.

She finally understood what Mr. Knapp meant when he told her she needed to write with more emotion and from the heart. Most people glossed over their pain or tried to make it go away. But as a writer, she needed to examine all that she was feeling, try to make sense of it, and transfer it into her story. Of course, she would never wish on anyone the heartache she'd experienced with Bellamy—loving him but leaving him. But at least she could find some use for it.

An ache pulsed in her throat just thinking about walking away from him, especially as he lay injured in bed. She'd wanted to be with him, wanted a relationship with him, wanted to spend every minute by his side. She'd probably wished for that all along, even before they'd entered into their fake relationship.

The trouble was, with each day that she didn't see him, the need for him only expanded so that she was missing him more than she'd believed possible. She wasn't sure if she could wait until tomorrow to see him when she returned the jewelry. A part of her wanted to go into town today.

She expelled a tight sigh, forced herself to step away from the jewelry, then sat on the edge of her bed.

Bellamy was being sweet in sending her the gifts. She could give him credit for that. He hadn't been belligerent about Kiernan and Da's insistence that he marry her, and he hadn't resisted their idea the way she'd expected. Instead, he'd been understanding, had even come to her defense with her writing when her da had belittled it.

At the thud of horse's hooves coming down the long lane in front of the house, she shot up and pressed a hand against her chest. It was about the time of the afternoon when Bellamy's messenger had come the past three afternoons. Was Bellamy sending another gift today?

She rushed to the window, threw aside the curtain, and fixed her gaze on the horse and rider. The swarthy skin, chiseled features, and dark hair belonged to only one man—the devastatingly handsome Bellamy McKenna.

Bellamy was coming. To see her? Why else would he make a trip out?

She practically threw the curtain back in place and plastered herself against the wall. What should she do?

Frantically, her gaze flew to the door. She wanted to rush down and greet him the moment he arrived. But she couldn't act too eager, could she? She had to behave with more caution. Because she was opposing him no matter what he might say to convince her that she wasn't trapping him into marriage, that her da wasn't forcing him, that the marriage was what he really wanted after all.

He'd told her the truth in the bank storage room after their kiss—that she wasn't the woman for him. She couldn't forget that, and neither the gifts nor his pleas could change the fact that if they hadn't spent the night together, he wouldn't be proposing marriage at all, much less so quickly. He was only doing it because he was a man of honor and believed he needed to save her.

Without moving from her spot against the wall, she waited as she heard him reach the front of the house, dismount, and race up the stairs. When his fist knocked firmly against the door, she drew in a quick breath. At the sound of the door opening and then voices, she closed her eyes.

Several moments later, the light taps of footsteps hurrying toward her bedroom told her Mam had sent a servant to fetch her. After the servant announced that she had a visitor, Zaira forced herself to count to twenty-five before leaving her room and descending the stairway. She expected to see Bellamy in the hallway or perhaps in the sitting room, but only her mam waited.

"He's outside on the veranda," Mam whispered, approaching and tucking a strand of Zaira's hair back into her chignon and then straightening one of the fabric-covered buttons on her bodice.

Zaira didn't want Mam making her presentable to Bellamy, hoping he would still want her and be willing to take her even though now she was blemished. The trouble was, she was already too flawed for Bellamy's taste, and having one more stain wouldn't make a difference.

Mam guided her forward. "I've sent the servant to bring you tea." She opened the front door and practically pushed Zaira out.

From the corner of her eye, Zaira could see Bellamy, but she shifted so her back faced him. Instead, she paused to allow Mam to follow her and act as a chaperone.

But Mam took a step back into the hallway. "Go on with

you now. You've kept Bellamy waiting long enough." With that, Mam closed the door firmly, leaving Zaira staring at it.

Apparently her parents didn't care anymore if she spent time alone with Bellamy, probably because they assumed the wedding would take place any day. Or maybe they both realized that after she'd spent an entire night with Bellamy, having a chaperone now was silly.

"Hi, Zaira." Bellamy's soft greeting behind her sent shivers up her spine.

Why, oh why did even the merest sound of his voice have to affect her this way?

She stared at the front door for a few more seconds, trying to pull her emotions into a semblance of normalcy. She could feel Bellamy watching her, waiting for her to turn. She couldn't put it off forever, even though she wished she could.

Dragging in a steadying breath, she pivoted to find Bellamy leaning against the porch railing. He was half perched on the beam, his arms crossed casually, his flatcap tilted at a rakish angle, and his dark eyes unreadable.

At the full effect of his handsomeness, her heart tumbled into an endless fall. She took him in, from the dark hair curling at the edge of his collar to the stretch of his vest across his chest to the long, lean legs crossed at his feet. Although his arm was in a sling, he didn't seem to be in pain or suffering in any way.

As she lifted her eyes to meet his, a smirk was playing at the corner of his mouth, almost as if he was enjoying watching her ogle him.

She narrowed her eyes into a glare in an attempt to rid herself of all the feelings for him that hadn't diminished and had only grown stronger. "Bellamy, you shouldn't have ridden out here with your injured shoulder."

His smirk only widened. "'Tis good to see you still care about me."

"You're the hero who saved my life. Of course I care about your well-being."

"Admit it. You care for more than just my well-being."

She pressed her hands to her hips, mostly to keep them from trembling. "I'd like to see you heal from your wound. That's all." If only that really was all.

He shrugged. "I came to tell you the two bank robbers were finally caught. Mr. Wright told the constables everything, and the two were apprehended getting off a steamboat near Hannibal."

"That's a relief." Maybe in the end she and Bellamy had been able to do some good after all, which would make all the trouble they were in worth it.

"I also came to tell you Seamus and Moya are doing well."

"I've missed them." And she'd been wondering how they were faring.

"Gavin crafted a special stool for Moya to stand on in the kitchen because she wants to be with Jenny and help her all the time."

Zaira couldn't contain a smile. "I'm glad they're getting on so well."

"Oh aye. Right well." His eyes were alight with a merriness she adored, one she couldn't resist, one she didn't want to go away. "I also came to find out if you liked my gifts."

"The gifts are very nice, Bellamy." She tried to keep her voice bland, nonchalant. "But if you thought they would win me over, then you're wrong."

"Is that a fact?" Bellamy pushed away from his post and swaggered a step toward her, his gaze homing in on her mouth.

Her whole body reacted with a shudder of pure delight.

When he took another step toward her, closing the distance so he was only inches away, she caught the scent of turpentine and paint. Had he been painting recently? Or was the scent left from the previous night?

"I need to return the jewelry to you."

"I'll not be taking any of it back."

"Aye, you must."

"Not yet."

"When?"

He shrugged. "Since the gifts didn't win you over, I know what will." His voice contained a cockiness she loved too.

Oh aye, he probably did know what would win her over, and easily. A kiss. She loved kissing him, and he'd figured that out.

"No, you may not kiss me, Bellamy." She held up a finger between them, as if that could stop him from bending in and stealing a kiss. Not that she would try to stop him if he tried.

Bellamy's grin kicked up one side of his mouth. "I see how it is. You've got kissing on your mind, so you do."

"No." She made a scoffing sound. "Of course I'm not thinking of kissing you."

"Good, then." He dropped his gaze to her mouth again, and his lashes fell halfway. "Because I wasn't planning on kissing you right now."

He was toying with her. That was becoming obvious. It was time for her to toy with him in return. She pressed her pointer finger into his sternum, then slowly walked her fingers up his chest over his shirt until she reached his collar. He wasn't wearing a cravat, and the top two buttons on his shirt were unbuttoned.

"Good, then," she imitated but lowered her voice into a whisper as she let the tip of her finger graze the narrow span of his chest showing there.

His nostrils flared just slightly, but that was his only reaction.

"I think it's for the best"—she drew a line from his chest to the base of his throat—"if you refrain from kissing me both now and anytime in the future."

His half-lidded gaze fell again to her mouth. He leaned closer, inching in, as though he had no intention of following her instructions.

Truthfully, she wanted him to toss aside all her objections, wrap his arms around her, and mesh his mouth to hers. She started to lean in, her whole body suddenly keening for his, needing to feel the long length of him, needing to have his hands on her, needing to have his mouth commanding hers.

With his lips only an inch away, her breath caught.

"Zaira?" His whisper was full of something equally raw and charged.

She started to curl her hand into his shirt to pull him in all the way. She was shameless. She wanted him more than keeping up appearances, more than her reservations, more than sticking to the boundaries she'd set.

But before she could kiss him, he took a step away, breaking her hold and breaking the moment. He began digging in the pocket of his vest. "It's here somewhere."

What was he doing? She couldn't think past the pounding of her pulse.

He dug deeper, tossing her another smirk.

He was still teasing her. And she'd played right into his ploy so that now he knew how she really felt about him—that she couldn't resist him, that she would be all too easy to convince to do his bidding.

"Ach, here it is." He tugged out a folded-up piece of paper.

"What is it?"

"Like I said. It's not a kiss." His smirk widened into a grin.

She released a huff while trying not to smile. Bellamy McKenna was impossibly wily. Any woman would be lucky to get to spend the rest of her life with him because things would never be dull. That was for certain. *She* just couldn't be that woman, although at the moment she couldn't exactly remember why.

He unfolded the paper and handed it to her. "I'd be honored if you would be one of my guests tomorrow evening."

As she took the wrinkled sheet, his eyes held a hesitancy, even a shyness, she'd never seen there before. What was this about?

She read the bold black print at the center. "'Please join Templeton & Evans Art Gallery in presenting the talented W. B. M. as he introduces himself and his newest landscape paintings.'"

She met Bellamy's gaze. "You're having a show?"

"Aye, so." He nodded as though he still needed to convince himself.

This was a huge step for him. No *huge* wasn't the right word. It was *gargantuan, immense, colossal*. Aye, *colossal* was a descriptive, solid word to describe this move Bellamy was taking. After he did so, he would no longer be able to keep his painting a secret from St. Louis. Everyone would know that Bellamy the matchmaker was also W. B. M. the painter.

"I hope you'll come," he said again, this time straightening his vest and backing up.

"Of course I'll come." She wanted to squeeze his arm in reassurance. But he'd moved to the top of the steps now.

"Then I'll be seeing you there. Come at eight."

"I wouldn't miss it."

"Bring your parents, if you'd like. And wear the jewelry."

She knew she needed to protest, but she couldn't find it within herself to do so. Instead, she nodded.

His grin this time was happy, even excited. As he bounded down the steps and toward his horse, she was happy and excited for him. Even though revealing her secret writing life had been difficult and she was still uncertain about how to proceed, a weight she hadn't known she was carrying had been lifted and she felt free now. Free from the lies. Free from the pretending. Free from having to live for her parents' approval. Free to live her own life as God had intended for her.

She could only hope Bellamy would find that same freedom.

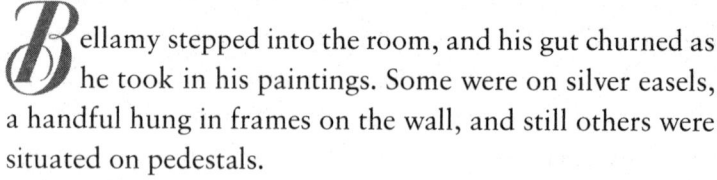

26

*B*ellamy stepped into the room, and his gut churned as he took in his paintings. Some were on silver easels, a handful hung in frames on the wall, and still others were situated on pedestals.

The Templeton & Evans Gallery was spacious, with large windows overlooking an elaborate garden with a maze. The evening sun was dropping low and casting a burnished glow over the shrubs and flower beds, and it slanted through the windows, adding an amber light to the lanterns lit strategically to showcase the paintings.

Several guests, older women, appeared to have arrived early, and they were already near one of the paintings and were discussing it while sipping champagne from crystal flutes. Mr. Davenport, the curator who had been working with Bellamy over the past months and helping to sell his paintings, was talking with the group but facing the door.

When Bellamy had approached him several days ago about

having a show, the curator had been all too eager to finally get to meet the talented W. B. M.

At the sight of Bellamy, Mr. Davenport nodded his way, then excused himself from the guests before sidling through the displays toward Bellamy. A tall, middle-aged man with lean features, Mr. Davenport wore a blue silk tailcoat over an embroidered velvet vest paired with light gray trousers. He carried himself with a stately elegance, one he'd probably perfected in order to be seen as a higher class than he really was.

Bellamy hadn't needed to pry much amongst the pub's customers to discover Mr. Davenport was from Pennsylvania and the son of a cobbler. He'd left home and lived in Philadelphia for a number of years, where he'd worked as a clerk for a local art collector. He'd eventually learned the trade and started collecting on his own.

"Mr. McKenna." Mr. Davenport's forehead creased with worry as he scanned the lobby, likely hoping for a glimpse of Mr. Moore. "Is everything all right?"

Bellamy removed his black felt hat, the best one he owned. "Everything is as it should be." Like Mr. Davenport, he was attired in his evening wear, except his was simpler with his black tailcoat matching his vest and trousers. He'd polished his leather shoes and slicked back his hair and given himself a fresh shave for the occasion, and he'd left the sling at home against Jenny's protests.

Even so, he guessed he would be underdressed compared to many wealthy patrons of the art. But he didn't mind. He wanted them to accept him as he was, a young Irishman, an immigrant matchmaker who owned a pub with his family. He didn't want to put on airs, didn't want to act differently, didn't want to try to impress anyone, didn't want to be anyone but himself.

Bellamy followed Mr. Davenport's gaze into the lobby with its high-vaulted ceiling. Fountains and plants and bird cages decorated the open area, along with the paintings and artwork of the more established artists of St. Louis.

Bellamy wasn't sure he'd ever rise to such ranks. However, fame and fortune weren't important. He hadn't painted to make a name for himself. And he didn't need the fortune, apparently not with Oscar's real estate investments. No, Bellamy had painted because it had connected him with his mam. He'd believed in bringing his paintings to life that he would be honoring her memory and her spurned efforts.

As it had turned out, her efforts hadn't been spurned. Oscar hadn't been the one destroying her painting career. She'd done it to herself through her choice to use drugs.

Over the past few days since Oscar's revelation about Mam's problems, Bellamy had thought a lot about her. She might have had a difficult life while growing up with a da and mam who'd been too busy fighting and drinking to love her, but Oscar had offered her his love and a better future. Why hadn't she chosen a new way, one filled with hope? Why had she clung so tightly to the pain of her past?

In thinking about her, Bellamy was realizing that being the matchmaker wasn't the problem, that he wasn't cursed because of being unlucky in love. Instead, he'd only be cursed if he continued to wallow in the past—like his mam had—and let the tangles of hurt bind him and hold him back.

When Bellamy had gone to mass a couple of days ago, he'd stayed longer, praying that God would help him to release the pain of his past—for never being enough for his mam, for her rejection, for her never loving him the way he'd wanted. He had to stop clinging to her brokenness and making it his.

As he'd left the cathedral, he'd still felt burdened by all he'd learned about his mam pushing away Oscar. Bellamy had feared that maybe he'd already pushed away the woman he loved, that maybe he was too late.

But here, now, he straightened his shoulders and prepared himself to let go of all fear and to choose a new way that was filled with hope.

His mam had made her choices, and it was time for Bellamy to make his.

His choices could be better, stronger, and wiser, starting with taking a stand for who he was and being proud of his Irish heritage.

Mr. Davenport was peering again through the lobby toward the wide front doors of the establishment. "I'd hoped Mr. Moore would be here by now."

Bellamy swallowed the last of his resistance, then whispered a prayer for courage. "Mr. Davenport, W. B. M. is here, and I am he."

The crease in Mr. Davenport's forehead deepened. "I don't understand."

"I am W. B. M.—William Bellamy McKenna, the painter of all of the works I've been bringing you."

Mr. Davenport stared for a long moment. "This cannot be."

"Oh aye, 'tis a fact if there ever was one."

Mr. Davenport cast a nervous glance toward the guests, then lowered his voice. "You said the painter was a reclusive Englishman."

"I regret that I presented the painter under false pretenses, so I do. But would you have given me a chance if I'd told you the paintings were mine?"

A sheen of perspiration began to form on the gentleman's hairline. "As the Irish matchmaker, I doubt anyone will take you seriously."

"If they don't, then I will remove my paintings from your gallery and repay you for any losses you incur."

One of the guests was approaching, a gray-haired lady wearing enough jewelry to fill the shelves of Chaseman's Jewelry Store. Each finger was covered in rings, multiple bracelets decorated her wrists, and pearls along with other necklaces dangled around her neck.

She was smiling, her lined face filled with anticipation. "Mr. Davenport, is this the talented artist?"

Mr. Davenport hesitated, his eyes flashing with panic.

Bellamy gave the woman what he hoped was one of his most charming smiles. "Aye, I'm the artist, so I am."

She stopped in front of Bellamy and surveyed him from his head to his toes, her expression growing sultry. "Mr. Davenport, where have you been hiding this handsome young man?"

Mr. Davenport cleared his throat and started to answer, but Bellamy spoke first. "I've actually been the one hiding. Mr. Davenport has been pressuring me to have a show for some time now."

"Well, I, for one," the woman purred, "am very pleased you came out of hiding."

Mr. Davenport's mouth was hanging open, and he closed it.

Bellamy let some of the tension ease from his shoulders, the pain from the gunshot wound having dulled. All it would take was a few wealthy patrons, like this woman, to accept him. Then the others would find it easier to overcome the social barriers that relegated the Irish to an underclass.

The woman batted her lashes at Bellamy. "Mr. Davenport, you must properly introduce me."

"Of course." Mr. Davenport finally spoke, clearing his throat as he did so. "Mrs. Chamberlain, this is . . . this is . . . our fine artist."

Mrs. Chamberlain? Everyone in St. Louis knew of the Chamberlain family, since they were one of the wealthiest in the city, even more so than the Shanahans. Mrs. Chamberlain had lost her husband about a year ago. He'd been among the first industrialists to make St. Louis his home, building a dozen different successful factories and businesses over the years.

Bellamy took the woman's offer of her hand and kissed the back. "I'm pleased to meet you, Mrs. Chamberlain. Please call me Bellamy."

"Bellamy?"

"The full name is William Bellamy McKenna."

"Oh, I see. I thought it was William Moore. I was mistaken."

A part of him wanted to let her think she'd been the one to misunderstand. But another part of him knew he had to be honest. "'Twas not your mistake, ma'am. Up until now, I've used the pseudonym Moore instead of McKenna. But tonight, I've decided to reveal my true name."

She cocked her head and gave him another once-over. "Very well, young man."

He waited for her to question him further, to at least make a comment about him being Irish, which was obvious with his accent and now his name. But she linked her arm through his and tugged him closer. Not only did she wear an extraordinary amount of jewelry, but she also was wearing an entire bottle of perfume, or so it seemed. "I would love for you to take me around to each of your paintings and explain your inspiration. I'm of the inclination to purchase them all."

"You can't purchase them all, Charlotte," said another older woman who stood nearby and had been eavesdropping on their conversation. "You must save some for the rest of us."

Mrs. Chamberlain dismissively waved one of her jeweled hands, the rings and bracelets clinking. "I was introduced to Bellamy first, which means I get first claim on his paintings."

With the women practically fighting over him, Bellamy smiled at Mr. Davenport. The curator smiled back nervously, then turned to greet another older lady who was breezing into the gallery with her husband.

Bellamy let Mrs. Chamberlain monopolize his attention for a short while, grateful for her words of praise over each painting—praise the other guests could hear. She continually stopped to introduce him to newcomers, more important and wealthy people from among the upper echelons of society.

A few raised their eyebrows when she explained that the initials stood for McKenna and not Moore. But her acceptance of him seemed to be all the permission everyone needed to put aside his Irishness and focus on his paintings.

After the first hour, all the paintings had sold—most to Mrs. Chamberlain, but a few to her friends. Mr. Davenport had already placed Sold signs on each painting, which only served to heighten the interest.

Bellamy knew the evening had been successful, probably more so than Mr. Davenport could have imagined. The worried lines and perspiration had disappeared from the man's forehead. Instead, he was smiling broadly as he took orders for more paintings, his eyes alight and his praise of Bellamy flowing smoothly, as if he'd never imagined another outcome of the evening.

Bellamy pulled out his pocket watch. The top of the eight o'clock hour was almost upon them. He glanced into the lobby, hoping for a sight of Zaira. At that moment, a barouche halted in front of the lobby doors.

The Shanahan barouche.

His pulse picked up speed. He excused himself from the couple he'd been talking to and stepped out into the lobby, straightening his cravat as he did so.

The coachman was opening the door of the barouche, and Bellamy's breath snagged in his chest.

Oscar had said he'd come and help with the plan to win over Zaira, and now Bellamy wished he'd taken up Oscar's offer to be there.

Bellamy had sensed the turn in his relationship with Oscar for the better, but he'd decided he had to atone for his past mistakes and dishonesty without anyone coming to his rescue. And repairing his relationship with Zaira was something he had to do on his own.

James Shanahan was the first to step down out of the barouche. He lifted a hand to aid his wife next. As James extended his hand again, Bellamy held his breath, the anticipation inside him swelling.

He'd gone nearly mad staying away from Zaira for the past week. Not only had he missed seeing her and talking to her, but he'd been worried that she would think he didn't care about her.

Oscar had assured him the gifts would alleviate any doubts

she might have. He'd also insisted that the time apart would help her to see her own feelings more clearly so that when she came to the gallery, her heart would be tender and she would be ready to forgive him.

Bellamy hoped Oscar was right.

As she placed her foot onto the carriage step and took her da's hand, he was able to get a full view of her. His racing heart slammed to a halt, his breathing ceased, and every thought evaporated. Except one.

Zaira Shanahan was absolutely the most spectacular woman in the world.

She was wearing a flaming garnet–colored gown. The color matched her hair, which was arranged halfway up and contained under a small matching bonnet with the rest of it hanging down in a cascade of ringlets.

She paused in the carriage doorway and pressed a hand against her throat, touching the garnet necklace there.

She'd worn the necklace he'd given her. That had to be a good sign.

As she stepped down to the ground, she released the necklace and straightened, giving him another perfect view of her striking beauty. Not only was the color the perfect match, but the gown showed off every elegant curve of her body and also contrasted with the silky cream of her skin.

Even though he had the urge to rush to her and draw her into his arms, he made himself remain where he was. He had to stick to the plan. This was his chance to show her he'd always loved her and always would . . . and that he really did want to marry her and not because anyone was pressuring him to.

He could only pray his and Oscar's plan would work.

27

Zaira couldn't believe Bellamy was really having an art show in the gallery. She was amazed at his bravery and prayed it would go well for him, better than the revelation of her identity had gone.

As she started toward the door of the building, she halted. She'd invited her parents, as Bellamy had requested. But the whole way from Oakland into the city, she'd resorted to her usual docile manner, pretending everything was as it should be.

The truth was, she still needed to admit to her parents that she hadn't stopped writing and publishing the way they wanted. At one point during the ride, she'd known she needed to have that conversation even if it pushed her farther away from them. Yet, she'd silenced the inner voice, telling herself she didn't want to have a disagreement with her parents on Bellamy's special night.

Of course, she'd informed them all about Bellamy's painting. She'd had to in order to invite them to the gallery with her. While they'd been surprised, they hadn't been put off by the news. They probably thought it was a hobby and nothing he was too serious about.

But she knew better. It was much more than a hobby for Bellamy. He was an exceptionally good artist, and he would someday be famous. Or at least her fanciful heart hoped so.

Regardless, she was frustrated at how readily her parents had accepted Bellamy's painting but how easily they'd squelched her writing.

Behind her, Mam gave her a nudge. "Go on with you now, Zaira. This is the perfect opportunity tonight to show yourself as the poised and proper lady that you are."

Zaira's spine only stiffened. Tonight wasn't about trying to repair her image or her family's reputation. It was about Bellamy and the strength he'd displayed to reveal his paintings, no matter the consequences, no matter what anyone thought, no matter what the future held.

She had to do the same.

Drawing in a deep breath, she pivoted and faced her parents. Both were wearing stylish evening attire and had seemed eager to do something in the city after having so few social activities that summer so far.

Da had been in the middle of whispering in Mam's ear. The flush on her face and soft smile meant he'd been complimenting her or sharing words of endearment.

Zaira opened her mouth to tell them the truth but then stopped. Could she really? Not when they both looked so happy.

She spun and took two more steps.

If Bellamy could be forthright and brave, then she would have to be as well.

Once again she halted. This time she spun and spoke at

the same time. "I'm still writing my weekly column for the *Daily Republican.*"

With fading smiles, her parents stared at her, their expressions startled.

She forced herself to continue. "I'm sorry you don't like my writing. But it's important to me. And I hope someday you'll accept me for who I am and not who you think I should be."

Without waiting for them to respond, she turned around and raced toward the doors, needing to get away before they reacted. She wasn't sure she could bear any more of their disappointment and disapproval, especially not tonight.

As she pushed open the doors and flew inside, her gaze seemed to have an internal compass that could always find Bellamy no matter where he was in a crowd. She immediately located him standing in the lobby just outside a busy room filled with people milling around paintings.

His eyes were riveted to her, so dark and intense and magnetic.

She stopped abruptly and let herself take him in from his wavy dark hair down the hard length of his body. He'd shed his sling for the night and was holding his injured shoulder stiffly. Even so, in his suit, he was a devastating heart-stealer. For better or worse, he'd stolen her heart, and she knew she'd never get it back. He had it forever.

As a tall gentleman came up to Bellamy and spoke to him, Bellamy didn't see or hear the man. He had eyes only for her, as if she was the only one who currently existed in the world.

As he smiled at her, a sweet pulse of pleasure raced through her, and she smiled in return. Oh aye, she loved this man. She loved him more than anyone or anything. And she wanted to be with him more than anyone or anything.

Since his visit yesterday, she'd thought of him even more, attempting to make sense of his gifts. Had he been sending the message that he cared about her? If so, he was wearing down her resistance. Was that what he'd been trying to do? Could she let him?

Bellamy walked away from the man at his side and began to cross to her. With each footstep closer, her heart pounded harder. What would he do when he reached her? Would he draw her into an embrace?

She had half a mind to fling herself against him, but she could hear her mam and dad entering the building, and she had to show some restraint. It was actually for the best if she kept Bellamy at arm's length and didn't allow herself to get carried away with him.

When he was but a foot away, he stopped, his charming smile melting her heart again. "You came."

"Aye, I wanted to be part of this special night." She glanced behind him toward the display room, mostly because his dark eyes were simply too handsome and if she looked into them for much longer, his intensity would turn her body into liquid. She would have no choice but to flop to the floor in a melted puddle.

The older gentleman had followed Bellamy. "Mr. Shanahan?" He stepped forward to greet Da. "I'm Mr. Davenport, and I'm the one in charge of the exhibition tonight."

Da shook the man's hand.

"I'm pleased you are here," Mr. Davenport continued, "although I regret to inform you that all of Bellamy's paintings sold within the first hour of the showing."

"Is that so?" Da peered at the room now with more interest.

"Bellamy!" Zaira reached for his hand. "I'm thrilled for you."

As soon as their hands connected, the heat was instantaneous. She felt the connection all the way to a place deep inside. From the way Bellamy's eyes widened, she guessed he'd felt it too.

Mr. Davenport had stepped back and was waving them toward the display. "If you do see any landscapes you particularly like, Bellamy has offered to paint on commission."

Bellamy finally seemed to notice the gentleman, and he tore his attention from Zaira to speak to the man. "Mr. Davenport, if the Shanahans are interested in any of my paintings, I will gladly give them anything they're wanting. They'll not be paying me a single cent."

"I see." Mr. Davenport's brows rose.

"It's time." Bellamy gave the man a knowing look.

He seemed at a loss for a moment, then he nodded. "Oh yes. I'll do it right away."

"Thank you."

Mr. Davenport scurried away, on a mission of some sort.

Bellamy made small talk with her parents for a few minutes before smiling again at Zaira, then slipping his fingers through hers. The pressure was intoxicating. She wanted to pause and examine every nuance of every finger that was intertwined with hers. She wanted to imprint the memory of all the sensations it evoked so she could write about it later. But as he led them toward the gallery, she knew now wasn't the time. This was his special night, and she couldn't focus on herself.

Several other guests attempted to garner his attention as

he passed by, but he didn't stop to talk to anyone. His attention was fixed solely upon her, his eyes brimming with something that made her breathing stutter.

Was it affection? Attraction? Or something else?

Her imagination all too often got the best of her, and she didn't want to get carried away. She needed to stay realistic.

As they reached the display room, he paused, glanced in, nodded—presumably at Mr. Davenport—then he stepped back out. "Close your eyes."

She did his bidding, letting her lashes fall. She loved surprises, and she would gladly play along with him if he had a surprise for her.

He guided her forward again.

She kept her eyes closed and let him lead. "What is it?"

"There's something I need to show you."

She could feel the attention of the guests, the conversations tapering to silence, the curiosity of the others now mirroring her own. What was Bellamy doing?

He halted and positioned her, then took a step away but didn't let go of her hand.

She supposed she ought to disentangle their fingers, but she loved the feel of his palm against hers, the firmness of his hold, the confidence in his stance. With him, she felt as if she could do anything.

"Ready?" he whispered.

"Aye." More than ready for whatever he was doing.

He waited several heartbeats as if fortifying himself for her reaction. Then he spoke. "Open your eyes."

She lifted her lashes and found herself positioned in front of three easels, each containing a landscape painting but with a woman in the background. A young woman with long red hair. Her.

The first painting was familiar. It was at Dover's Pond, and she was sitting on the bank in the tall grass with a stack of papers in front of her and was looking up at someone and smiling playfully.

The second painting was along the Mississippi River, and in this one, she was riding upon a horse, glancing over her shoulder at someone, again with a teasing glint in her eyes. Had that been the day when they'd gone to the immigrant camp to hunt for the children?

The third painting was of the shrubs that graced the property of her family's home, flowers in bloom, insects in the air, the summer sunshine hazy with coal dust. She was walking away, giving someone a sideways look, another smile, this one filled with mischief.

He'd portrayed her so beautifully, so gently, and so thoughtfully, showing unique aspects of her personality and different views of her body and face.

And he'd painted her with such accuracy that she could have been looking at herself in a mirror. Every curl of her hair, the dimple in her chin, the curve of her shoulder, the way she parted her hair.

How had he done this? How had he replicated her without having her there to pose for him?

Zaira stood breathlessly, taking in the paintings again, trying to make sense of them, trying to understand how Bellamy had been able to create them.

He was still holding her hand and looking at the first painting, his head cocked. "The name of the Dover's Pond painting is *The Woman I Desperately Love*."

Zaira sucked in a sharp breath.

Bellamy shifted his attention to the second painting. "The name of the Mississippi River painting is *The Woman I Desperately Can't Live Without.*"

Her heart started beating at double the speed. What was he doing?

He nodded at the final painting. "The name of the Shanahan garden painting is *The Woman I Desperately Need.*"

Hot tears pricked her eyes.

He met her gaze, his eyes dark. "I painted these over the past week and wanted you to see them tonight so you know you're a part of my heart and soul and body and that I'll never, never be able to get you out of my mind. Every aspect of you is seared into my memory. My lifeblood flows with your breath. My heartbeat beats with your name."

Oh dear heavens, Bellamy was the epitome of romantic perfection in that moment. She couldn't imagine coming up with better words herself, not in real life and not even in fiction. He was winning an award for the most romantic man on earth.

She opened her mouth to tell him she loved everything he'd just done for her, but before she could, he was lowering himself to one knee in front of her.

She inhaled sharply as gasps resounded throughout the room, echoing hers.

He peered up at her, his expression more serious and sincere than she'd ever seen it. "Zaira, I've loved you from the day I first saw you at church and you stuck out your tongue at me."

She laughed lightly. He'd loved her then? That long-ago day when she'd been just a child enamored with the handsome new boy?

His eyes were glassy. "I loved you all the way through every holiday and occasion that I saw you over the past ten years."

Her heart was about to burst with the emotion swelling inside, and she couldn't contain several tears that trickled out and rolled down her cheeks and caught in the lines of her smile.

"I've loved you now when we are all grown up." He cleared his throat. "Even when I tried not to love you, I failed at it utterly, because I can't cut my love for you out of my life without cutting out my heart completely."

"Oh, Bellamy." She was about to swoon with the sweetness of everything he was saying. It was beyond heavenly.

He pulled something out of his pocket and held it up to her. It was a garnet ring that matched the other jewelry he'd already given her. "The moment I saw this jewelry with its flaming red jewels, I knew I had to give it to you. You're the only woman who could ever wear it. And you're the only woman I will ever want."

But what about everything he'd told her that night in the bank?

As if hearing her silent question, his eyes pleaded with her. "I know now that you're the perfect woman for me and that I'm the one with all the imperfections—"

"No, Bellamy—"

"Aye, I realize I was letting my imperfect past take away from the beautiful future I could have with you. I'm sorry for that, and I'll always say I'm sorry when I let my imperfections get the best of me."

She couldn't stop herself from reaching for his cheek and pressing a hand there. Neither of them was perfect, and their match wouldn't be perfect either. But maybe they could both learn to forgive each other's imperfections and in doing so grow stronger together in the process.

"I love you, Zaira Shanahan." Bellamy was still holding up the garnet ring. "And I will love you all my days until my dying breath."

"I love you too, Bellamy." In fact, she loved him more than she could express.

His eyes filled with relief, as if he hadn't been sure if she could love him in return.

"I've always loved you too," she assured him. "And it was always hard to pretend that I didn't."

"It was my fault for pushing you away."

"It's also your fault for being so irresistible."

He took a deep breath. "You would make me the happiest man if you would agree to live out all your days by my side."

"Yes." She could hardly get the word out in her excitement. "Yes, a thousand times yes."

His handsome grin made an appearance, and he slipped the ring on her finger as the people around them clapped, including both of her parents, who stood nearby smiling.

As Bellamy climbed to his feet, his gaze held hers and was filled with all the love she'd ever dreamed he would direct her way but never believed would happen.

She studied his handsome face, wanting to run her fingers over his features to ensure herself that he really was here and really was in love with her. "Am I living in a story-world and just imagining this?"

His charming grin cocked up on one side. "Do you need some proof that this is real?"

"What kind of proof?"

When his gaze dropped to her lips, she knew exactly what he had in mind.

With a smile, she wound her arms around his neck and drew him down at the same time he bent in. As his lips passionately collided with hers, he left her no doubt just how real their love was.

28

*H*e was a married man.

As he turned the door handle of the pub, Bellamy paused and kissed Zaira's forehead gently. Oh, how he loved her. He loved her so much his chest ached from the loving.

Laying her head against his arm, she released a soft sigh.

He was learning what her sighs meant, and this was one of contentment. In a pink silk gown decorated with dozens of pink rosettes, she was picture-perfect. Her hair was fashioned in an elegant chignon, and a wreath of a dozen more of the pink rosettes graced her head. In his mind, he'd been painting her all morning.

"Are you ready for this?" he asked, unable to stop himself from kissing her forehead again.

She had both hands linked through his arm and was pressed against him as though his side was the only place she wanted to be. She smiled up at him, her eyes alight with happiness. "I'd like another kiss first."

They'd kissed for most of the carriage ride back from the cathedral where they'd gotten married an hour ago. Even after the carriage had come to a halt outside the pub, they'd kissed again. He'd been so swept up in their kissing that he'd lost track of time until Kiernan had banged on the carriage door and told them they had to stop and come inside because everyone was waiting for the celebration dinner.

Bellamy wouldn't mind skipping the celebration, sweeping Zaira off her feet into his arms—even with his injured shoulder—and carrying her up the outside stairway to their apartment above the lawyer's office across the street from the pub.

He'd offered to buy her a home of her own, even to build her a new home if that's what she wanted. With the money from all the paintings he'd sold, he had more than enough to purchase anything she wanted.

But she'd insisted on finding something close to the pub because she knew he wanted to continue to help his family. Not only that, but the pub was the best place for him to mingle with people who wanted the services of the local matchmaker.

Zaira had claimed that just being with him was enough for her, that she didn't care where they lived as long as they were together. And he felt the same way.

When he'd started inquiring into accommodations in the area, the first place they'd visited was the apartment across the street. Zaira had loved it from the moment they'd toured it because it had a second bedroom he could use as a studio and she could use for her writing.

She'd spent the first couple of weeks of August since the night of his gallery show cleaning and fixing up the apartment as well as purchasing furniture and rugs and decorations. Her mam had even come to help her from time to time.

Although Zaira's relationship with her parents would never again be the same, she seemed to be forging a new path forward. While they still weren't happy about her publishing venture, they loved her enough that they would eventually set aside their traditional views on a woman's role and accept her and her writing.

Traditional ways weren't a bad thing. After all, he was the matchmaker, and that was about as traditional as things could get. But there were areas, especially when it came to women's abilities and talents, that traditions needed to grow and expand.

"I love kissing you, Bellamy." Desire darkened her green eyes to a shadowed woodland, and as she trailed one of her hands down his arm, heat speared his stomach.

He needed to kiss her now. Swiftly, he took her lips captive, tasting her and devouring her but never getting enough of her. He knew he never would, not as long as he lived. But he would sure enjoy trying, especially since all he'd gotten over the past couple of weeks was a stolen kiss here and there.

The door of the pub swung wide. "I told you they would be kissing again." The wry statement came from Kiernan.

Cheers and whistles from their family and friends greeted them.

With a breathless laugh, she broke the kiss.

Oscar had invited everyone to come back to the pub, closing it to the public. Jenny and Gavin had been busy all the previous day making enough roast and colcannon to feed all the guests, and now the waft of the potato-and-cabbage dish filled the air.

The Guinness was already flowing freely, with Oscar behind the bar counter pouring drinks. With the newspapers making the announcement last week that the worst of the cholera epidemic was over, the ban on beer had ended. People had started to return to their homes, and normal life was resuming.

In fact, Bellamy had received a message yesterday from Senator Whitcomb, who'd returned to the city a few days ago, and the senator had asked for the matchmaker to set up a match between Deirdre and Zach Meier. Bellamy had shared a smile with Zaira over the news. He had the feeling his wife would be a great asset to his role as the matchmaker.

With Zaira's hand securely in his, they entered the pub and accepted the hugs and well-wishes from all the guests. Even though he wanted to be alone with Zaira, he was still grateful to everyone for their support and that so many had come out to celebrate.

Zaira's family was there, except for Sullivan and Enya who were still in New Orleans and nearing the time when Enya's baby would be born. Riley, who was still working in positions of leadership in the city, had his arm around Finola and his hand on her gently rounded abdomen.

Kiernan and Alannah were as happy in love as always. Kiernan had made arrangements for a new house to be built out by his brickyard on land he'd purchased. Over the past weeks as the cholera had started to decline, the brickyard had begun to thrive as more St. Louis businesses had gotten back to the work of rebuilding.

Georgie McGuire sat at the bar counter among many other of their closest customers and friends. Jenny and Gavin were busy bringing out platters of food. Seamus was hustling after them, eager to help with everything. Moya, on the other hand, perched on her special stool behind the bar counter next to Oscar and chatted with anyone and everyone who would listen to her.

With no more leads on where their father was, Seamus had stopped talking about trying to find him. The two children were no longer emaciated, frightened waifs but loved being a part of Jenny and Gavin's family. Even Oscar seemed to have adopted them as his grandchildren and enjoyed their company.

More of the orphans around St. Louis were being placed in homes, thanks to Riley's committee's efforts and Bellamy's connections. Zaira had offered additional suggestions, like screening the homes of interested families, coming up with questions that could better pair children with like-minded families, and providing ways for both children and families to communicate with the committee if things didn't work out.

They were praying that perhaps this new placement of orphans in homes would offer an alternative to the orphanages that would be more suitable for everyone.

So far it had worked well for Seamus and Moya, and Bellamy hoped the arrangement would last a long time.

"Attention, everyone!" Oscar bellowed from behind the bar counter. "I've got an announcement to make, so I do."

Oscar's gaze landed upon Bellamy where he was sitting beside Zaira at one of the tables closest to the bar counter. They were surrounded by Zaira's family, including her two youngest brothers, Madigan and Quinlan.

Oscar's smile had never been brighter than it had been all day. He'd stopped Bellamy early that morning before they'd left for the cathedral, and he'd shaken Bellamy's hand and told him that in all his days as a matchmaker, the match with Zaira was the most fitting he'd witnessed.

"I've never seen two people more in love than the two of you," Oscar had said as he'd blinked back tears. "Remember, there's no luck involved in love. Instead, 'tis what you do day after day that counts, first growing in God's love yourself and then growing in love toward her. If you do that, you'll be having a marriage that will never fail."

Bellamy bent toward Zaira and placed another kiss upon her forehead. She squeezed his hand in return.

"Today is not only the marriage of my son, Bellamy, to the love of his life, but it's also the day I officially resign as matchmaker and hand over the duties to Bellamy."

Bellamy nodded at Oscar, knowing the older man had been right all along to require more from Bellamy before being ready to take over the role. He'd thought he knew enough about love and relationships and would be wise enough without experiencing love for himself.

But he'd been wrong. Now, after falling in love with Zaira, he was infinitely more prepared to be the matchmaker and explore all the nuances that came with love and marriage. He'd learned an incredible amount about himself, and in doing so, he would be much more compassionate and empathetic to others.

Oscar pulled something out from a shelf, then began to make his way around the counter. As he rounded the corner, Bellamy got a glimpse of what Oscar was carrying—his big leather matchmaker book.

Bellamy's heart swelled with the emotion and responsibility of this momentous occasion. At Oscar's approach, Bellamy pushed back from the table and stood, releasing Zaira's hand. Even though he wasn't holding her hand anymore, he could feel her presence, her love, and her encouragement.

Oscar stopped beside him and held out the leather book that had been passed down through generations of matchmakers to record the names of couples and families who'd been blessed to have the matchmaker's assistance.

Bellamy clasped one end of the book with worn pages.

Oscar seemed to swallow hard, then he grasped Bellamy with his other arm and drew him into a half hug. "I'm proud of you, son."

"Thank you . . . Da." Although the word *Da* was a little rusty coming off Bellamy's tongue, it felt right.

As they pulled away, the door of the pub swung open, and bright midday light spilled inside. A thin man in ragged clothing with sallow skin and sunken cheeks stood in the opening.

Silence fell over the guests, and all eyes turned to the newcomer.

He blinked several times and then took a rapid step back as if he hadn't expected to be the center of attention. "Pardon me. I thought the pub was open to the public, but I can see I'm interrupting a gathering."

Something about the man set Bellamy suddenly on edge. He placed the leather matchmaker book onto the table at his spot, then faced the newcomer. "Can we help you?"

The man hesitated, glancing around the pub as though looking for someone. As his gaze alighted on Seamus, who was now sitting at the bar counter beside Moya, he seemed to breathe out his relief. "I'm looking for Seamus and Moya O'Reilly."

Both children turned wide eyes upon the man.

Since Mr. O'Reilly had immigrated well ahead of his wife and two children, it had been a year or more since they'd last seen each other. They all would have changed by now, perhaps so much that he wouldn't recognize them anymore. As young as the two were, they probably only had vague recollections of their father.

Jenny, who had just stepped back into the pub from the kitchen, set a tray down on the counter, clattering the dishes. Her face had turned ashen, and her hands trembled as she reached for Gavin, who was entering behind her. Gavin slipped his arm around her and drew her close, both of their expressions filling with apprehension.

They'd grown too attached to the children. It was one of the risks of placing the orphans in homes. Riley and his committee had brought that up as a drawback, but they'd pushed forward with the new program regardless. The children needed the love and attention of families, even if the arrangement didn't end up being permanent.

"I'm Seamus." The lad hopped down from his stool at the bar counter, his eyes never leaving the man's face. "Are you my da? You don't look like him."

The man's face was filled with sadness. "I'm sorry, Seamus. I'm not your da."

Seamus halted, and his expression turned wary. "If you're not our da, then who are you?"

"I'm Patrick Leary. I was your da's friend, and we worked together at the stone quarry in Grafton."

Was? Worked? Bellamy guessed what had happened before the man could explain more. Mr. O'Reilly had died.

Patrick Leary removed his hat to reveal thinning hair. "He asked me to come and check on you and your mam if anything happened to him."

Seamus didn't say more. Jenny let go of Gavin and crossed

to the boy. She stood behind him and placed a hand on his shoulder.

At her touch, he backed into her, needing her presence and her strength.

"I'm real sorry to tell you that your da passed away earlier in the summer from an accident at the quarry."

Seamus only nodded, as though he'd already expected the bad news. Jenny wrapped both arms over his shoulders, holding him tighter.

"Soon as the letter arrived from your mam that you were in St. Louis, I planned to come down and look out for you." Mr. Leary's eyes filled with tears. "But my wife took sick with cholera, and then two of my younguns followed her to the grave."

Seamus clearly didn't know what to say. Thankfully Jenny responded. "We're sorry for your loss, Mr. Leary. This has been a very difficult time for so many."

He nodded and wiped his eyes. "I'll take Seamus and Moya with me back to my home in Grafton. My two older daughters can look after them. It's what their da would've wanted."

The room was entirely silent, and all eyes were fixed upon Mr. Leary. All except Moya. She released a sudden and piercing cry. "No-o-o!"

Gavin was at the little girl's side in the next instant, lifting her into his arms. She went to him willingly, wrapping her arms around his neck and burying her face into his chest.

Mr. Leary hesitated, looking as though he wanted to run away rather than deal with a crying little girl. "I'm glad to see they're doing well here."

"We found them living on the street after their mam passed." Bellamy broke into the conversation. "We brought them here so they could have a place to live until we found their da."

"Thanks be." Mr. Leary's voice was soft and kind. Since he had a steady job and a home and two daughters, no doubt Seamus and Moya would be well looked after. "I'm in your debt, and I know their da is looking down from heaven and is grateful too."

"Aye." If Mr. O'Reilly had given custody of his children to Mr. Leary, then the two would need to go with him. But what if the fellow could be persuaded into allowing the children to decide where they wanted to live?

Mr. Leary nodded to a wagon out on the street in front of the pub. "I guess I'll be loading them up and heading out."

"No-o!" Moya cried again, clinging to Gavin. "I wanna stay with Jenny and Gavin. They're my new mam and da."

"Jenny and Gavin"—Bellamy nodded to his sister and her husband—"they've grown fond of the two children, so they have."

Jenny was blinking back tears. The children hadn't called them Mam and Da before, and Bellamy guessed that the occasion was monumental for Jenny.

"If the children want to stay with us," she managed in a wobbly voice, "we would love to have them."

At her emotional declaration, Seamus glanced up at Jenny, searching her face.

She pressed a hand to his cheek and peered down at him tenderly, even as tears slipped down her cheeks. "You've become like a son to me, Seamus. And Moya is like a daughter. If you've a notion to stay, Gavin and I have already decided that if we couldn't find your da, we wanted to make you our children and adopt you."

"You want to make us yours?" Seamus pulled away from her, his expression already losing the wariness and filling with excitement.

"Would you like that?" Jenny asked, caressing his hair.

"Yes!" Moya piped up from Gavin's arms, the tears still streaking her cheeks but her eyes now bright. "Will you adopt me and Seamus today?"

All eyes turned to Mr. Leary, still standing in the door of the pub watching the exchange. He seemed to be taking everything in, weighing the situation, and attempting to make the right decision.

Bellamy liked him for his caution. The fellow didn't want to abandon the children to just anyone. He wanted to make sure they would be happy and well taken care of. It showed that he'd cared about Mr. O'Reilly and fulfilling his promise to his friend.

Zaira stood and slipped her arm around Bellamy, leaning into him just the way he loved. He stooped and kissed the top of her head. He didn't care that he'd already done so a dozen times or that Mr. Leary was watching. After all, this was still his wedding day, and she was still his bride.

"Mr. Leary," Zaira said with a smile, "you can rest assured that here in the McKenna house, there is enough love for everyone. More than enough."

Mr. Leary offered her a tired smile in return. "I can see that."

"Then you'll let Moya and Seamus stay?" she asked.

He looked from Moya to Seamus and back. Both children

had such hopeful expressions that he could do nothing but nod. "Of course."

Moya released a happy cry, and Seamus gave a shout of jubilation. Gavin, with Moya still clinging to him, strode to Jenny and gathered all of them together into his arms so that in the next instant they were hugging and crying together with happiness.

Bellamy could only look down at his wife, his love for her swelling so strongly that it nearly brought tears to his own eyes.

"Bellamy McKenna," she teased softly, "are you about to cry?"

He blinked. "Not even a wee bit."

"'Tis okay if you are."

"And if I am, what will you be doing about it?"

"What I'll be doing for the rest of your life." She lifted her lips and kissed him sweetly. "I'll be loving you, Bellamy McKenna. That's what I'll be doing about it."

"And I'll be loving you too." He drew her into his arms and raised a grateful prayer heavenward. Oh aye, there might not be such a thing as a perfect match. But he'd come very close to it.

Keep reading
for a sneak peek of

A COWBOY FOR
KEEPS

Available now wherever books are sold

CHAPTER

1

Colorado Territory
August 1862

"Stop or we'll shoot!" A dozen feet up Kenosha Pass, three robbers with flour sacks over their heads blocked the way, their revolvers outstretched.

Walking alongside the stagecoach, Greta Nilsson didn't have to be told twice. She froze—all except her pulse, which sped to a thundering gallop.

Next to her, the Concord jerked to a halt.

"Come out and put your hands up where we can see 'em," called the lanky robber at the center, peering through unevenly cut holes in his mask.

Greta raised her gloved hands and hoped they weren't trembling. Likewise, the two gentlemen hiking near her wasted no time in obeying.

Before she'd left Illinois, everyone had warned her of the

trouble she might encounter on the route to the west, including the growing problem of stagecoach robberies. Over the past eight weeks of traveling, she'd braced herself for the possibility, had mentally rehearsed such an encounter and what she'd do.

But today, on the last day of the journey, she'd finally allowed herself to relax and believe that for once things might work out in her favor, that she hadn't made a big mistake in moving to Colorado.

Apparently, she'd assumed too much too soon.

At the rear of the stagecoach, several men had been pushing it the final distance to the top of the pass, and they now eased out into the open, their arms up. The driver sitting on his bench atop the stagecoach set the brake, then released the reins controlling the two teams of horses that had been straining to pull them up the mountain. He, too, cautiously lifted his hands.

She guessed, like her, the other passengers were well aware of the tales of murder and mayhem along the wilderness trails. And they weren't taking any chances either.

At least Astrid was inside the coach. After trekking uphill for the first hour, the little girl's poor lungs hadn't been able to handle the exertion. As much as Astrid had loathed returning to the bumpy conveyance, she'd been able to have a seat to herself since everyone else had gotten out to lighten the load.

Last time Greta had peeked through the open windows, her sister had been sprawled out asleep, and now Greta prayed the precocious child would stay that way.

The middle robber inched toward them, his revolver swinging in a wide arc. His leathery hands and dirt-encrusted fingernails contrasted with the ivory handle of his revolver. "Nobody move."

Morning sunlight filtered through the aspens, their white bark and green-gold leaves making the trail feel more open and airy than other parts of the mountainous road. A cool, dry breeze rattled the leaves, swishing like ladies' skirts brushing against grass.

Just minutes ago, Greta had been marveling at how different the dry and cooler climate was from northern Illinois, where oppressive humidity plagued the summers and made every chore feel like a burden. What she wouldn't give at this moment to be back there shucking corn or snapping beans, even if she was dripping with perspiration.

"Anyone left inside?" one of the other robbers asked.

"No," Greta said quickly. "Everyone's out."

Just then the stagecoach door inched open.

The lanky robber with the uneven eye slits swung his revolver toward the door and clicked the hammer.

"No!" Greta threw herself between the robber and the stagecoach, shoving against Astrid's strong push.

A short distance away beyond the trees, the mountainside overlooked the sprawling grasslands of South Park, nestled between the Front Range in the east and the Mosquito Range in the west. Their destination was within eyesight. If only it was also within shouting distance so they could call for help.

The bandit shifted the barrel's aim to Greta, his arm stiff, his fingers taut. "Woman, unless you want to find yourself eating a bullet, you'd best step aside and let that person out."

Inside, Astrid cried out in protest and once again attempted to open the door. But Greta flattened the full length of her body against it.

"Move on outta the way, woman," the robber said, louder and more irritably.

"It's her little sister." One of the other passengers moved to stand beside Greta, a middle-aged man who'd introduced himself as Landry Steele yesterday morning when they boarded the stagecoach in Denver. He'd spent the majority of the journey conversing with the other gentlemen. However, during the few brief interactions she'd had with him, he'd always been considerate.

"The girl is ill and is of no concern to you." Beneath the brim of Mr. Steele's bowler, he shot Greta an apologetic look, as though realizing she'd wanted to keep Astrid hidden away and out of the conflict.

"That so?" The gunman's revolver didn't waver. "If she's of no concern, then let her on out."

Greta pressed against the door harder. She hadn't brought Astrid all this distance to have her die at the hand of a robber. "She's only eight years old—"

"I'm nine," came Astrid's indignant voice.

"Allow her to come out," Mr. Steele said with a quiet urgency. "You don't want her to end up an orphan, do you?"

Astrid an orphan? Never in Greta's plans had she counted on dying before Astrid. The truth was, Astrid's days were numbered, and Greta hoped to lengthen and make them as pain-free as possible. But she couldn't do that if she let the robber kill her.

Swallowing hard, Greta stepped away from the stagecoach. The door flew open with a *bang*, and Astrid tumbled out. She landed with an *oomph* onto the grassy road but then bounded up as nimbly as a barn cat. Though the consumption had emaciated the girl so that she was thin and petite for her age, somehow she still retained a fresh and vibrant spirit that made up for her physical frailty.

Her big silver blue eyes, so much like Greta's, took in the scene—the robbers, their guns, and all the passengers standing motionless with hands in the air. Astrid's hair was also the same color as Greta's, a golden brown now sun-streaked from so many days of neglecting her bonnet. Astrid had refused to allow Greta to plait her hair when they'd arisen at half past four in the morning for a hasty departure from the stagecoach station, and now it hung in tangled waves.

Even so, Astrid was the picture of perfection. She had dainty porcelain but beautiful features that drew attention everywhere she went. Greta had never considered herself to be a beauty, not like some of the other young women back home and certainly not like Astrid.

But too many people to recall during the journey west had exclaimed how much she and Astrid looked alike. The admiring glances and flattery had been strange but not unwelcome. At times, she wondered if maybe she was prettier than she'd realized, if maybe she'd been hasty in accepting the first mail-order bride proposal that came along.

Astrid took several steps in the direction of the closest robber. "Why are you wearing a sack over your head?"

"Astrid, come here this instant," Greta whispered in her sternest tone.

The thief's gaze darted over to the passengers, revealing a crooked, lazy eye that didn't focus. "It's what robbers do, kid."

"W-e-l-l." Astrid drew the word out and cocked her head. "It makes you look kinda silly, like a scarecrow."

Greta lunged for Astrid, but the girl dodged away and skipped toward the robber.

His gun wavered, as though he was considering turning the weapon on Astrid.

"Astrid!" Horror rose in Greta's throat, threatening to strangle her. "Don't you dare go a step closer."

Astrid halted and held out her hand. "Here's some money, Mister. It's mine, but you can have it since you need it more than me."

The man's lazy eye shifted to Astrid again. "Drop it on the ground."

Astrid released a crumpled wad and a few coins. They bounced in the grass near the robber's feet. "My sister has more—"

"No!" Greta couldn't let these bandits discover her secret stash since she'd taken pains to sew the cash into the lining of her coat after the passengers had been warned not to carry valuables.

It was her jam money. Her earnings from picking and preserving the wild berries that grew on the farm. The accumulation of two years of working every spare minute.

Astrid turned her pretty eyes upon Greta. "They have to wear flour sacks instead of hats. Guess that means they need the money more than we do. Right, Mister?"

"Right, kid." This time the robber's voice hinted at amusement.

The thieves made quick work of emptying the locked box next to the driver and then divested each of the passengers of anything of value. Within a few minutes they ran off into the woods with their loot.

Greta stood with the others, surveying their belongings

strewn over the grass surrounding the stagecoach. Astrid had lost interest in the robbers and was intent on picking a bouquet of wildflowers.

"We got lucky." The driver broke the silence, his voice shaky as he closed the now-empty box next to him. "Last time the Crooked-Eye Gang struck, they killed three men—"

Mr. Steele cut off the driver with a glare and a curt nod toward Astrid.

The driver clamped his mouth closed, and everyone set to work repacking their bags and trunks.

Greta fingered the frayed coat hem. Although Phineas Hallock, her intended, had informed her he had plenty of money since he was part owner of a gold mine, she couldn't keep dismay from weighing upon her.

She'd corresponded with Phineas by letter on several occasions last year, and she sensed in him genuine kindness, especially since he'd so readily agreed to take care of Astrid. He also made all the arrangements for the trip, including paying for their fare.

Though the small daguerreotype he'd sent in his last letter the previous autumn had shown him to be a plain-looking and somewhat older man, his face held a look of integrity as well as honesty. Maybe he wasn't handsome or young, but that didn't matter. What she needed was a husband who was reliable, dependable, and able to provide for her and Astrid.

Besides, after making up her mind, Greta had wanted to move as quickly as possible to get Astrid to the healing air of the Rockies. Why waste time corresponding with other men when Phineas had been so eager and ready to help her?

Maybe she'd acted rashly. But what was done, was done.

She was on her way to marry Phineas. She would, in fact, wed him by the day's end.

Still, she blinked back tears. All of her savings were gone. If only Astrid knew how to obey better. If only the little girl had a real mother and father to raise her. Instead, she was stuck with a mere half sister who clearly didn't know how to keep her in line.

Greta sat back on her heels and watched the young girl with a mixture of frustration and helplessness.

"Don't be too hard on her." Mr. Steele bent next to Greta and retrieved a shiny leather shoe.

"She's a handful."

"She saved us from meeting our Maker today."

"She did?"

The gentleman removed his bowler and smoothed back his dark hair, which had hints of gray at his temples and streaking his long sideburns and mustache. "The gang leader liked her and showed mercy on us as a result."

Mercy? Each of the passengers had lost everything of value. But she supposed that was better than losing their lives.

"I have a son about Astrid's age." Mr. Steele replaced his hat, watching Astrid wistfully.

"You must be looking forward to seeing him when we arrive in Fairplay."

He focused on the child a moment longer, his expression filled with sadness. "Unfortunately, I won't be seeing him anytime soon. He lives in New York with his mother."

"I'm sorry." Greta didn't know what else to say.

Mr. Steele shook his head, as if by doing so he could shake away his morose thoughts. "Tell me again why you're moving to Fairplay."

Greta hadn't told him anything yet, since he hadn't asked. But she wouldn't be so impolite as to say so. Instead, she gave him the rehearsed line she'd spouted to everyone else who'd wanted to know. "My fiancé lives in Fairplay, and I'm traveling there to marry him."

"Your fiancé? Is that so?" Mr. Steele's eyes lit with interest. "May I ask who the lucky fellow is? I'm mayor and have gotten to know many men in the area."

All the misgivings she'd had since agreeing to marry Phineas soared. What if she'd made a mistake in coming west and agreeing to marry a stranger? What if he wasn't who he had claimed to be? What if he mistreated Astrid?

Just as quickly as the doubts assailed her, she tossed them aside. If Phineas wasn't the man he'd portrayed in his letters, then she'd have no obligation to stay with him. In fact, perhaps Mr. Steele would be able to advise her regarding the true nature of Phineas's character. Then if her fiancé had any glaring faults, she'd be well aware of them before arriving in Fairplay.

She cast a sideways glance at the other passengers, who were in the finishing stages of stowing their belongings and were thankfully heedless of the conversation. "I haven't actually met my intended."

Mr. Steele, in the process of picking up another shoe, paused.

"We've written to each other."

He straightened and gave her his full attention. "You wouldn't happen to be Phineas Hallock's mail-order bride, would you?"

Something in his tone made the skin at the back of her neck prickle with unease. "Yes, Mr. Hallock is my fiancé. Do you know him?"

The gentleman shook his head, his features creasing. "I knew him well. He was a good man."

Her heart began to patter fast and hard. "Knew?"

"I'm sorry, Miss Nilsson. Phineas Hallock is dead."

"The mine owner Phineas Hallock, originally from Connecticut?"

"Yes, he left for California last October. Said he was traveling there to purchase supplies for his new bride and that he planned to be back by late spring. When the thawing came and he didn't return, we all thought he was delayed. Until a body was discovered on Hoosier Pass."

"His body?"

"As far as we can tell, after so many months of being exposed to the elements . . ."

She stared at Mr. Steele, but somehow he faded from her vision. All she could see was the black-and-white photograph of Phineas.

In his last letter, he'd mentioned his trip to California and his excitement over picking out additional furniture and items for their home. He expressed his desire to have the newly built house well-stocked and ready for her arrival. She hadn't heard from him since and assumed he hadn't had the opportunity to send further correspondence. Even if he had, mail delivery via the Pony Express and stagecoach wasn't reliable. Letters were sometimes lost or stolen.

Besides, she'd been busy preparing for the trip, sewing clothes for Astrid and her, packing their belongings, and saying good-byes. She'd never in her wildest imagination believed Phineas Hallock hadn't written again because he was dead.

He was dead.

She swayed, her vision growing fuzzy.

Mr. Steele's grip on her elbow steadied her. "I'm truly sorry, Miss Nilsson."

With a deep breath, she tried to bring the world back into focus. The sunlight streaming through the aspen branches above splashed across her face as though to wake her from a nightmare.

The man she'd come west to marry was dead. Every penny of her savings had just been stolen. What would she do now? How could she, a lone woman with a sick child, survive in the wilderness knowing no one and having nothing?

CHAPTER

2

The cold barrel of a revolver jammed into the back of Wyatt McQuaid's neck and stopped him short in the middle of Fairplay's dusty Main Street.

"Quit stealing my business." The voice—and the sour body odor—behind Wyatt belonged to only one man: Roper Brawley.

"I ain't stealing your business—"

"Jansen's steers were mine." Brawley dug the steel into Wyatt's flesh, bumping and loosening his hat so it tumbled to the street.

Against the black felt, the chalky line from dried sweat was all too visible and encrusted along the brim with dust, grease, and mud spots. The center was dented where a heifer had recently trampled it. And the hatband of braided horsehair hung loose.

Even if his hat wasn't pretty, it was still his pride and joy. And he wouldn't stand for anyone knocking it from his head.

With a jab backward, Wyatt elbowed Brawley's stomach,

forcing the man to double over. With the pressure gone, Wyatt spun, latched on to Brawley's gun arm, and slammed it down hard against his knee, giving Brawley little choice but to release the revolver.

The weapon flew several feet, landing in the gravel, far enough away that Brawley couldn't easily reach it.

"This here is a free country." Wyatt swiped up his hat and situated it on his head. Although the sun was on its evening hike down to Sheep and Horseshoe Mountains, the rays were still strong and hot. "The miners can sell their oxen to anyone in the blazes they want to."

Nursing his stomach, Brawley straightened. A black patch covered a missing eye but couldn't hide the thin, white scars scattered across his cheek—wounds he'd gotten fighting Indians. "Me and my men were here in South Park first."

That was debatable. Wyatt had arrived in the summer of 1860 and tried gold mining like thousands of other prospectors. After scraping by and managing to pan only enough nuggets and gold dust to fill his pockets, he'd tried his luck at something different—ranching.

With the passing of the Homestead Act earlier in the year, he'd been one of the first to file an application and pay the registration fee at the land office in Denver. He'd gotten himself the one hundred sixty acres allowed under President Lincoln's new legislation fair and square.

His pasturelands spread out to the southeast of Fairplay. Wyatt had spent the spring and summer laboring from sunup to sundown, building a house and a barn on his claim. He and Judd had buckled down and made the place livable for both man and beast. And over recent weeks, he'd started adding more steers to his small herd.

And now, Roper Brawley was determined to keep him from succeeding.

Brawley crossed his arms and nodded at several cowhands loitering outside Cabinet Billiard Hall. At their boss's signal, they sauntered toward Wyatt, their spurs jangling, their hands resting on the handles of their six-shooters tucked into their holsters.

Wyatt made eye contact with Judd, who stood next to the livery guarding the two bone-thin steers Wyatt had just purchased. The white-haired man limped forward too. He didn't reach for his Colts—didn't have to. Judd was the fastest gunslinger in the Rockies. He could shoot iron quicker than the twitch of a cow's tail.

Fortunately, Brawley and his men knew it. They stopped a dozen paces away, feet spread, hands at the ready.

Brawley spit a stream of tobacco into the street, then wiped his sleeve across his mouth. "This place ain't big enough for the two of us, McQuaid."

"If that's the way you feel, then I guess you oughta be moving on."

"You're the one needing to move on." Brawley's bottom lip rounded out from the chew stuffed inside, and his thin, scraggly beard and mustache were stained with the juice. Brawley probably wasn't much older than Wyatt's own twenty-three years, but his lean, leathery face and somber eyes spoke of hardships that had aged him too soon.

"Come on now, Brawley." Wyatt attempted to dredge up some empathy for the man. After all, he knew a bit about hardships himself. "This land here in South Park can handle more than one ranch. Let's aim to live in peace—"

"Peace?" Brawley scoffed. "You buying up all the cattle and leaving me with none ain't aiming for peace."

Wyatt almost snorted but held himself back. Brawley had things backward. He was the one buying up the weak and worn-out oxen as rapidly as the miners and teamsters came over the passes.

The rumbling of wheels and the pounding of hooves from the northeast end of town cut off their discussion. *Discussion* was too kind a word for Brawley's attempt to intimidate Wyatt into leaving. It wasn't the first time the rancher had made threats, and it probably wouldn't be the last.

As the stagecoach rolled closer, the clatter and dust rose higher. Brawley bent and retrieved his revolver and then headed toward his men. Across the street, Judd watched with unswerving intensity, his bushy white eyebrows narrowed and his white mustache pursed until the men disappeared into the billiard hall. Once they were gone, Judd tipped the brim of his hat at Wyatt before he shuffled back toward the newly purchased steers.

Wyatt rolled his shoulders and tried to release the tension. At the rate he was going, he'd never make enough profit to send for his ma and siblings. Even if he could help his family with the costs of traveling to Colorado, how would he support them once they arrived?

What he needed to do was purchase a herd of purebred Shorthorns from the breeder he'd met in Missouri during his days transporting livestock for Russell, Majors, & Waddell. Beeves like that would thrive on the buffalo grass, wheat grass, and moss sage.

He peered beyond the buildings that lined the street to the grassy plains that spread out to the distant Tarryall mountain range in the east. Since the grass was endless and free, he'd have no trouble fattening up the cattle for butchering. The miners always had a hankering for beef, tiring easily of the fish they caught in local streams or the canned goods they bought for exorbitant prices.

In fact, if Wyatt could purchase a big enough herd of Shorthorns and start his own breeding, he'd be able to send a stream of beef to the markets in the east. Eventually, he might make enough from sales to buy up more of the surrounding land and expand his ranch.

The trouble was, he didn't have a tail feather left, not after pouring every penny of his savings into the start-up costs of his place. He could hardly afford the worn-out oxen that newcomers were practically giving away. Besides, he couldn't rely on that supply forever, especially with Brawley's hackles rising every time Wyatt made a purchase.

As the stage rolled to a jerking halt in front of the Fairplay Hotel, Wyatt expelled a pent-up breath. What he needed was an investor, a partner who'd be willing to help him build up his herd.

The gold mines in the mountains surrounding South Park had made millionaires out of numerous men. Would any of them be willing to invest in his ranch?

Wyatt scanned the buildings lining Fairplay, most having the typical false storefronts that made the businesses appear bigger and more significant to draw men in. Set at the center of the flat grasslands along the intersection of Beaver Creek and the South Platte, Fairplay had earned its name from its first prospectors who'd vowed that their mining camp would be different from the others in the area, that they'd operate with integrity and fairness.

Although the town had its share of taverns and dance halls, it was a shade tamer than some of the other colorful mining towns that had sprung up in the area, towns like Buckskin Joe and Tarryall.

Of all the mining towns Wyatt had lived in and visited, he liked Fairplay best, mainly because he liked and respected the men who ran it.

Men like Landry Steele . . .

Steele stepped down from the stagecoach, wearing his usual dark suit coat, vest, and matching trousers. He turned around and offered his hand to a woman in the stagecoach door.

The woman accepted the help descending. The brim of her bonnet hid her face, but from the litheness of her movements and the womanliness of her form, she was awful young to be Steele's wife. In a blue dress, the woman was also too plainly attired to be Steele's fancy eastern wife. Besides, Steele had yammered on more than once about his wife refusing to live in the Wild West.

As the woman planted both feet on the ground, Steele reached up to the doorway again and, this time, offered his hand to a little girl.

Wyatt couldn't contain his surprise and released a low whistle. Maybe Steele's wife had decided to come west with their child after all, although hadn't Steele talked about a son, not a daughter?

The girl bounded down, her bonnet pushed back, revealing long, loose hair the color of a newborn fawn. Petite and pretty, the child smiled her thanks to Steele before skipping away.

"Astrid, stay close." The woman spun after the child and revealed her face. Her hair was the same light brown as the child's, and her features were just as pretty but fuller and slightly rounder.

Astrid didn't heed her mother and frisked away from the stagecoach in the direction of Simpkin's General Store.

"Astrid, please." The woman grabbed a fistful of her skirt and picked up her pace, then cast a glance over her shoulder at Steele.

Steele smiled and waved her on. "Go and explore. You know where to find me."

She nodded, her expression emanating gratefulness, before she hustled after her child.

Stroking his mustache, Steele watched the young woman until she disappeared into the store behind the little girl.

Wyatt needed to stop staring, but his curiosity got the better of him. If this woman wasn't Steele's wife, then who was she? Couldn't be his mistress. Steele had never struck Wyatt as the type of man who'd cheat on his wife, no matter how much he had a hankering for a woman.

As if sensing the scrutiny, Steele's gaze swung to Wyatt, where he still stood in the middle of the road. Steele touched the brim of his bowler in greeting.

Wyatt repeated the action.

"Don't look at me like that, McQuaid," Steele called.

"Like what?" Blast it all. Why hadn't he walked away before Steele had caught him staring?

"Like I'm doing something I shouldn't be."

"She ain't your wife, is she?"

"No, of course not." Steele huffed.

"I took you for a God-fearing man who took his marriage vows seriously."

"And I am."

"Then what are you doing with a pretty lady like that?" Wyatt glanced at the dusty window of the general store but couldn't see inside past the grime to the woman in question.

Steele pressed his lips together and crossed toward him. "Do you think she's pretty?"

Wyatt hadn't seen her long, but it had been enough to know she was a real beauty. "A man'd have to be blind not to think so."

Steele halted in front of him. The dust from the journey lightened the black of his suit coat to a charcoal gray. "Good. Then I want you to marry her."

Jody Hedlund is the bestselling author of over fifty novels and is the winner of numerous awards. Jody lives in Michigan with her husband, busy family, and five spoiled cats. She writes sweet historical romances with plenty of sizzle. Visit her at JodyHedlund.com.

Sign Up for Jody's Newsletter

Keep up to date with Jody's latest news on book releases and events by signing up for her email list at the link below.

JodyHedlund.com

FOLLOW JODY ON SOCIAL MEDIA

Author Jody Hedlund   @JodyHedlund   @JodyHedlund